THE REINCARNATION

OF

THE ASSASSIN

I0586961

DOUG McPHILLIPS

Also by Doug McPhillips:

Other Visionary Stories:

NOVELS.

From Darkness to Light.
Awake to my Gutted Dream.
The Sword of Discernment.
Santiago Traveller.
I'Prophet.
Masters at my table.
The Guru of Jerusalem.
We is me Upside Down. (Biography)
The Wicklow Way.
The Adventures of Ace McDice,
Stretch Deed & Moonshine Melody.
Instant Karma & Grace.
The Credo.
Reflections of an Old Man.
A Camino Guide Book.
Country Camino. (Album)
Santiago Traveller. (Album)

Doug McPhillips April 2023

ISBN. 978-0-6458862-0-7

National Library of Australia Catalogue- in -publication data:
Holy Bible, New International Version, Hodder & Stoughton 1984.
Assassinated! Steven Parissien, Quetiius, 2008.
Google research- wikipedia.Org, historytoday.com- Authors Unknown.

Content

To those searching for belief in a God
of their own understanding,
and for saving grace against the forces of evil.

Introduction.

It matters little in the telling of this tale as to the reader's belief in the science of creation, the biblical account of the plan and aftermath or the doctrine of evolution. Each philosophy of the beginning lead ultimately to one conclusion, the nature of man as a consequence of what took place in the heavens at the appointed hour; a war that followed between those on the side of the agency of the infinite intelligence plan and that of the angel who was cast down from the heavens. The one known as Lucifer is the personified of all the evil that has since transpired in the hearts of man and befallen the earth as a consequence. This once-chosen angel is responsible for the evil wrongdoing in the use of free will of defects of character infused in the heart of humanity since the fall and thereafter. This story enters the hearts of humanity in the telling.

For it was the Infinite intelligence who created human nature with the intent of abundantly living His plan. "Be fruitful and multiply, and fill the earth, and subdue it, and rule over the fish of the sea and over the birds of the sky and over every living thing that moves on the earth." This Infinite intelligence whom we may choose to call God has always had a built-in essential plan of salvation, an agency if you will of rules and regulations to be carried out by his creator likeness known to be a man and by his action of free will, as dictated by divine law, this plan's reliance for the growth and betterment of the world would be learned experience progressive to God infused goodness, and by Godly grace mankind's success could be guaranteed. For this God of all had his plan for mankind in the stewardship of achievement of his plan for all the living, with mankind as his highest creation of earthly representation. It is due to these realities that each of us has an inner sense of God's original intent. These ideas were built into the song of creation, and we still have echoes of that melody bouncing through our existence.

So it came to pass Lucifer, or Satan if you will, as punishment for his disobedience and the grave dishonouring of his angelic post in manipulating the natural order of God had established in an attempt to raise himself higher than God in a complete reversal of his entire being and status. According to God, one cannot become more than they already are. Lucifer was a spirit son of God who rebelled against the plan's reliance on the ability and privilege God gives us to choose and act for ourselves. God's agency is essential in the plan of salvation, without this plan's reliance, we would not be able to learn or progress or to follow God's plan. The Infinite intelligence of God was naturally privy to Lucifer's intent and thus created another son to be our Saviour whose sacrificial act, as we of Christian belief acknowledge, is our saving grace. Lucifer, or Satan if you will, as punishment for his disobedience and the grave dishonouring of his angelic post was cast out of heaven with an army of angels who followed him. "How you are fallen from heaven, O Lucifer, son of the morning! how art thou cut to the ground which didst weaken the nations!" Isaiah14:12.

And God in his wisdom creation of all gave man dominion over earth. So in His Infinite Intelligence, he provided Adam with the first of men and women as partners that he might provide his seed to increase and multiply in accord with His plan. And in the heavens, God sent an angel of his intent to impregnate a woman of pure heart with the seed of mankind's salvation after the fall. And Lucifer the dragon was wroth with the woman, and went to make war with the remnant of her seed, who choose to control their defects of character in preference to keep the original of God, and have the testimony of him, the one who was to be acknowledged as Jesus, the chosen one of God."

So it came to pass that from the the time of the great fall, the dividing line between the spirit of natural grace within the heart of man's intent is always at war with what the divine spirit offers of the throne of heaven, and that of human inner knowledge of the ways of the evil. For one leads to Godly intent whilst the other leads only to destruction and death. "He that saith, I know him and kept not his commandments, is a liar, and the truth is not in him" (1 John 2:4). As the Apostle Paul related in his writing:" It is evidence this covenant that I will make with them after those days, saith the Lord, I will put my laws into their hearts, and in their minds will I write them," (Hebrews 10:16).

Even the prophet Daniel recognised this division of forces when he wrote, "And such as do wickedly against the covenant shall he corrupt by flatteries: but the people that do know their God shall be strong, and do just exploits," (Daniel 11:32). Yes, as Lucifer flattered the angels in heaven with the thought they were naturally good, so he seeks to flatter people today. But the people that do "know their God" will not be fooled or deceived, but will do mighty things for God, and for the redemption of many. Whose side are you on? God or Satan?

Many can be heard repeating the lie that we do not need to obey God in order to be like God. Even in Christian circles, the lesson is taught that God's law is obsolete, and one need not obey to be like Him in character. Just as a great multitude of heavenly angels fell for Satan's lie, so now millions of people carry the same philosophy and therefore place themselves in rank with the forces of Satan. Adam and Eve were sold the same lie, "You can be like gods," without obeying God. They fell for it. As a result, humanity became rebels of the kingdom of heaven. "For to be carnally minded is death; but to be spiritually minded is life and peace. Because the carnal mind is enmity against God: for it is not subject to the law of God, neither indeed can be," (Romans 8:6-8). But God introduced the plan of salvation, a plan designed to lead mankind back to the throne of God through obedience to His law, and all who stand for the government of God place themselves squarely against Satan and his army. This is the dividing line between those who will be loyal subjects of the throne of heaven and those who refuse to acknowledge and strive to live by God's law. For within the heart of man is both his good nature and those of his defects of character which God alone knows and allows repentance through the sacrificial act of Jesus Christ who died on the cross so that mankind may be saved.

Suffice it is to say that the world offers much for a man to follow his own nature and use his defects of character for his betterment and not destructive purpose. But more often than not those very same defects that render him to fall from grace through the desires of the evil one. That characteristic of his seven deadly defects of the character of pride, covertness, lust, anger, gluttony envy and sloth that so often brings man to destruction an ultimate death of the spirit and physical demise without the grace of God. It is the goal of Lucifer and his army of fallen angels who administer this route to destruction and death that this story tells. Whilst the path taken could be told in the collective of those who bring about mass murder, a coalition of the willing who buy the lie of world domination and damnation of the collective souls of mankind, or the ultimate untimely final war of a catastrophic Armageddon as depicted in the Book of Revelations. The story here tells a different tale, for it delves in the minds of the ones who accept the evil within them and use their defects of character in the mistaken belief that they have a duty to kill. It is the reincarnation of the Lucifer within those who are trained to lie in the name of the common welfare of mankind. These men come to be known as assassins from the time of the fall.

Assassins.

Do you hear the words of the poet,
music in the stories he tells,
do you see the signs in the sky now,
how the climate is changing as well.

Do you feel the vibrations of the instruments,
the planes that are dropping your bombs,
can you see the mushroom cloud now,
the killing and maiming that's done.

Do you listen to raw emotion,
the voice in the Wildness Ride,
have you joined the unit of Legions,
feeding on flesh with the carrion crows.

Cease the bombing and killing of children,
in the name of the Father of Peace,
give up on the lying and cheating,
call your Assassins home for a rest.

Oh! Hash is the drug of deception,
for your killers given the job,
to take out the home of subculture,
the souls that oppose your mob!

You're moving the souls by the thousands,
to the legions of your all-seeing eye,
so please change your war of deception,
just let us the people try.

Now the poet's run out of writing,
his voice has turned to decay,
the words of his songs and his music,
somehow they are fading away.

Presidents and Prime Ministers,
contemplating the hole in the wall,
praying to the Prince of Darkness,
whilst the elephant's still in the room.

Cease the bombing and killing of children,
in the name of the Father of Peace,

give up the lying and cheating,
call your Assassins home to rest.

CHAPTER 1.

LUCIFER'S ASSASSINS.

The biblical story is told of an angel named Lucifer, who was described as a "covering cherub, "an angel that stood in the very presence of God, covering the ark of the testimony, in which lay the agency- the Law of God, above the ark, was God's mercy seat. So earthly replicas were designed to teach heavenly realities- show us the foundation of God's throne (the mercy seat) in heaven which was His law (ark of the covenant), and Lucifer was once an angel that stood closest to the throne of God, guarding and protecting the law of God. This was his position in heaven and all was peaceful until immortality was found in Lucifer. For it was a fact of his character to commit dishonour of God's plan by the transgression of the law. Lucifer, the angel that was to guard the law of God, the foundation of God's government, turned against that very law which resulted in the introduction of sin into the heavenly atmosphere. Hence, the first war was over the law of God. Lucifer, like a master politician, argued that heavenly angels had no need for a law because they were already holy. Lucifer said, "I will be like the most High without obeying His laws." In other words, Lucifer, now Satan, had introduced the principle of self-righteousness righteousness by one's own standard versus the universal standard of God's law. The argument was a deceptive one and one that still deceives the masses today.

So it was that the war that followed saw Lucifer losing his status in the heavens and being cast to earth with his army of followers, who like him rejected the law of God's agency. The majority of the heavenly spirits of creation remained with God's natural order and plan for the universe. However, there were many of mankind's earliest inhabitants who were enlisted to the ways of Lucifer. The first of these in the order of the beginning of the earthly universe is mentioned in rabbinic literature as Lilith, who is variously depicted as the mother of Adam's demonic offspring following his separation from Eve as his first wife. Whereas Eve was created from Adams's rib according to Biblical text, some accounts hold that Lilith was the woman implied in Genesis 1:27 who was made from the same soil as

Adam. She is depicted as the female figure in Mesopotamian and Judaic mythology, alternatively the first wife of Adam and supposedly the primordial she-demon. Lilith is cited as having been "banished" from the Garden of Eden for not complying with or obeying Adam, finally refusing to lay with him.

The Bible mentions Lilith only once, as a dweller in waste places (Isaiah 23:14), but she is depicted as a seducer or slayer of children which has a long history in Babylonian religion. She was sexually attracted to Lucifer as his first human earthy wife and was found in a cave bearing children by three angels. She refused to return to God's grace and in revenge is said to rob children of life and is responsible for the deaths of stillborn infants and crib deaths. In Isiah 34:14 in various Bible translations, interpreters often envisage the figure of Lilith as a dangerous demon of the night, who is sexually wanton, and who steals babies in the darkness. Lilith later wedded Eblis, the prince of the devils, and became the mother of demons and spectres and in vengeance upon her rival, Eve the mother of mankind, became the special enemy of babies. As for Lucifer's offspring, his daughter, known as the Angel Liberty was created by God from a feather left behind from a wing of Lucifer in the process of his banishment from heaven. All this myth and storytelling of the beginnings of the Universe speak of a fall but it equally tells of the outcome of human defects of character over Godly intent. More to the point is the acceptance of humanity in the rejection of supernatural grace given to humanity by God for our betterment.

Lucifer set out from the very beginning of his earthly realm to temp and deceive, not only those who were obedient to God's agency but those who by their own will and defects of character fell under his evil spell and those of his army of angels of death who at their fall took on human form. For Lucifer to win the kingdom that God created on earth he knew that his influence over humanity would bring soul darkness and ultimately death. By the indoctrination of dark deeds, his mission of death and control of all would be assured. Mindful of God's good orderly direction Lucifer knew that in the Garden of Eden, there was a tree of knowledge that was to be left until the appointed hour for man to know of its power and opportunities. Initially, it was Eve whom Lucifer tempted by appealing to her curiosity. Biblically speaking he tempted Eve to encourage Adam to eat the fruit from the tree of knowledge despite God's rule to the contrary. We can only assume that the symbolic apple temptation by Eve to Adam may well have been some sort of depravity of a sexual kind, or maybe the deception that man could be as powerful as his Maker by eating off the forbidden fruit. Well as we know Adam did partake with Eve of the fruit of the tree of knowledge and all hell broke loose thereafter. For their punishment, the Infinite Intelligence banished them from the Garden of Eden thus forcing them to a life of hard work and further temptations off the flesh by Lucifer. This initial sin is the route of all evil that enters man's hearts from the moment of the first man and woman's defiance of God. So as punishment for their great error, Adam and Eve were banished from the Garden of Eden, then after Adam and Eve were forced to leave they decided to start a family. While the exact number of children they had is unknown, the Bible tells us that their first two were boys named Cain and Abel. When they grew older, Cain worked in the fields, planting and harvesting crops, and Abel became a shepherd. As they began to reap the benefits of their new occupations, they decided to give offerings to God to show their gratitude. For his offering, Abel brought God the "fatty portion" of his flock, which pleased Him. However, when Cain presented God with some of his harvest, He was not pleased.

Yet God still gave him the chance to redeem himself. "Then the Lord said to Cain: Why are you angry? Why are you dejected? If you act rightly, you will be accepted; but if not, sin lies in wait at the door: its urge is for you, yet you can rule over it."Instead of making amends, Cain took out his anger on his brother. After he spoke with God, Cain took Abel for a walk in the fields and murdered him. Shortly after, God asked Cain where Abel had gone, and Cain tried to evade the question. But God knew the sin he committed against his brother, and punished him. Genesis 4:10-12 says:"God then said What have you done? Your brother's blood cries out to me from the ground! Now you are banned from the ground that opened its mouth to receive your brother's blood from your hand. If you till the ground, it shall no longer give you its produce. You shall become a constant wanderer on the earth." Cain was even more distressed after hearing what his punishment was to be. However, he didn't express remorse for his actions – he was only concerned that others might want to kill him for what he had done. In his mercy, the Lord put a mark on Cain, so that the angels of death would not have him killed. Cain was exiled to Nod, the land east of Eden, where he later started his own family. Cain's sacrifice implies that he did not offer God the best of his crop.

While both Cain and Abel presented a portion of their gains to God, Cain was insincere in his offering. Rather than having a contrite heart and seeking to determine why God was not gratified with his offering, Cain jealously turned against Abel. Cain's failure to respond in humility ultimately came from his unwillingness to admit his mistakes. The devastating results serve as a reminder of the consequences of giving in to defects of character – the consequences of being too proud to admit when we are wrong and change our ways. Cain lost his brother, was banished from his home, and was forced to wander the earth for the rest of his life. Yet even Cain's exile was a reflection of God's boundless mercy. After Cain murdered Abel, God allowed him to start a new life in a different place and marked him to prevent him from being killed by others. Through these acts of mercy, God reminds us that even in spite of our weakness – or outright depravity – God is a God of grace and second chances.

Lucifer had his game plan in play having had his way with the hearts and minds of the first human parents and that of their eldest offspring. So he set forth to cause mass death and destruction to the human race through killing fields of war and natural disaster. It was his focus to cast his spell over humanity, but to achieve this he needed an army of angels of death to carry out his plan of total control in a final Armageddon in the future. Meanwhile, he watched and waited as leaders rose through the evolution of man to rule earthly kingdoms.

It was to these great leaders of the world of their times that Lucifer used his angles of death to enter their hearts to destroy mankind and ultimately destroy the leaders themselves. Let us not forget that his mission's dependence has always been to rule and divide by death. So it came to pass as great leaders rose, the power of Lucifer entered their minds and hearts as much as the killers whom he used to destroy them. These killers of renown came to be known as Assassins, for their motives, ambitions and goals their acts encompassed have existed since communities were first organised and the children of the offspring of Adam appointed leaders. For they were conditioned by the influence of the evil one and the angels of death to premeditated killing in the interest of some cause more often than not vilified by a litany of lies from those orchestrating the killings or the conditioning of the Assassin's interpretation as to the need for the murder to be done. Sometimes to quieten the mind overrule their conscious hearts and steady their resolve they were often given a cannabis plant extract called hashish to smoke prior to the killings.

The word "Assassin" derives from a secretive murder cult in the 11th and 12th centuries called the "Hashishin", meaning "hashish eaters".While much of the origin of this cult has been lost, the original leader was Hasan Ben Sabah, a prominent devotee of Isma'ili beliefs. Hasan's group was a cult of the Isma'ili sect of Muslims. The name itself is from a possibly fabricated tale (perhaps fabricated by enemies of the Hashishin, as a way to explain how Sabah got his followers to be willing to be sent to their deaths so readily) that Hasan would have men kidnapped and brought to his stronghold. There they were drugged up with hashish and put into a hypnotic state. After this trance-like state was induced, the men were offered sensual pleasures- beautiful handmaidens and harem girls and made to believe they were in heaven. When they came out of the trance, they were sent out on gangland-type missions. The men were told that if they attempted to kill prominent targets and things went sour, they would be given a quick return trip to paradise in order to make them fearless in their mission.

Prior to the popularisation of the word Assassin killings of leaders were carried out as premeditated, more often than not politically motivated acts and must be distinguished from contract killings which may well have a more personal reason for the need to kill. Assassinations have helped the cause of Lucifer from their very inception and mostly changed the course of history. The moral status of the assassinated victim varies of course. How can one compare the cold genocidal killing of a Nazi leader to that of a Civil Rights leader for example? For a time after the assassination of a particularly inspiring figure, it seems all is lost and the last hope of freedom and liberty be extinguished. But somehow the resilience of men of Godly intent invariably bounces back from even the most tragic of circumstances.

Assassinations are depressingly still with us. Indeed assassination, rather than dying out, is becoming an increasingly common feature of modern political life. Governments, sects and perhaps more than ever – are still prepared to waive elementary rules of social responsibility, personal integrity, democratic accountability and freedom of speech in order to eliminate political opponents never more so than in the 20th Century and sadly continuing in these first two-plus decades of the 21st Century. The brutal assassinations of the 20th Century embraced Presidents, Princes, Princesses, Politicians and Political activists, journalists, diplomats, and elected officials. Hardly a decade went by that there wasn't a killing or at least an attempt at one. Not a great deal has changed from the 20th Century to the times of this millennium.

So in the mind of Lucifer and his angels of death, we must understand the character of the ones selected to be Assassins in order to tell the histories and stories of those who become influenced by the cause. Lucifer therefore set down a breakdown of the requirements of those selected to do his dirty work. In his own words, Lucifer dictated:. "The assassin needs the usual qualities of a clandestine agent. He should be determined, courageous, intelligent, resourceful, and physically active. If special equipment is to be used, such as firearms or drugs, it is clear that he must have outstanding skill with such equipment. Except in terroristic assassinations, it is desirable that the assassin be transient in the area. He should have an absolute minimum of contact with the rest of the organisation and his instructions should be given orally by one person only. His safe evacuation after the act is absolutely essential, but here again, contact should be as limited as possible. It is preferable that the person issuing instructions also conduct any withdrawal or covering action that may be necessary."

Then Lucifer set a game plan for the members of the human order assigned to arrange the killings. In most assassinations, the assassin must be a fanatic of some sort. Politics, religion, and revenge are about the only feasible motives. Since a fanatic is unstable psychologically, he must be handled with extreme care. He must not know the identities of the other members of the organisation, for although it is intended that he die in the act, something may go wrong.

The earliest recorded assassination attempt was against the Pharaoh of the Middle Kingdom of Egypt, Amenemhat 1, around 2000 BC. Known by many as the "Mountain Chief" and by the crusaders as the "Old Man of the Mountains," he is the first identifiable leader of the assassins and, under him, an assassin named Bu Tahir Arrani had their first notable success in killing the vizier named Nizam al-Mulk Tusi.

Meller, a German archaeologist discovered the remains of the victim and by examination of the bones and modern-day DNA he reported to a German Newspaper his findings: "The prince had at least three severe injuries to his body, with a sharp dagger deep into his stomach and spine, splitting his collarbone." Meller noted "...his injuries are where Roman gladiators would have aimed. It must have been a trusted person close to him. Perhaps a relative, friend or bodyguard," he also told the German newspaper. "The ruler was unsuspecting and surprised by the attack. It could well be that he, like Julius Caesar in ancient Rome, was the victim of a conspiracy."

To understand the mood of the assassin and the influence of the angels of death over the whole being in their mission to kill we need to track back through history. It seems that governments, sects and factions are always prepared to waive elementary rules of social responsibility in order to eliminate opponents. It applies even more so today, those fundamentalist extremes that God and politics have been reconnected to deadly effect. it appears from historic records that that Lucifer is winning and great discernment of understanding needs to be investigated to lessen the cause of this energy. In such a savage world of predatory environment, who can be safe?

The earliest recorded assassination by a known group of collaborators was carried out in the deathly attack in 44BC during the 'Ides of March,' on the 15th of the month, the 'ides being the midpoint. saw the end of the life of **Gaius Julius Caesar**, Dictator of Rome, appointed for life was one of the most successful generals of the Roman Republic; and was the subject of Shakespeare's famous play. The plot thickened for the assassination and the stage was set for the murder most perfect Enter the Soothsayer who warned Caesar before the Ides to " Beware the Ides of March " but at the appointed hour as the great dictator passed the Soothsayer Caesar remarked to him: "The Ides of March have come", and in reply the Soothsayer responded: " Aaw! Caesar but not gone." In the brutal aftermath of the assassination, the foundation stone for the mighty Roman Empire that lasted over four centuries had begun and it marked a profoundly influential of all historic assassinations.

It was at the beginning of the year 44BC that the Roman Senate; those who ultimately took part in the assassination, named the 55-year-old political-general as 'dictator for life.' Caesar's military record could not be faulted, for in the previous decade from 55BC had pacified the Gauls and subdued the Balgae, those who inhabited the area known as modern France. He then conquered Armorica, present-day Brittany and invaded Britain.

Caesar's way to overtaking territory was by no means a softy-does-it approach. It is estimated that as many as 1 million people died in Gaul as a result of Caesar's "pacification." another 1 million were enslaved, 439 tribes subjugated and 800 cities destroyed. Caesar had made enemies at home as well as abroad. In 50 BC the Senate led by his arch-rival Pompey, ordered Caesar to return to Rome and his army on the expiration of his term as proconsul. Caesar judged, perhaps correctly, that if he entered Rome without the immunity enjoyed by a consul, or without the power of his army behind him, he would be at the very least politically neutered and at worst imprisoned or even murdered. Pompey publicly accused Caesar of insubordination and treason, making an accomodation between Caesar and his senatorial critics look impossible. Accordingly in 49 BC Caesar crossed the Rubicon River at Italy's northern boundary and with one legion he committed an illegal act for a Roman subject, thereby he lit the torch of the Romans first civil war in the decades.

So Pompey, now nervous about plunging the republic into a bloody anarchy, allowed Caesar, with his just one legion, to seize the initiative. With Caesar hot on his heels Pompey fled by sea to Spain. So Caesar left Italy in the hands of his allies, Marcus Aemilius Lepidus and Mark Anthony, and pursued Pompey into Spain and defeated his army. But the elusive general escaped to Greece and then subsequently into Egypt. Pompey hoped that King Ptolemy, his former client, would assist him, but the Egyptian king feared offending the victorious Caesar. On September 28, 48 BC, Pompey was invited to leave his ships and come ashore at Pelusium. As he prepared to step onto Egyptian soil, he was treacherously struck down and killed by an officer of Ptolemy. The first of early recorded assassinations of a Political General of the Roman Empire

Caesar secured his position as dictator of Rome and plunged his efforts into civil strife along with the help of Ptolemy's sister, wife and co-ruler, Cleopatra V11, Caesar defeated Ptolemaic forces and installed Cleopatra as sole ruler of Egypt. So an affair over the next 14 years took place and a son Caesarion was born. They never married as Roman law forbade a foreign powerful ruler to marry. During this time Caesar crushed Pompey's remaining supporters in Africa and Spain. He then returned to Italy in 45 BC with the known world seeming at his feet. As The dictator of Rome, he appointed his adopted son Octavian his sole heir; and overhauled the old Roman calendar, creating a regular year and bringing months roughly into line with the seasons. He introduced far-reaching economic reforms, regulated the price of grain to prevent rampant inflation and instituted a massive programme of public works centred on Rome itself- which soon had the formidable name of Caesar at its heart.

So why was it that the majority of the Senate plotted against him and plotted his assignation? Well had been appointed Rome's dictator for life and consul for ten years. It seems to them that the honours and power heaped upon him had gone to his head. He never rose to meet his senators was the custom of the time, but sat in the fashion of an Egyptian pharaoh. The Senators were also worried that he might appoint himself King; a custom that had been dispensed with centuries before, and overthrow the Senate and rule as a tyrant. Thus the plot thickened and the Senate conspirator's imagination perceived a headlong fight, so an allegiance was formed between Senators led by Caesar's former close friend Marcus Junius Brutus and his brother-in-law Cassius led a group calling themselves the 'Liberators,' resolved to murder Caesar before he could effect his alleged popular coup. [notation from Assassinated! Steven Parissien 2008].

So on the 15th March 44 BC, the group of senators led by Brutus called Caesar into the Forum to read a petition demanding he hand back the power to the Senate. Mark Anthony was privy to the Senate conversation the night before and realised the petition was a fake. Fearing the worst Mark Anthony went to warn Caesar about the plot to kill him but he was too late. The group of Senators had intercepted Caesar on the steps of Pompey's theatre to request he step into a portico and presented him with the bogus partition. As Caesar began to read, Tillius Cimber, one appointed as an Assassin, pulled down on Caesar's tunic and produced a dagger, ineffectively stabbing the dictator's neck. Caesar spun around and grabbed the arm of Casca, a nearby co-conspirator, demanding to know what he was doing. The petrified Casca shrieked for help whereupon the entire group of 'liberators,' including Brutus, produced daggers and were stabbing Caesar indiscriminately. Caesar attempted to escape but fell on the portico steps and his Assassins continued to stab him as he lay there. He had been stabbed 23 times before he died.

Once rumours of Caesar's assassination had begun to spread, Rome's people preferred to lock themselves in their houses to avoid ensuing bloodshed. Whilst a people's uprising failed to materialise, an angry mob set fire to the Forum and the city narrowly escaped further burnings. Caesar had been highly popular with the middle and lower classes, and it was this popularity that Octavian and Mark Anthony, Caesar's heir and right-hand man respectively, sought to harness. Mark Anthony made a dramatic eulogy that won over their Roman crowd. His ensuing hold on the citizens made many of the plotters and spoilers of the Senate fear that one king would now be replaced by another. The months and years that followed were plagued by civil war. Caesar's assassins were declared enemies of the state, and many of them were hunted down and excited. Octavian as heir apparent consolidated his hold on Italy, whilst Mark Anthony having fallen out of favour with Octavian established a power base in Caesar's old stamping ground of Gaul. Brutus still remained at large and encouraged by the rift between Octavian and Mark Anthony decided to march on Rome with a sizeable army of 17 legions.

Although initially successful against Octavian's forces, he failed in his attempt when Octavian and Mark Anthony combined forces and overcame Brutus' at Philippi in 42 BC. Brutus evaded capture but committed suicide rather than submit to an inevitable show trial and execution. Thus the last hopes of the Roman Republic died. The constitutional balance of power shifted from the senate when Octavian, known as Augustus became the first Roman Emperor.

Over the next decade, Octavian successfully marginalised Lepidus and drove Mark Anthony into self-imposed exile with the same Cleopatra who had bewitched Caesar in Egypt. In 31 BC the combined fleets of Anthony and Cleopatra were crushed by Octavian's naval fleet and the ill-fated lovers subsequently followed Brutus example and committed suicide.

So the senate plot to kill Caesar amid fears that he would be king and overrule their power base as a tyrant proved a reality under the rule of his appointed heir to the throne Octavian the Emperor King.

It will be seen that throughout the history of assassinations that follow, in the main it's the collective who assigns the killing of powerful leaders that are the real enemy. For the assassin, i is just a pawn in their game plan. The assassin accepts the assignment to kill without any emotional regard to his victim or his own soul or he is instinctively brainwashed by his own belief in the justification to kill which in some cases seems necessary.

CHAPTER 2.

THE ELITE AND ASSASSIN PAWNS

Throughout history, there have been leaders who were villains who have toppled celebrated heroes from their pedestals of high places in the pecking order as leaders. Sometimes it seems justifiable that those elites who plot the assassination of an evil ruler are in the right to do so. Perhaps Lucifer in his wisdom sees such a leader as impossible to deal with as such a ruler of mankind taking control of the legions of angels of death within at the expense of the power of the devil Lucifer himself. It therefore means the elite plotters take the best course of action to rid themselves of one who rules on earth deceiving themselves that he or she is incapable of being rehabilitated to their purposes thus assassination is their plan for the greater good.

One such was the **Roman Emperor Caligula** for whilst the sordid evidence of his life and character is scant, he did receive enough bad press to endorse his just desert in his violent death. 'Caligula' was his nickname from he was born to Emperor Augustus's adopted grandson, Germanicus, an immensely popular general who might have conceived himself to be Augustus's heir apparent. The boy born **Gaius Julius Caesar Germanicus** in 12 AD was the third of six surviving children and often accompanied his parents on military campaigns in Germany, during which time he became the mascot of his father's army and was often dressed in miniature soldier uniform with military boots and all. In this way, he acquired his affectionate nickname 'Caligula' literally meaning ' little boots.'

Caligula's upbringing was far from a happy one. His father was poisoned by Germanic assassins of his rival, Augustus's son Tiberius, and freed up as a hostage in the home of Tiberius's mother, the machiavellian schemer Livia, and later in the home of his grandmother Antonia. He was deliberately kept indoors and away from the world at large. It is during these years that acts of incest are reported for he was allowed to indulge himself liberally. It is from these years that accusations originated of his incest with his three sisters, his sole companions during that period.

The young future leader's morals took a further downturn into debauchery in 31 AD when he was given over to the care of Tiberius on the Mediterranean island of Capri. Here he was encouraged to indulge in any perversion he desired. Such practices engrained in such a young child together with the many killings he witnessed as a boy mascot riding into battle with his father no doubt set in motion the dark side of legions of evil angels of Lucifer for the remainder of his life.

When his so-called guardian Tiberius was smothered to death with a pillow by a prefect of the Praetorian Guard in 37 AD, it hastened Caligula to proclaim himself Emperor. Over the ensuing months after Tiberius' demise Caligula took care to keep public opinion on his side. He arranged the execution of Tiberius' hated lieutenant Sejanius and many allies of his appointees. Caligula worked swiftly to end Tiberius's treason trials, reformed the tax system, revived free elections and ironically banished sex offenders from the empire.

In the pattern that followed throughout the history of the Roman empire, he staged lavish spectacles for the public. Then soon after his accession, he ordered the construction of a temporary two-mile floating bridge across the Bay of Naples, using ships as pontoons from the resort of Baiae, the city later known as Naples, to the neighbouring port of Puteoli, an Italian Community. In the character actor he had been conditioned to as a child he proceeded to ride his favourite horse Incitatus, across the straits, wearing the breastplate of Alexander the Great- both to rival Persian King Xerxes crossing of the Hellespont and to defy a recent prophecy that he had 'no more chance of becoming emperor than riding a horse across the gulf of Baize.'

After recovering from a serious illness in 37AD Caligula's personality took a turn for the worst. His behaviour grew more erratic and violent. Perhaps the pedophile training he got as a small boy and being held in isolation affected his better nature and the legions of defects of character came to the fore. Thus in 39 AD Caligula removed a replaced Rome's consul without consulting the Senate, and publicly humiliated several senators by forcing them to run alongside his chariot in their full robes. He subsequently dressed up Gauls as German prisoners to provide proof of his vast but fictional military victories. On another occasion veteran Roman troops were ordered to collect sea shells as spoils of the sea, to illustrate victory over Neptune, the god of the sea. The retiring g to Rome, Caligula declared himself now a living god, thus ensuring that Augustus 'Cult of the Deified Emperor' now centred entirely on him. He began to take on the role of a character actor appearing at the Forum or the Temple of Castor dressed as a Dog and demanding that those present worship him. Then to add insult to past Roman ' gods' he had their heads replaced with replicas of his own likeness, even those of female deities.

Stories of Caligula's increased deranged behaviour circulated around the empire. None more so than the continual incest of his sibling sisters and the murder of his favourite Drusilla by his own hands. It is rumoured also that she l was in cahoots with another servant to kill her brother, so the deranged angered Caligula had no qualms about killing her. Apart from his rumoured attempt to deliver his sister's baby by caesarian section whom he had fathered may have been the cause of her death. There were a multiple number of strange rituals giving cause to his insanity None more so than having his favoured horse, Incitatus installed as a priest and giving the beast a house to reside in,- complete with a marble stable, golden manger and jewelled necklaces. It is said he intended to make the horse a member of the Senate was most likely a fable.

Caligula was in every way deranged and dangerous. There was widespread testimony of his impressively sized genitalia which he exposed and happily manipulated at public games. A much more serious event was the opening of a brothel in the palace which he populated with Senator's wives, who were required to perform while the hapless patricians looked on in horror. Week in and out his behaviour became more unpredictable, and when there were not enough convicts to fight the lions in the arena, he threw spectators in to make up the numbers.

For years the behaviour of the Emperor's increased insanity was protected by his German bodyguards and by the Roman Praetorian Guard. It is said he made it a crime to look down on him from above and to leave him everything in one's will. It was only when the Praetorians' senior commander, another Cassius, had enough after he received a series of wounds to his groin during long years of devoted service that things came to a head. Caligula had often mocked Cassius for his injury decreeing that he was a eunuch whenever Cassius Chararea was on duty. So on the 24th January 41 AD Cassisu Charerea and another guardsman accosted Caligula whilst he was addressing an acting troupe of young men during a series of games being held in the honour of the 'Divine Augustus.' Cassius approached Caligula requesting an order of duty taking the opportunity to attack him. After the first blow, Caligula cried for help, prompting fellow conspirators too strike as well. Suetonius the Roman historian recorded at least thirty wounds, several of them delivered to the despised Emperor's genitals. Another soldier conspirator then sought out Caligula's wife and daughter and murdered them.

Back at the arena Caligula's enraged German bodyguards arrived at the scene of the assassination too late; stricken with grief and rage, they responded with a vicious attack on innocent Senators and arena spectators. In the ensuing mayhem, Caligula's half-forgotten uncle, **Claudius** was dragged away to safety whereupon the praetorian guards declared him emperor.

The Roman Empire experienced numerous assassinations in its history and little good came from its four hundred years of worldly control to benefit the public. Lucifer had his way as did his army of evil angels of death during those times. Under **Claudius's** rule 41 AD- 54 AD, the Roman Empire had the most major of expansion of territories since the reign of Augustus. Thrace, Judea and other territories were added to the empire at the east end of the Mediterranean. In North Ad Africa, Caligula's annexation of Mauritania was completed. However, the most important new conquest, both politically and economically was the area known as Britannia at the empire's northern extreme.

Whilst Britain had been invaded by Julius Caesar in 55 BC, no permanent Roman settlement had followed. Now Claudius intends to claim this rich prize for his empire. The disunited British tribes failed to ally against the might of the Roman legions, allowing the Roman legions to overpower them all one at a time. Claudius in his haste to join the fray sailed to Britain with additional legions and to the amusement of the British with a herd of Elephants. When the only British general who offered any real opposition, Caracas, was finally captured by the Romans in 50 AD, he was granted clemency by Claudius and he lived out his days in a captive curiosity on land provided by the Roman state.

Claudius worked hard at his job, starting work at midnight every day. His efforts began to pay off and he made major improvements to Rome's judicial system, passed laws protecting sick slaves, extended citizenships and increased women's privileges, and may have done a lot more good for the Roman Empire had he not been assassinated. He is remembered for expanding the Roman Empire- the construction of many roads, aqueducts and other infrastructure. Ancient historians agree that Claudius was murdered by poison – possibly contained in mushrooms or on a feather – and died in the early hours of 13 October 54. Nearly all implicate his powerful wife, Agrippina, as the instigator. Her motive was to install her son Nero as emperor. Well, we all know how that went. Nero is known as one of Rome's most infamous rulers, notorious for his cruelty and debauchery. He ascended to power in AD 54 aged just 16 and died at 30. He ruled at a time of great social and political change, overseeing momentous events such as the Great Fire of Rome and Boudica's, the Queen of the British tribe's rebellion in Britain So what did he accomplish during his reign? Well, Nero built a grand palace, the Golden House, which was apparently magnificent, but it was so resented by the public and by his successors that it was almost completely dismantled. His armies put down rebellions in Britain as well as doing some good. He brought down taxes in Rome, reduced the price of food and often performed on stage singing and dancing for big crowds and was patron of the arts. However, Nero was no less insane than Caligula, with his most spectacular act being the burning of Rome under his command like it was a theatrical event.

In my contemplation, I was reminded of the words of the great Alphonse de Lamartine, French poet, historian and statesman who achieved renown for his lyrics, which established him as the key figure in the Romantic movement in French literature. "I shall teach my readers by facts, by events and by the hidden meaning of those great historic dramas of which we perceive only as scenery and the actors, while their plot is contrived by a hidden hand." I was coming to some understanding now of my purpose in writing of Lucifer and his evil angels of death infiltrating the minds of his assassins in my writings, uncovering the plot of Lucifer, the hand in the dark and that of the hidden hand within Judaism and Christendom itself.

Lucifer and his army of angels of death seem to be wining the way of the human heart and mind to this time but let us fast forward to the story of King Henry 11 of England and the tragedy of Thomas Becket, the Archbishop of Canterbury c.1118-1170 to uncover the work of the Assassins of that time in killing of a good man for the sake of evil intent.

Thomas Becket, also known as Saint Thomas of Canterbury, Thomas of London and later Thomas à Becket served as Lord Chancellor from 1155 to 1162, and then notably as Archbishop of Canterbury from 1162 until his death in 1170. According to a study, the addition of the 'auto Becket's name is based upon Robin Hood characters such as George a' Green and Alan a'

Dale, which were popular in the 1590s, with the name designed to make Becket into a sort of rustic figure of fun by Protestants. Thomas Becket, a London merchant's son, was a complex person – in his youth, he was a normal ebullient young man, stormy and proud, selfish and arrogant, vain, and anxious to please, but in later life, became one of the most pious and devout Archbishops of the 12th century.

As a boy, he attracted the attention of the Archbishop of Canterbury Theobald. He saw in Thomas a clever boy and being the 12th century social mobility was really only possible through the patronage of the Church. Thomas was aware of this and won favour with his subsequent rise from obscurity to high office was meteoric. Theobald quickly sent him on missions abroad, employed him as a clerk and ultimately appointed him Archdeacon of Canterbury. It was fashionable then for those of unique ability to be educated to the priesthood as a means of understanding the world at large and religious theology. So it was not long before Becket was appointed into the king's orbit of celestial grace. Henry 11 had assumed the throne in 1154 amid two decades of bitter civic war between throne rival claimants, Stephen and Henry's mother Matilda. Henry declared as his primary mission to establish a strong and stable government. To that end, he wanted a reliable lord chancellor who would be accepted by most of the powerful vested interests in the kingdom. This he found in Archbishop Theobald's' nominee: Thomas Becket. The king noted Thomas's close links with the City of London's rich business leaders with a great deal of political influence. His own father was highly influential in London and reasonably well off and of Norman background, and with the Archbishops endorsing the young protege this pleased the king too. What the king didn't bargain for was their relationship would grow into a close friendship. Becket soon became known as Henry's hard-fisted right-hand man.

He brutally endorsed Henry's authority in the extensive French territories, the Angevin Empire, that endorsed the king's marriage to Eleanor of Aquitaine in 1152. He busily reversed the tax system to the fury of the nobles for the first time full tax had been imposed on them in 20 years. And he became Henry's most indispensable courier, advising Henry on social events, palace etiquette as well as legal, fiscal and military matters. King Henry sent his eldest son and heir, Prince Henry, to live in Becket's household. The outcome of this unusual fostering, however eventually drove a wedge between Henry11 and Becket, for the young Prince later reported that Becket had shown him more fatherly love than his own father ever did in his life.

In 1161 Archbishop Theobald died, and Henry, after some hesitation, installed his friend Thomas as Theobald's successor. This had the effect of removing Becket from the king's and his councillor. Becket was unhappy and saw his promotion to the primacy of England as a means of neutralising his political influence. He turned to the Pope for support just at the time when Henry was seeking to reduce papal influence over the English Church. He provocatively opposed the king's new tax proposals, insisted that barons do homage to him for a land connected with the Archbishop of Canterbury, and upheld the Church's indecent legal system thereby preventing the secular authorities from prosecuting clergy who had committed a crime. In short, Becket metamorphosed from a royal political fixer into a self-appointed defender of the Church. Henry had mistaken his man for he had expected his loyal chancellor to rally the Church beyond the throne and not distance the Church from the state and publicly challenge the king's authority. King Henry known for his bad temper was enraged at Becket's opposition and resolved to remove him as archbishop to ensure his humiliation. A court case on a land dispute saw Becket at Northampton Castle for a royal council meeting in October 1164 but the king refused to see him. So Becket applied to the king to leave England, but before the king gave his decision Becket fled the castle and the country.

Becket's flight quickly became an international incident. He arrived at the court of Henry's greatest enemy, French King Louis V11 who was already harbouring the pope. His melodramatic appeal to Alexander 111 won him papal support. By 1165 Alexander 111 was denouncing Henry's actions, and the following year he appointed Becket as his papal legate from England. Meanwhile, Henry did himself no favour with Rome by mean-spiritedly dismissing Becket's allies and appointees. More positively he allied himself with the Popes' enemies in the Holy Roman Empire and consolidated all his territories in what is now Western France. Henry had decided to have his son Prince Henry reign as joint king, but a legitimate coronation could only be conducted by the Archbishop of Canterbury.

By 1168 Beckets' presence in France was becoming an embarrassment to Louis V11, preventing him from putting out peace feelers in the wake of Henry's armies. Even Pope Alexander, far more of a diplomat than his ambitious Archbishop of Canterbury, restrained Becket from more intemperate action while secretly trying to heal the breach with the king. Louis and

Alexander brokered a series of wide-ranging negotiations at Montmirail in January 1169. Both Henry and Becket were invited and both accepted. However, their attempted negotiation ultimately failed because of Becket's righteous pride, and Henry went ahead with the coronation of the Young King anyway in the Archbishop's absence.

Pressured by the French, Becket finally agreed to a reconciliation with Henry in July 1170. On 1st December 1170, Becket's ship docked at Sandwich in Kent, but he had already scored a major goal before leaving France. He had with the pope's connivance, excommunicated the Archbishop of York, the other English Church province, for officiating at the Young King's coronation. The timing of this act was poorly conceived and would ultimately cause Becket's assassination. To the enrage Henry it seemed nothing had changed. Becket was still the same self-centred, overground and vain prelate. In the end, tensions between the two men would only be solved by an act of violence.

He had considered ridding himself of Becket the year earlier. but this time, however, there were four knights willing to take the King at his word.

On 29thy December 1179 Reginald Fitzurse, Hugh de Moreville, William de Tracy and Richard Le Breton were eager to win the king's favour, but not over-endowed with intelligence. sets out to confront the archbishop at his cathedral. Becket. They were offered dinner and then followed him into the Church for vespers. They considered murdering Becket with his own cathedral cross. However, in an alcoholic state, one struck him with the flat of his sword declaring ' Flee, you're a dead man.' The archbishop faced them with calm and dignity and resigned them to do their worst. This they did and Becket fell in a reign of sword blows. The life of the man ended and remorseful kings began to regret sanctioning Becket's death warrant.

To absolve themselves of the Killing of a priest the knights made their way to the Pope in Rome, who commanded them to go on pilgrimage to the Holy Land. All four are believed to have died either in Jerusalem or on their way there, or perhaps they were reassigned to be Knights of the Templar protecting pilgrims on The Way and given this penance as part of their absolution from their sin.

The life and death of another great man of Britain that parallels that of Thomas Becket was another saintly disposition. **Thomas More** was born in London on February 7, 1478. His father, Sir John More, was a lawyer and judge who rose to prominence during the reign of Edward IV. His connections and wealth would help his son, Thomas, rise in the station as a young man. Thomas' mother was Agnes Graunger, the first wife of John More. John would have four wives during his life, but they each died, leaving John as a widower. Thomas had two brothers and three sisters, but three of his siblings died within a year of their birth. Such tragedies were common in England during this time.

It is likely that Thomas was positively influenced from a young age by his mother and siblings. He also attended St. Anthony's School, which was said to be one of the best schools in London at that time. In 1490, he became a household page to John Morton, the Archbishop of Canterbury and Lord Chancellor of England. Archbishop Morton was a Renaissance man who inspired Thomas to pursue his own education. Thomas More entered Oxford in 1492, where he would learn Latin, and Greek and prepare for his future studies. In 1494, he left Oxford to become a lawyer and he trained in London until 1502 when he was finally approved to begin practice.

Thomas More married his first wife, Jane Colt in 1505. They would have four children together before her death in 1511. Their marriage was reportedly happy and Thomas often tutored her in music and literature. After Jane's death in 1511, Thomas quickly remarried Alice Harpur Middleton, who was a wealthy widow. Alice was not particularly attractive, and her temperament was less docile than Jane's. The wedding took place less than a month after Jane's passing and was poorly received by his friends. It was rumoured that Thomas married her because he wanted a stepmother for his four children, and she was a woman of wealth and means. It is believed the pair knew each other for some time prior to their marriage. They would have no children together. Thomas accepted Alice's daughter from her previous marriage as his own.

 Thomas was considered a doting father, and he often wrote letters to his children when he was away at work. He also insisted that his daughters receive the same education as his son. His daughters were well-known for their academic accomplishments. In 1504, More was elected to Parliament to represent the region of Great Yarmouth, and in 1510 rose to represent London. During his service to the people of London, he earned a reputation as being honest and effective. He became a Privy Counsellor in 1514.

More also honed his skills as a theologian and a writer. Among his most famous works is "Utopia," about a fictional, idealistic island society. The work is widely regarded as part satire, part social commentary, and part

suggestion. Utopia is considered one of the greatest works of the late Renaissance and was widely read during the Enlightenment period. It remains
well-read by scholars read today. From 1517 on, Henry VIII took a liking to
Thomas More, and gave him posts of ever-increasing responsibility. In
1521, he was knighted and made Under-Treasurer of the Exchequer.

The King's trust in More grew with time and More was soon made Chancellor of the Duchy of Lancaster, which gave him authority over the northern portion of England on behalf of Henry. Thomas More stopped in good
stead with King Henry for over the next decade. More became Lord Chancellor in 1529. and was immediately effective, working with speed and precision which is admired today. He was likely one of Henry VIII's most effective servants and was fiercely loyal to the king.

During his tenure as Lord Chancellor, More prosecuted those accused of
heresy and worked tirelessly to defend the Catholic faith in England. This
was an arduous, but achievable task as long as he enjoyed Henry's favour.
However, in 1530, as Henry worked to obtain an annulment from his wife,
Catherine, More refused to sign a letter to the Pope, requesting an annulment. This was More's first time crossing Henry. The relationship between
More and Henry became strained again when seeking to isolate More, Henry purged many of the clergy who supported the Pope. It became clear to all
that Henry was prepared to break away from the Church in Rome, something More knew he could not condone.

In 1532, More found himself unable to work for Henry VIII, whom he felt
had lost his way as a Catholic. Faced with the prospect of being compelled
to actively support Henry's schism with the Church, More offered his resignation, citing failing health. Henry accepted it, although he was unhappy
with what he viewed as flagging loyalty. However, In 1533, More refused
to attend the coronation of Anne Boylen, who was now the Queen of England. More instead wrote a letter of congratulations. The letter, as opposed
to his direct presence, offended Henry greatly. The king viewed More's absence as an insult to his new queen and an undermining of his authority as
head of the church and state. Henry then had charges trumped up against
More, but More's own integrity protected him. In the first instance, he was
accused of accepting bribes, but there was simply no evidence that could be
obtained or manufactured. He was then accused of conspiracy against the
king, because he allegedly consulted with a nun who prophesied against

Henry and his wife, Anne. However, More was able to produce a letter in which he specifically instructed the nun, Elizabeth Barton, not to interfere with politics.

On April 13, 1534, More was ordered to take an oath, acknowledging the legitimise of Anne's position as queen, of Henry's self-granted annulment from Catherine, and the superior position of the King as head of the church. More accepted Henry's marriage to Anne, but refused to acknowledge Henry as head of the church, or his annulment from Catherine. This led to his arrest and imprisonment. He was locked away in the Tower of London. He faced trial on July 1 and was convicted by a court that included Anne Boylen's own father, brother and uncle, hardly an impartial jury. Still, More had one thing going for him. He could not break the law of which he was accused if he remained silent. However, he had no defence against treachery, and several dubious witnesses were able to contrive a story that he had spoken words that had the same effect as treason. Despite a brilliant defence of himself and persuasive testimony, grounded in truth and fact, More was convicted in fifteen minutes. The court sentenced him to be hanged, drawn, and quartered, which was the traditional punishment for treason.

Henry was pleased with the outcome, although likely upset that one of his favourite advisers refused, even upon pain of death, to sanction his annulment and break from Rome. Henry was a Machiavellian king and while he may have regretted the loss of More, he was more intent upon retaining his authority. As a final act of mercy, Henry commuted More's punishment to mere decapitation.

More ascended the scaffold on July 6, 1535, joking to his executioners to help him up the scaffold, but that he would see himself down. He then made a final statement, proclaiming that he was "the king's good servant, but God's first." It is reported that the executioner did not want to proceed to cut off the head of Sir Thomas and said something to the effect. " You must do the duty of your King, for do not be afraid of your occupational requirement." Following his death, it was revealed that More wore a hair shirt, a garment destined to be itchy, and worn too as a sign of atonement and repentance. It became obvious to all that he was a man of deep piety, asceticism, voluntary self-discipline, and penitence. More's decapitated body was buried in the Chapel of St. Peter ad Vincula at the Tower of London, in an unmarked grave. His head was put on display, but his daughter Margaret possibly bribed someone to take it down. The skull may be in the vault of a church in Canterbury. Whilst More's death can not be assumed an assassination, it rates high in the course of a good man doing his duty in the Agency of God's plan as opposed to that of Lucifer and in that sense, it should remain here in the telling of this tale.

The real appearance of the Arabic 'hash' injecting killers came with numerous stories of a group of Muslim drug-entered madmen that date back centuries. These contracted assassins were shown the kingdom of the heavens as a reward for their tasks in contract killing on the belief of the order of their leaders of the day. The stories that emerged where they were ordered to attain a heaven-on-earth state may be an old wives tale, but the invention has had astonishing success to the present day in the world of assigned killings. On the reliance of mind-altering drugs, it is believed that Assassins can be encouraged to foolhardy murderous attacks and often suicidal ones.

CHAPTER 3.

THE ANGELS OF DEATH REIGN.

The Assassins were an offshoot of the Ismaili community, itself a sect of Shia Islam. They first appeared at the end of the 11th century in Persia and Syria, led by their charismatic revolutionary leader Hasan-Sabah. His member followers having seized a series of castles in eastern Persia used them as their base to erode the integrity of the Seljuk Empire to the west. The tragic murders of leading Seljuk commanders and prominent members of the Sunni Muslim faith, initially at Hasan's behest, began around 1100. But it was their murder of a Western potentate in 1192 that brought them to the attention of the wider world.

The perfect example of the man who seemed to have everything was **Conrad of Montferrat,** crusader leader c1145-1192. He was famously handsome, world rich and by birthright well connected being the cousin of the Holy Roman Emperor, Frederick 1 'Barbarossa', to King Louis V11 of France and to Duke Leopold V of Austria. He was celebrated across Europe as the epitome of chivalry and courage, and Christendom's most illustrious warriors. Conrad had been trained as a diplomat and, skilled military leader, defeating Emperor Frederick's army at Camerino in 1179. When he appeared in Byzantine court in 1180, he was observed as of 'beautiful appearance with a spring in his step, speaking with courage and intelligence and his body flowered with much body strength.'

In 1187 this man of exceptional military talent set off to join his father in the kingdom of Jerusalem, which had been established by Crusaders in 1099 but was currently under the threat of the legendary Kurdish-born Sultan Saladin. Conrad arrived to find the crusader had been crushed by Saladin at the battle of Hattin, and the King of Jerusalem, Guy of Lusignan was Saladin's prisoner as was his own father Duke William V of Montserrat; as the city of Jerusalem and fortress of Acre were with Saladin. So Conrad set sail to the besieged port of Tyre with the idea of rescuing the prisoners and further protecting the city. Saladin assaulted Tyre by land and sea and offered to release Conrad's father if he gave up Tyre. Apparently, the old man had told his son to stand firm even when threatened with death, and Conrad replied to the Seljuk leader that his father had already lived a long life and confronting Saladin aimed his won crossbow at him. This prompted Saladin to remark; " This man is an unbeliever and very cruel.' He then agreed to release William V to his son's custody. Then at the end of December 1187, Conrad launched a bold attack against the besieged Seljuks and routed Saladin's Egyptian navy and his landward troops. Tyre was saved at least for the present.

Conrad was the only Christian general who appeared to offer any hope of saving the embittered kingdom of Jerusalem. Saladin released Guy of Lusignan, who duly appeared at Tyre and demanded that Conrad owe him tenant rights and hand over the keys of the city to him. Unsurprisingly Conrad, who had a more impressive military record than Guy's limited resume refused, and declared that Guy had effectively lost the throne at the battle of Hattin. Conrad even refused permission for Guy and his Queen to enter the city until the matter had been arbitrated by the Holy Roman Emperor. Conrad then cemented his own claim to the kingdom by marrying the only major claimant after Guy, Isabella of Jerusalem. Whilst Isabella was happily married at the time, her ambitious mother cheerfully colluded to have her marriage annulled on the spurious grounds that she was underage. The less-than-happy couple were thus joined in matrimony on 24th November 1190.

Guy of Lusignan then sought guidance from the newly installed Richard 1 King of England whom he knew had his eyes set on restoring Christian fortune in the Middle East. Guy won Richard's support, who pledged to restore Guy's throne and demobilise Conrad. Richard then set sail for the Holy Land to do battle. Meanwhile, Conrad had further strengthened his winning hand by raking back the key fortress of Acrem, which had been taken by Saladin two years previous in the siege. The two commanders then came to an agreement and Guy of Lusignan was reconfirmed as King of Jerusalem with the promise that Conrad was to be made sole heir as well as the governor of the cities of Tyre, Beirut and Sidon.

The shrinking village of Jerusalem was not big enough to have two prima donna commanders, so it was inevitable there would be fallout. In 1911 despite the Seljuk hostages captured by French forces, Richard 1 had the hostages killed and Conrad took refuge in Tyre in fear of his life. Saladin meanwhile rightly surmised that he did not need to move against the Cr Christian army when so much in-house fighting was happening. In 1192 Saladin was surprised to find Conrad in open negotiation with him. Meanwhile attempting to broker an alliance with him against Richard. Unbeknownst to Conrad, Saladin had already approached Richard to broker a marriage between his brother and Richard's widow sister.

Weary of the internal strife, the Crusader barons pressed for a rapid solution to power the vacuum in the kingdom, and in April 1192 the crown of Jerusalem was put to the vote. To Richard's horror, the nobles elected Conrad as head. So Richard arbitrarily awarded Guy of Lusignan the island of Cyprus as a consolation prize, which he ruled nominally until his death in 1194. Unfortunately, Conrad's triumph was tragically short-lived, When he returned from a visit to his friend and kinsman, Bishop of Beauvais, he was attacked by two assassins who stabbed him twice in his back and side. His guards killed one of the attackers and captured the other, but Conrad died shortly afterwards. He was appropriately buried in Tyre, in the Church of Hospitals. Under torture, the surviving Assassin claimed that Richard 1 was behind the killing. It is quite unlikely Saladin's senior officials were involved as the Sultan was no friend of the assassins.

Much of the European elite believed Richard was guilty of Conrad's murder, and as a result, he was a marked man. Returning home from the Middle East overland, Richard was recognised in disguise by Conrad's nephew captured and imprisoned him. Accused of Conrad's murder by one of the late King of Jerusalem's cousins Leopold V of Austria, Richard requited the Assassins leader to vindicate him. A letter purportedly came from the Assassins leader, Rashid al-Din Sinan, appeared to do the trick, but it is now believed that was a forgery. Leopold certainly didn't believe it and instead, he handled his illustrious prisoner to the New Holy Roman Emperor, Henry V1, who demanded an enormous ransom for Richard's release. and a host of taxes decimated clergy and laity in England and Richard's Angevin Empire raised the 150,000 marks to have Richard released in February 1194.

The 12th-century Assassins thrived for another eighty years or so. In the 1270s, assassination attempts on Western European crusaders such as the Count of Tripoli and Prince Edward of England, later King Edward 1, together with Philip de Montfort in Tyre in 1270 were unsuccessful. Whilst the reputation lived on in myth and legends for centuries, their political powers were extinguished by the invading Mongols, who swept over their Persian homelands and erased assassin mountain strongholds.

So the next major Assassination plot did not transpire until the assassination of **Lord Darnley,** Henry Stewart consort to Mary Queen of Scots in February 1567. Henry's life may have passed relatively uneventfully and lasted a lot longer, were it not for the fact that before his 20th birthday, he married his relative and most eligible woman in Scotland, and thereby entered the turbulent personal and political dramas that constituted the life of Mary Stuart, Queen of Scots. Before two years were up, Darnley fell victim to an assassination plot, but not before conspiring in a murder plot of his own.

Mary Stuart was born in 1542, the daughter of James V of Scotland and French wife Mary Guise. Six-year-old princess Mary became Queen of Scotland when her father died at age thirty and she was crowned the fi following year. It could not have been the worst time of monarchial instability: the Scottish army had recently been defeated at the battle of Solway Moss, and Scotland risked England's takeover. Mary had been betrothed to Edward, son of Henry V111 to enable heirs to the kingdom of Scotland and England. When Mary of Guise soon made it clear that she would not abide by the treaty, Henry V111 launched a series of raids on Scottish territory, resulting in a full-scale invasion in 1544. Despite the Scots' overwhelming defeat at the battle of Pinkie Claugh in 1547, Mary of Guise ensured the toddler queen always evaded arrest.

Mary of Guise then turned to the traditional alliance between Scotland and France with French King Henry 11 proposing the two kingdoms unite by marrying the infant Mary to his newborn son Francis. On 7th July 1548, whilst English forces were devastating the Scottish Lowlands, a marriage treaty was signed by Mary and dispatched to the French court. Eleven years passed until the vivacious, pretty and clever Mary Stuart impressed the court, dismayed by the macho posturing of the king, became an accomplished linguist and musician, and mastered horsemanship, falconry, and needlework.

Mary married Francis on 24th April 1558, and on this accession a year later became Queen of France, as well as the Queen regnant of Scotland. That same year her cousin Elizabeth 1, acceded to the English throne, and Mary became Elizabeth's natural heir apparent, notwithstanding that Henry V11s had explicitly barred the Stuarts from the succession.

However, Francis, who had always been a sickly young man, died on 5th December 1560 after only 15 months on the throne. Mary was now diplomatically isolated. Five months previously on her mother's death, the French tamely undertook to withdraw troops from Scotland and recognise Elizabeth 1's sovereignty in England which Mary refused to ratify. However, when France was wracked by civil strife she had no alternative but to return to Scotland.

On arrival in Scotland on 19th August 1561, she soon realised she had merely exchanged one developed civil war for another. Scotland, was like France being torn apart b with fighting between Catholic and Protestant factions, the latter of which was being led by Mary's illegitimate half-brother, the Earl of Moray. Much to the Catholic rage, however, Mary chose a compromise path, balancing the breach between the two faiths and attempted to do likewise by healing the wounds between Scotland and England. A crude diplomatic gesture of inviting Elizabeth to her kingdom backfired when Elizabeth refused the offer with a suggestion that Mary should instead journey to England. So Mary sent an ambassador to England to press her case as heir to the throne of England. The response predictably was a swift rejection by the English Queen and parliament. Two years later, in the face of the parliament's growing unease about the succession, Elizabeth agreed to consider Mary's claim, provided Mary married a man of Elizabeth's choosing. Her choice was her current favourite, the self-important protestant aristocrat Robert Dudley, Earl of Leicester. Not surprisingly Queen Mary dismissed such a suggestion. To add fuel to the fire, Mary, in July 1565, rashly married the Catholic Lord Darnley, whom she had met in France four years beforehand. Consequences of the marriage followed swiftly and Elizabeth broke off diplomatic relations, and the Earl of Moray joined with other protestant nobles in open rebellion.

Mary, never a good judge of men's character, had troubles with Darnley who proved immature, prone to possible violent effects of syphilitic illness, and had no less political sensitivity than his wife. He demanded he be made sovereign, but instead content with the role of consort. Mary became pregnant but was even less safe from Darnley's physical attacks. He once tried to force a miscarriage and became increasingly estranged from Mary. Darnley focused his jealousy on her private secretary, the Italian-born David Rizzio and plotted with his former Protestant enemies.

Rizzio had arrived at the Scottish court in 1561 on the staff of the Duke of Savoy's ambassador. He was handsome and liked Mary as an accomplished musician. By 1564 he was not only the queen's secretary but also her principal adviser. On the 15th March 1566, Darnley's thugs assassinated Rizzio by stabbing him in the presence of the pregnant queen at the palace of Holyroodhouse. Not only Mary but the whole court was deeply tainted by this appalling public and clumsy murder. May gave birth to son James a few months later, but before the boy's first birthday, his father was dead. On 10th February 1567, the bodies of Darnley and his servant were discovered in the garden at Edinburgh house in which they had stayed. Darnley had been recuperating from an illness possibly brought on by an advanced stage of syphilis. A violent explosion had occurred that night in the house, yet the evidence pointed to Darnley having escaped that assassination attempt, only to be strangled when he ran outside.

Suspicion had fallen on Mary's latest, the Protestant 4th Earl of Bothwell, as Mary found herself out of the frypan and into the fire. An enquiry she set up to investigate Darnley's murder exonerated Bothwell, but it convinced no one. On 24th April she saw her son for the last time. Then the notoriously violent and unpredictable Bothwell' abducted the suspicious queen and took her to Dunbar Castle where, apparently, he raped her. Under severe duress, Mary agreed to marry him. On 6th May 1567, barely three months after Darnley's assassination, the unlikely couple returned to Edinburg and were married according to Protestant rites.

By mid-June 1567, just weeks into the marriage. Mary found herself in prison in a castle on an island in the middle of Loch Leven. She had miscarried twins have coincided them with Bothwell, so she abdicated the Scottish throne in favour of her one-year-old son James who was under the regency of the ubiquitous Earl of Moray. On 2nd May 1568, Mary escaped from Loch Leven and managed to raise a small army. This was to be her last stand as government forces decimated her army. She fled to England on 19th May, only to be imprisoned at Carlisle.

Elizabeth 1, to her credit, refused to try Mary for the murder of Darnley, hoping to protect some of her fellow sovereign's majesty. An enquiry uncovered eight letters purportedly written by Mary to Boswell which incriminating passages but they were later proved to be forgeries. Elizabeth sought to avoid our right 'guilty' verdict, but Mary was in fact condemned by association. In point of fact, Mary was considered too much of a risk to be set free at a time when her candidacy for the English throne could been used by the power of the Catholics of continental Europe, notably the King of France or Spain, as a pretext for invasion or usurpation. Mary's remaining 18 years of her life were spent in England under house arrest. To the more extreme sort of disaffect Catholic plotter, Mary was always a potential replacement for Elizabeth on the throne of England, and this was to seal her fate.

The discovery of the Catholic plot in 1586 to dethrone the English queen forced Elizabeth to act. The plan was to assassinate Elizabeth and install Mary as queen with the help of Philip 11 of Spain and the Catholic Guise factions of Mary's maternal family in France. Mary may not have been aware of the ploy but she was put on trial for treason. She denied the accusation and was spirited in defence but ultimately convicted. A reluctant and vacillated Elizabeth was finally persuaded to sign the death warrant and Mary was beheaded at Fotheringay Castle in Northamptonshire on 8th February 1587. Even in death, her luck had failed her, for it took three blows to hack off her head, the executioner resorting to using his own axe as a saw. Her body was embalmed and buried in a leaded coffin in the place of her execution then buried at Peterborough Cathedral in 1588. The Coffin was exhumed in 1612 when her son James 1 of England ordered that she be reinterred at Westminster Abbey.

The shadow of the mind of assassins always finds some justification for the deeds they commit on behalf of the plotters, and religious or political power causes are often at the heart of the plan. William of Orange was the Protestant founder and ruler of the modern nation, the Netherlands. A French zealot Balthasar Gerard, born in 1557 as a French Catholic got caught up in the Reformation. He was attached to the prospect of eradicating a high-profile enemy of Catholicism and gaining a sizeable cash incentive being offered by Philip 11 of Spain to kill the 'outlaw' William. Gerard vowed to travel to the Netherlands and do the deed himself.

In May 1584 Gerard presented himself to William, posing as a French nobleman who would guarantee the support of French sympathisers to both the besieged French Protestants and those who feared that their country was about to be surrounded by the Spanish. William loved the story and sent Gerard back to France as an intermediary. He returned to the Netherlands again having brought pistols on his return voyage, and on 10th July made an appointment with William of Orange at the latter home in Delft.

Upon hearing Gerard had arrived William left his first-floor room and descended the stairs to the hall. Barely had he set foot in the hallway when Gerard shot him in the chest at point-blank range and fled. According to a traditional Dutch account, Williams's last words were: *"Lord, My Lord, have pity upon me and my people."* William 1's assassination was a setback to the Dutch nation which was then fighting for independence from Spanish overlords. It was a blow from which the Dutch almost didn't recover. It was only after 64 years of that intermittent slaughter of William of Orange that the Dutch were finally awarded their complete independence.

William of Orange was born in 1533 at his family seat of Dillenburg in Nassau, then a Dutch province. He was the son of the Count of Nassau, raised as a Lutheran, he inherited the title of 'Prince of Orange' from his cousin when only 11 years old. William's nominal overlord was the Holy Roman Emperor Charles V, Protestantism's most implacable opponent, and he not only imposed himself as the province's agent but also insisted William be educated as a Catholic. The young prince obeyed and rose to be one of Charles V's most trusted Dutch advisers and most effective military commanders. In 1555 Charles V, to the astonishment of Europe, succumbed to his morbid fear of death and began the process of abdicating his many lands and titles. The sovereignty of the Netherlands was passed to the eldest son Philip, who then became Philip 11 of Spain. Philip too relied on William's advice and authority and viewed him as a trustworthy bulwark against the rising tide of Protestantism. He appointed William governor under his own authority of the Northern Netherlands province of Holland, Zealand and provided him with an independent Dukedom that passed to Habsburg in 1477. Phillip however chose to rule the Netherlands from Madrid, and in his absence, the tensions caused by the spread of Protestantism and the heavy taxes imposed by the Spanish escalated to widespread violence. Full-scale warfare erupted in 1568, a date which the Dutch regard as the first year of the Eighty Year War, the titanic conflict that finally led to Dutch independence in 1648.

William already had signalled sympathy from the nobles including his brother Louis who presented Philip's regent, Margaret of Parma, with a partition demanding toleration for Protestants. He also distanced himself from the cherished religious beliefs in icons 1566, when Calvinist mobs ransacked the churches and shrines. Guided by William and his fellow moderates, Margaret's inclinations were compromised. She soon found her authority strenuously undermined by Phillips Spanish hawks, who opposed any concessions to the Protestants.

As order deteriorated throughout the province Philip 11 announced the despatch of a fanatically Catholic Spanish general, the Duke of Alva. William astutely recognised that the time for compromise or his characteristic circumspection had passed, and he withdrew to this seat in Nassau. The Duke of Alva's administration of the province proved disastrous. In August 1567, the Duke established the Council of Troubles, also known as the 'Council of the Blood,' to assess those suspected of involvement with Protestant violence. In an act of total stupidity and complete political misunderstanding, he alienated William by including him in a list of 10,000 to be summoned before the council. Wisely William chose not to appear, and the Chief magistrate was thus deprived of his title and properties and declared an outlaw by Phillip.

So almost overnight William successfully transformed himself from the austere pillar of Spanish establishment into a fiesta, pragmatic leader of Dutch rebels. He then used his considerable wealth to fund the Protestant naval groups who raised the coastal settlements and he helped raise an army led by his brother Louis, in the northern province. In May 1568 the army defeated a Spanish force under the Duke of Aremberg who was killed in the fighting at Heiligerlee. Alva countered by executing a Dutch nobleman he had assembled as a hostage, including important counts of Egmont and Hoorn. He then assumed personal command of his army and annihilated Louis's Dutch troops. at the battle of Jemmingen in July 1568. William, with his back now to the wall, led a second army south, but it was soon disintegrated.

By 1572 it looks like the Dutch Revolt was finally crushed. William was restricted to issuing anti-Spanish pamphlets from across the German border. In April of that year, however, the rebel's cause was reunited by the Protestant pirates unexpectedly capturing the coastal garrison of Brielle. Oppressed by Alva's heavy-handed retribution, other cities in Northern Netherlands cheerfully opened up the gates to the Protestant rebels. Once more William had a cause to lead. The rebel States general met with William and acclaimed him leader of Holland and Zeeland.

Over the next few years, the tide of battle went one way then the other. William's low point was reached in 1573 when the Spanish regent, Don Luis de Requestens decisively defeated the troops of Orange at the battle of Mookerheyde, and William's brothers, Louis and Henry were killed. The Protestants starved of complete defeat by breaching the dykes to save the city of Lieder. Thereafter the Spanish forfeited moderate support when unpaid soldiers went on the rampage in what became known as the 'Spanish Fury.' Starved of cash, the new regent, Don John of Austria, signed a Perpetual Edict in 1577, which seemed to assure religious tolerance and the departure of Spanish troops. But it proved to be a false dawn when Don John retook the offensive, capturing Namur, whilst William took the capital of Brussels. So the fighting went on.

In 1579 alarmed by the radical calvinism of some of William's northern followers, the more Catholic provinces of Southern Netherlands surrendered to the Spanish at the treaty of Arras. In response, the predominantly Protestant provinces signed the Union of Utrecht, binding themselves to continue the struggle. William had no choice but to back the Union, but for the rest of his life, he still hankered to reunite all the provinces of the former Spanish Netherland under his rule.

Concluding the union was no guarantee of victory, William was desperate for foreign support and turned to the French prince Francis, Duke of Anjou and Alencon, brother Henry 11 in France. In 1851 declared himself 'Protector of the liberty of the Netherlands', and effectively installed himself sovereign of the Netherlands, in place of Phillip 11. The Duke of Anjou proved inept and relied heavily on William for advice and authority. He attempted to take Antwerp in 1883 and narrowly escaped with his life from the city.

Assignation was on the horizon for William when on 18th March 1582, a deranged Spanish soldier, Juan de J'auregui, fired a pistol at William's head while offering him a petition. He was lucky to survive, the bullet pierced his neck below the right ear and passed out through the left jaw. Aided by his wife, Charlotte, J'auregui was killed by William's bodyguards. Two years later William's luck had run out. G'eralds pistol shot ensured he died instantly. Mourned by the whole of the Netherlands, William of Orange was buried in the " New Church" in Delft. From the 17th century onwards, Dutch monarchs have been buried beside him.

CHAPTER 4.

LUCIFER SPREADS HIS WINGS

A little bit more background may help the cause of understanding the plot of assassinations at the time. In 1584 the stake of the religious wars was raised further, when the king's youngest brother and heir, Francis, Duke of Anjou and Alencon, died. This meant that King Henry 111, of the Pyrenean kingdom of Navarre and de facto leader of the Huguenots, became the new heir. Whilst Navarre was Protestant, it was the pretext for the Catholic League to start an all-out war, long called the 'War of the Three Henries.' Three regimes now ran France simultaneously: one Catholic, one Huguenot and one enfeebled royal administration. Guise did the unthinkable then with the secret treaty of Joinville naming his family ancestors with the Spanish. Thus Philip 11 of Spain committed himself to support the Catholic cause by providing arms and money; and in return, Guise pledged he would eradicate heresy in France, by exterminating the Huguenots and installing his elderly relative Cardinal of Bourdon to the throne in place of the rightful heir, Navarre.

Henry of Guise or The Scarred, French Henri de Guise or le Balafré, (born December 31, 1550—died December 23, 1588, Blois, France), popular duo of Guise, the acknowledged chief of the Catholic party and the Holy League during the French war of religion. Henri de Lorraine was 13 years old at the death of his father, François, the 2nd duke (1563), and grew up under the domination of a passionate desire to avenge his father's death, for which he held the Huguenot admiral Gaspard de Coligny responsible. In 1566 he went to Vienna hoping to gain military experience by fighting the Turks, but the war ended before he could go into action. He returned home to take part in the further wars of religion and performed deeds that were as daring as they were useless. Nevertheless, he won the love of the people of Paris.

In 1572 Catherine de Médicis turned to the Guises for help in getting rid of the admiral **Gaspard de Coligny**, who was pressing the King to adopt poli-cies at variance with her aims. After an attempt on the Admiral's life had failed, Guise attended the secret meeting (August 23) that planned the Mas-sacre of St. Bartholomew's Day . On August 24 he personally supervised

Coligny's murder, thereby avenging his father's death, but otherwise took no part in the massacre and even sheltered about 100 Huguenots in his house. By the following year, he was without a serious rival as head of the Catholic party; Catherine de Médicis came to depend on him to protect her from the intrigues of her son François, duc d'Alencon and later duc d'Anjou, and Henry of Navarre.

At Henry 111's accession (May 1574) the duc de Guise occupied a unique position at court as well as in the affections of the people of Paris. In October 1575 he calmed the anxieties of the Parisians by defeating a German army at Dormans, receiving a wound and scar that won him his father's nickname of "le Balafré-Small Scar." Fearing Guise's growing popularity, Henry III made peace with the Huguenots (May 1576). Guise, angered by what he regarded as a betrayal, formed the Holy League of nobles in defence of the Catholic cause; Henry III countered the move by placing himself at the head of the movement. His relations with Guise deteriorated further the cause of peace (September 1577). While the king fell under the spell of new favourites, Guise strengthened the ties that existed for some time between his family and the Spanish monarchy and from 1578 onward had a pension from Phillips 11 of Spain.

In 1584 **Henry of Navarre** became heir presumptive to the crown, and the League was revived in order to exclude him from the succession. Guise himself became ambitious for the crown. In the War of the Three Henrys he again drove the Germans out of France and, when invited to the capital, ruled there unopposed as a kind of "King of Paris." On May 12, 1588—the Day of the Barricades—the people rose against Henry III, but instead of seizing the throne, Guise helped to appease the mob, and Henry III was able to escape to Chartres. By the Edict of Union (July) the king surrendered to the League's demands, and on August 4 Guise was appointed lieutenant general of the kingdom. Soon after, Henry III decided to destroy Guise. On December 23 Guise fell into a carefully laid trap. As he left a Council meeting in answer to a royal summons, he was set upon by the king's bodyguard and stabbed. His body and that of his brother Louis II cardinal de Guise, who was murdered the next day, were burned and the ashes thrown in the Loire.

Henry 1V is lauded as the most gifted monarch France ever had. He was brave in leading troops into battle, he was also cruel and authoritarian, and used flogging as a means of punishment, even on his own children. He was known for his many mistresses, and his frequent adventurous trips for playing his favourite game of tennis. More importantly, he was a clever man and politically astute, leading France to an impressive recovery after the haemorrhaging of 30 years of conflictive religious wars. He was no religious fanatic, making peace with Catholics, and maybe for appearance's sake converting in 1593 when it seemed politically clever to do so. Yet he continued to guarantee the Huguenots, largely Calvinist, generous freedom of worship and civil rights. Never a martyr to religious dogma, although a Catholic by birth he was raised a Protestant by his mother Jeanne d'bert, who declared Calvinism the religion of the Navarre, the land-locked kingdom perched on the Pyrenees between France and Spain. [This kingdom would later feature in the Song of Roland [French: La Chanson de Roland) is an 11th-century story based on the Frankish military leader Roland at the Battle of Roncevaux Pass in AD 778, during the reign of the Carolingian king Charlemagne. It is the oldest surviving major work of French literature and the first lyrical song of a battle cry recorded.]

As a mere teenager, Henry left his hometown of Pau, the Navarre capital, and joined the Huguenot forces in the French Wars of Religion, fighting alongside the Prince of Conde' and Admiral Coligny during the battles of the later 1560s. In 1562 Henry's mother died leaving him as King Henry111 of Navarre. On 18th August he married Antione de Bourbon, the sister of Charles 1X, King of France, in a bid to end religious killings. However, Charles 1X's unscrupulous villain of a mother, Catherine de Medici, an utter Catholic supporter had schemed with the Duke of Guise to ensure the marriage would not last. So six days after the weddings, the royal family authorised an orgy of silence against the Protestant community, massacring thousands of Huguenots across France and Henry himself very narrowly escaped death by pretending to convert to Roman Catholicism. He was imprisoned, but escaped in January 1576, rejoining the Protestant armies in the field.

In 1584 Henry of Navarre became the legal heir to the French throne upon the death of his brother Francis, Duke of Anjou and Alencon, and brother of the French King, Henry111. The latter had no choice but to recognise Navarre as his legitimate successor. as under under Salic Law a female dependent could not claim the title. Henry of Navarre's claim was slender, but as he was a direct descendent on the male line from King Louis 1X, who had died in 1270, it was impossible to deny or refute. Thus Henry of Navarre became Henry 1V of France, the first of the Bourbon kings to rule France, on and off, for the next 141 years.

In 1593 he renounced the Protestant faith in favour of Catholicism, al-legedly declaring' *Paris vary bien une messe*- Paris is well worth the Mass'. His pragmatism won him the support of the most war-weary Catholic population, the Catholic cause having been indelibly cemented with his overly close association with the predatory foreign policy of Phillips 11 of Spain, who consistently overturned Salic law by installing his daughter Isabella as queen. Henry was crowned at Charters Cathedral in February 1594, with his forces finally occupying Paris. The acceptance of the Sorbonne recognised Henry as the legitimate sovereign, but it didn't prevent a Jesuit student, Jacques Chastel from attempting to assassinate him in December of that year.

In 1595 Henry felt confident enough to declare war on Spain and allied with the Dutch and England made a threat to evaporate the Spanish treasury to bankruptcy. The 30th April 1598 threats evaporated with the Spanish treasury's guarantee to allow limited tolerance of the Protestants of France. Henry's programme for the recovery of France after almost forty years of civil war was bold, in imaginative and, by modern-day standards, liberal. His goal was to raise the standard of living for all his subjects. By the time of his death in 1610 he had overhauled trade and agriculture, and the na-tion's dependence on luxury goods was reversed, and France enjoyed a health surplus. His minister Sully presided over an ambitious programme to drain swamplands in order to create productive areas for agriculture, pro-tect forests from devastation, build a new system of tree-lined roads, and construct new bridges and canals. Paris itself was adorned with the 'Pont Neuf' bridge and grandiose additions to the Louvre palace. France seemed to enter a new Golden Age.

Abroad Henry 1V wisely preferred to subsidise his allies rather than costly wages and risky wars himself, to rely on judicious use of aggressive threats. and empower alliances to encourage his opponents to ease their position. In 1610 however, the police failed. and Henry found himself on the brink of war with Holy Roman Emperor, Rudolf 11, over the succession to the dukedom of Julich-Cleves. Never one to shrink from challenge Henry mo-bilised his forces, and on May 14th rose out to take personal command of his army. It was on his way to the command post that he was stabbed to death by Ravaillac, the fanatical priest who had been rejected by the Jesuits leapt onto the King's coach and stabbed him to death. He had laid an obstacle on the trail to get the carriage to stop. The king's guard seized him and transported him to nearby Hotel de Retz, to avoid a mob killing. During the course of his trial, the radical priest was tortured in an attempt to make him identify his accomplices, but he always declared that he was working alone and that he simply sought to stop Henry from' making war on the pope.' The fortuitous combination of knowing the king's route and the timely blockade caused feverish speculation as to who the mastermind had been. Henry 1V was buried ceremoniously traditional resting place of France's sovereigns, the parish church of St S Denis. By contrast, Ravaillac suffered the punishment meted out to Assassins in France; he was tortured one last time, publicly scalded with burning sulpha, molten lead boiling oil and reuse, then slashed with steel pinches before being pulled asunder by four horses, Before his death Racaillac declared: 'I have no regrets at all about dying, because I've done what I came to do.' Thereafter his family were forbidden to use the name " Ravaillac' ever again.

As for another English Royal favourite, **George Villiers** was a courtier who became a favourite of King James I. The King became infatuated with him and made him Viscount in 1616, Earl in 1617, Marquis in 1618 and **Duke of Buckingham** in 1623., and at the ripe old age of 31, he had it all. Out manoeuvring his rivals the Howards, Villiers was appointed Lord High Admiral in 1619. Buckingham was not only a good-looking young man but groomed for success in the court, and his homosexuality manipulated the lovestruck King James to gain unprecedented control over royal patronage, rewarding himself and his family generously. He married his relations into the most important families in England. His own marriage was to Lady Catherine Manners, the only daughter of the wealthy Earl of Rutland. Buckingham accompanied Prince Charles (later Charles I) to Madrid in 1623 in an attempt to arrange a marriage between the Prince and the Infanta Maria, sister of Philip IV of Spain. It was during this journey that Buckingham transferred his main loyalty from King James to Prince Charles, and that Charles came to rely heavily on Buckingham's advice and support. The Spanish match was extremely unpopular with English Protestants and ended in humiliation for Buckingham and Charles when negotiations broke down. They returned to England determined to wage war on Spain in retaliation, thus undoing all of King James' efforts to maintain peace. Charles and Buckingham largely directed foreign policy during the last two years of James' reign. However, he handled things so badly in Spain, that the Spanish Ambassador asked Parliament to excuse him for his behaviour on his return from Madrid. Buckingham cannily forestalled any potential fallout from diplomatic disaster by immediately calling for war with Spain, which had, James 1 accession, been England's traditional enemy.

Buckingham remained in favour when Charles I succeeded James to the throne of the Three Kingdoms in 1625. He made himself unpopular with Parliament by negotiating Charles' marriage to the Catholic princess Henrietta Maria of France and compounded his unpopularity by his monopoly of royal favour and patronage. Buckingham was held responsible for the failure of Count Mansfeld's expedition to recover the Palatinate and for the mismanaged attack on Cadiz in 1625. The Parliaments of 1625 and 1626 threatened Buckingham with impeachment, but King Charles dissolved them prematurely rather than allow his favourite to come to trial. In 1627, Buckingham personally led an expedition to relieve the Huguenots of La Rochelle who were threatened by the forces of King Louis XIII of France. Through a combination of bad management and misfortune, the expedition failed disastrously. Although Buckingham had become intensely unpopular, King Charles continued to support him. In August 1628, Buckingham was at Portsmouth preparing another expedition to La Rochelle when he was attacked and stabbed to death by John Felton, a discontented army officer.

More recent historians have blamed Charles's 11-year 'personal rule' of 1629-40, when the king dispensed with parliament altogether, and indirectly, the outbreak of the English Civil War in 1642. On Buckingham's assassination. certainly, a number of MPs approved of the murder, whilst some were even drawn to communicate with Felton. The Parliament that had assembled in March 1628 had already been programmed to pursue a forceful approach against Buckingham. That autumn some parliamentarians expressed hope that the death of the duke would augur a new era of a more positive relationship between the Crown and the House of Commons.
Charles however, clearly felt that parliament was at the very least guilty of condoning the murder of his favourite. Parliament was only finally recalled on 20th January 1629; the Catholic rancorous session that followed encouraged Charles to dissolve both houses only for a few weeks. It was only in 1640 that, faced with the pressing need for parliamentary revenue, cost and unnecessary military action to enforce religious conformity in Scotland-

Parliament was summoned once more. This time the MPs were determined to exact vengeance for the humiliations of 1629; furthermore, the intervening decade had allowed a host of other grievances against Charles's church policies and his royal advisers to fester. From the minute Commons assembled, the nation began to slip inexorably down the road toward civil war.

Buckingham was buried in Westminster Abbey, in a splendid marble tomb designed by the royal sculptor Le Sueur and completed in 1634. Occupying a prominent site, it was the first non-royal tomb to be inserted into Henry V11's Chapel, a sure sign of Charles 1's lasting devotion to his, and his fathers's unpredictable favourite. Felton the discounted army officer was hanged on 28th November 1628. His body was subsequently exposed in chains at Portsmouth.

Gustav was a vocal opponent of what he saw as the abuse of political privileges seized by the nobility since the death of King Charles X11.. Seizing power from the government in a coup d'état, called the Swedish Revolution, in 1772 that ended the Age of Liberty, he initiated a campaign to restore a measure of Royal autocracy, which was completed by the Union and Security Act of 1789, which swept away most of the powers exercised by the Swedish Parliament during the Age of Liberty, but at the same time, it opened up the government for all citizens, thereby breaking the privileges of the nobility.

In 1700 Sweden was one of the major powers of Europe. Its armies minted not only the Baltic region but vast areas of Germany too. As the continental nations prepared to embark on a cataclysmic War of the Spanish Succession, arguably the planet's first genuine world war all waited to see what side the powerful Swedes would join. It was only a year later that Gustav 111 was crowned King. Gustav III reigned as the King of Sweden from 1771 until his assassination in 1792. During this time he became one of the key proponents of a policy known as "enlightened absolutism", where he espoused the ideals of the Enlightenment while increasing his own power and autocracy. To this end, he became a patron of the Swedish arts, curtailed the power and corruption of the nobility and introduced reforms to liberalise the economy. At the same time, he amassed enormous personal power and cracked down on press freedoms.

Sweden had lost its Baltic dominions during the Great Northern War with Russia in the early 18th century, and though he had some military success, Gustav failed to recapture the territories in a war with Russia in 1788-90. In other areas of foreign policy, Gustav was the first neutral head of state in the world to recognise the independence of the United States in 1782, and militarily assisted the rebels. In foreign policy, Gustav tried Sweden to hide. France. As a result of his adoration or her was a granted 300,000-pound subsidy from Louis XV, a Caribbean island of Saint Barthelemy. and an invitation to visit Paris once again, which Gustav duly did in 1784.

To bolster his foreign ambitions, Gustav also increased the size of the navy, creating galley-based fleets designed to cope with treacherous shallows and inlets of the baltic at Stockholm and prudent day Helsinki, and a British-style battle fleet based on sailing ships of the lien at Karlskrona. Gustav embarked on an ambitious spent considerable public funds on cultural ventures, which were controversial among his critics, as well as military attempts to seize Norway with Russian aid, then a series of attempts to recapture the Swedish Baltic dominions lost during the Great Northern War through the failed war with Russia. Nonetheless, his successful leadership in the Battle of Svensksund averted a complete military defeat and signified that Swedish military might was to be countenanced. Gustav also embarked on ambitious building programmes, using Franco-British neoclassicism as his model for a variety of royal structures. An 'English' park and palace were planned, complete with a Kew garden-style Chinese pagoda and fake medieval stables a neoclassical theatre was built at Gripsholm; and an homage to Versailles's Petit Trianon was erected north of Stockholm. Increasing royal expenditure and the subsequent rising tax burden, however, caused disquiet in the middle of the 1780s.

It was then that Gustav made his most critical mistake; he embarked on what he gambled would be short and victorious against Sweden's neighbouring arch-enemies Denmark and Russia. In 1788 he took advantage of Catherine the Great's preoccupation with the Turkish War to invade Russia-administered in Finland, using Swedish soldiers dressed in Russian uniforms. The campaign did not start with a good chance of success. In failing to obtain the consent of the estates of war, Gustav had violated his own constitution of 1772: it was a clumsy mistake that led to a serious mutiny by the ' Anjala Confederation' among his aristocratic officers of Finland Meanwhile, his hopes of victories failed to materialise. The only notable result was the capture of the Russian ship Valadislav which brought an epidemic of typhus to its new Swedish home., Kariskrina, where 5000 seamen died before the disease spread inland. On the bright side, he led his galley fleet to a crushing defeat of Russian naval forces at the Battle of Svenkund. Long regarded as Sweden's greatest-ever navy victory, it saw the loss of only 6 Swedish ships compared to Russia's 50 vessels. But in the subsequent Treaty of Varala with Russia in 1790 almost nothing was gained.: no territory, no compensation. As he curtailed the power of the nobles and enforced his absolute monarchy, many nobles in Sweden began to despise the king and actively plotted a conspiracy against him. On 16 March 1792, as the King was attending a masquerade ball at the Royal Swedish Opera, Assassin Jacob Johan Anckarström shot the king in the back from behind. Gustav died thirteen days later from septicaemia.

Jean-Paul Marat (1743-1793) has become one of the French Revolution's most identifiable figures, as much for his untimely death as the political contributions he made in life. Marat was born in Switzerland, the son of an Italian father and a French Huguenot mother. He left home as a teenager and travelled to Paris, where he undertook studies in medicine and set up practice as a doctor.

By the 1770s Jean-Paul Marat had also taken an interest in the Enlightenment philosophies, so he began writing works of political theory. He also spent several years in Holland, Scotland and England, where he studied the British political system and wrote prolifically on both politics and medicine. Marat returned to Paris in 1776 and set up a flourishing medical practice. He soon found himself in demand as a physician, his clientele including members of Parisian high society and Charles Philippe, youngest brother of Louis XVI. Desperate to penetrate the intellectual elites, Marat also continued both his scientific research and his political writing. He conducted experiments on the nature of light and optics; his findings were examined and commended by Enlightenment figures like Benjamin Franklin.

Despite this, Marat's research was rejected by the Académie des Sciences, possibly because of his lack of education and patronage. Marat's political writings were also ridiculed by Voltaire and his followers. By the late 1780s, Marat had become frustrated and resentful at this treatment. The onset of the French Revolution presented Marat with both opportunities and new ideas. The convocation of the Estates-General prompted Marat to take up his pen for the Third Estate. Between late 1788 and mid-1789, he wrote several essays urging constitutional reform and political equality for all French citizens. At least one of these essays was tabled in the National Constituent Assembly during its constitutional deliberations.

In September 1789, Marat began publishing his own newspaper, L'Ami du Peuple ('The Friend of the People'). In its first edition, Marat attacked the Second Estate and demanded that all nobles be expelled from the Assembly. In the second, he refocused his aim on bourgeois bankers and financiers, men who, according to Marat, "built their fortunes atop the ruination of others".

Jean-Paul Marat's newspaper, written single-handedly and published several times a week, was enormously popular with the working people of Paris. The appeal of L'Ami du Peuple was derived not from its political ideas but from its focus and tone. Every edition claimed to expose some scandal or conspiracy; every copy launched a scathing new attack on perceived enemies of the people.

Marat's targets shifted as the revolution evolved and radicalised. At first, he attacked the king and his ministers, the nobility, the high clergy and the affluent bourgeoisie. By late 1789, L'Ami du Peuple was haranguing the National Constituent Assembly for protecting feudal and bourgeois business interests, for not implementing universal suffrage, and for not going far enough. The Paris Commune, the National Guard and political moderates like Necker, Honore Mirabeau, Marquis Lafayette, Jean Bailly and Antoine Barnave were also frequent targets.

As might be expected, Marat's poison pen made him a target for liberals and moderates. Between the autumn of 1789 and late 1792, he was regularly subject to arrest warrants and government suppression. Marat spent October and November 1789 hiding in the sewers and catacombs of Paris, while the Commune and the gendarmerie sought his arrest. He returned briefly but fled again in late January 1790, taking refuge in England for four months.

Marat's return to Paris in May 1791 lasted until late July when L'Ami du Peuple was held accountable for Jacobin radicalism and the Champ de Mars Massacre, and its printing presses were destroyed by gendarmes. Marat spent yet another period of exile in England between December 1791 and March 1792. *L'Ami du Peuple* was a one-man operation so it ceased publication whenever Marat went into exile or hiding. By the summer of 1792, the revolution was becoming more radical and Marat and his ideas were gaining popularity. Now backed by the republican Cordeliers, Marat's articles spat venom at the monarchy, the Girondins, foreign spies and other suspected counter-revolutionaries. *L'Ami du Peuple* helped fuel the insurrection of August 10th 1792 which culminated in the invasion of the Tuileries.

Marat was also held responsible for the massacre of prisoners in Paris the following month, a charge he did not deny. In September 1792 Marat was elected to the National Convention. He spent the next six months bickering with Girondins within the Convention and attacking them in print outside. In April 1793, Marat was arrested and tried before Paris' Revolutionary Tribunal, on charges he had called for widespread violence and the suspension of the National Convention. He was acquitted after delivering a passionate defence. Two months later the Girondins, were expelled from the Convention. Marat, once the enemy of the revolution, had become one of its most important leaders, both inside the Convention and on the streets of Paris.

On July 13th 1793, Marat was murdered at his home on the Rue de Cordelier. Famously depicted in a painting by Jacques-Louis David, his death remains one of the revolution's most dramatic scenes. Marat's assassin was Charlotte Corday, a 24-year-old unmarried woman from Normandy. Raised in a convent, Corday was well-educated, politically astute and a keen student of revolutionary events. By 1792 she had become a follower of the Girondins, believing them the logical leaders of the new nation. Corday detested radicals in the Montagnard faction, particularly Marat. In mid-1793, she travelled to Paris, intending to assassinate Marat in public at the *Fête de la Fédération*. After discovering that Marat was too unwell to attend, Corday visited his house on the morning of July 13th but was refused entry. Undeterred, she returned to her hotel and penned a letter to Marat, offering information about Girondinist plotting in her native Normandy. She also changed her clothing and attended a hairdresser, hoping to appear more alluring.

Corday returned to Jean-Paul Marat's apartments at around 7 p.m. on July 13th. This time she was allowed to enter and found the radical journalist soaking in a bath. Marat was desperately unwell and, according to some sources, already close to death. Riddled with eczema and weeping skin lesions, he bathed constantly; unable to hold down solid food, he drank copious amounts of coffee.

After chatting with Marat and providing him with a list of names, Corday unveiled a five-inch kitchen knife, which she plunged into his chest. Marat's wife and attendants rushed in and desperately hauled him from the bath, though death was almost instantaneous. In the days that followed Marat was hailed as a martyr and immortalised in word, art and symbolism. His funeral was attended by thousands, his heart was embalmed and kept at the Cordeliers club, and his remains were entombed in the Panthéon. Corday was immediately sent to trial and guillotined on July 17th. Though she was almost certainly acting alone, Marat's murder touched off another savage wave of violence against counter-revolutionaries, royalist agents and Girondinists.faction While the murder of Marat did not directly cause the Reign of Terror, it certainly contributed to the paranoia from which it sprang.

If Jean-Paul Marat had died before 1788 he would have been known to the world as a Swiss-born French scientist and physician who, if not quite Newton or Descartes; certainly made a significant contribution to the scientific advancement. Indeed he might have been better known in Britain where he published most of his groundbreaking scientific papers. As it is, it was this political activity during the last five years of his life that he is best known. And perhaps more than any other assassin's victim, it was the manner of his death that has made him a household name to the world over the inspiration of artists and revolutionaries alike.

CHAPTER 5.

INTERMISSION: GODS AGENCY OR LUCIFERS

It is time to take a look back on the reasoning behind this little work of the reincarnation of the evil angels of Lucifer versus the Agency plan of God. Lucifer saw the free will in discord to that of the plan of God for humanity, For God made man in his own image and likeness and in that, he had given man free will to procreate with his principles according to a golden rule of goodness to carry out his plan to its ultimate conclusion. It matters little which myth, legend or biblical folklore that one might believe in or use to one's advantage in understanding the Godly plan. They all to my mind equally display the unique power of a God of one's own understanding. A seven-day miracle, an evolutionary creation or indeed a Big Bang theory all demonstrate a creator power. All fit into the dynamic of the mind of the believer who may choose as he/she so pleases. The non-believers, on the other hand, prefer to use science as the God of their understanding, and those of us of questioning mind cannot argue in that regard either. We who sit on the fence of both the believer and non-believer, battling with the ego mind and the spiritual presence within, are conscious of the light of the world's good as equally with the dark, of the evil fashioned by Lucifer at the fall. The choice that is within our own nature, since the so-called fall, allows us to follow our inner spiritual consciousness of good or the Satan within, so to speak.

The facts of history, biblical and non-biblical, documented the progress of our world and confirm more a world of darkness than of light, of one of not-so-perfect progress. A world progress that has evolved on the back of the blood of many through the cardinal vices of pride, greed, lust, envy, covertness, wrath and slot of the survivors. Those of humanity who created wars, those who kill and those who are killed, in the name of progress and domination for 'the good of all.' The eating of the forbidden fruits of this world in preference to the good virtues that are equally within us. The challenge of chastity versus lust, temperance over gluttony, generosity instead of greed, diligence in lieu of laziness, patience instead of anger, gratitude replacing envy and humility over pride. These are and have always been our choices from our first breath, and will be to our last one. Mankind from the so-called 'fall from grace,' to the present day, turned to take the power of the tree of knowledge and use it for their own advantage instead of the will of the one who creator them. This has resulted in the will of the darkness of the soul of man to live by the seven cardinal vices, traversing adversities, facing a world of carnal desires, frustration, illness, bondage and death.

If we lived by the Golden Rule we would not need governments and everyone would get along just fine without any human authority over us. Hillel, around the time of the birth of Christ, when asked to explain the Torah, the Jewish body of rules for life-based on the bible exclaimed "Whatever is hateful to yourself, do not do to others- all the rest is commentary." Jesus explained it in his command, "Love God and thy neighbour as thyself." Jesus's Sermon on the Mount was a compendium of moral instructions for people. It matters little in the context of this reading, whether you believe in his divinity or that he was mortal or even existed. I talk here only of the wisdom of his philosophy, as presented in the teaching. He added a further dimension to the Golden Rule that has been difficult for this man and my fellow man throughout the ages, since his reported death on the cross, his resurrection and ascension into heaven, to grasp and live by.

To "Love God above all else and our neighbour as our self."If the entire world lived by the Golden Rule, there would be peace on earth." Jesus added a caveat to the rule, a further dimension whatever the circumstance. He said that it was not about showing love and kindness to people who are nice to us, it is showing love and kindness when they are not. He gave us many examples: "Love your enemy, turn the other cheek; if someone asks you to carry something for a mile, carry it for two; if someone wants your coat, give him your jacket too. Remain at peace, whatever the circumstance.

The Golden Rule is considered an ethic of reciprocity in most religions whilst others treat it differently. It all boils down to the 'yen yang' of human good or defects of character (sin) of human nature. The maxim may appear as a positive or a negative governed by one's conduct. One should treat others as one would like to be treated (positive form). One should not treat others the way one would not like to treat oneself (negative form). What you wish upon others, you wish upon yourself (empathic or responsive form).

We do not in our own nature live by the Golden Rule. Humanity has been programmed to the Golden Rule, but our human nature is guided by our own needs and desires. We have been given this concept of the rule as codified in the tablets, in the code of Hammurabi, between 1754 and 1790. I has been ratified to be carried out through the ages, in the biblical text of the old and New Testaments, as a global ethic, endorsed by faiths of Buddhism, Christianity, Hindu, indigenous, inter faiths, Islam, Judaism, native American, Neo-pagan, Taoism, etc, endorsed as The Golden Rule by some 143 leaders of the world's major faiths as part of the 1993 code of 'Declaration Towards a Global Ethic." Whilst this 'do unto others' concept is, from a humanitarian ethic, an ideal rule for the masses of men, it is by no means a religious ethic. Belief in God is not necessary to endorse it.' Soothsaying Philosophers have historically objected to the rule on a variety of grounds. Like, how does one know how others want to be treated? Obviously, asking them makes sense, but what if they have not reached a particular or relevant means of understanding? George Bernard Shaw wrote "Do not do unto others as you would, that they do unto you. Their tastes may be different." This suggests that if your values are not shared with others, the way you want to be treated will not be the way they may want to be treated. Hence, based on this premise, the Golden Rule of "do unto others" is "dangerous in the wrong hands." One philosopher wisely stated, "Some fanatics have no aversion to death: the Golden Rule might inspire them to kill others in their suicidal missions."

Most ancient wisdom expressed the negative, advising what you should not do, rather than what you should. This bias favours a do-nothing inertia that has allowed Monarchs, the Church and Governments through the ages to allow bad actions and states of affairs to persist for far too long with ultimate negative consequences. On the contrary, formulating positive action in accordance with the Golden Rule can lead to a cycle of tit-for-tat reciprocity. Throughout the history of mankind the forces of positive or negative, good versus evil, have been accompanied by mechanisms that have resulted in good outcomes or death, defeat and decay. The Golden Rule, heavily qualified by other rules and regulations, with a maxim of forgiveness when things go wrong, should ultimately work in the favour of the common good. Of course, if such a 'Golden Rule' is carried out, influenced by the love and guidance of a Higher Power, belief or good understanding from within, it is more likely to have consequences to the benefit of all concerned. Therein lay the dilemma for the powers that be, in their guiding nature the enforcer of the Golden Rule. If it be a hand from the light that leads the way then we have nothing to fear. But as we have seen throughout

history, the force of Lucifer and our own defects of character has us conditioned to dark over light to be blinded by believing that progress of the
world to the betterment of humanity must have assassinations to keep peace
in the world. Our leaders have been living that lie in their egocentricity
since the first murder of Cain on his brother Abel, and man can only seem
to come to the light of reason by suffering to find his way to the light and
back to living by the Agency of God through the golden rules of his better
nature.

We, as the present living have the capacity to reason as individuals and col-
lectively, to let go of the desires that ultimately lead to living in the dark,
and slowly but surely be enlightened to both the evil within us, as equally
as the evil of the world. The choice is always ours, to follow the dictates of
the Golden Rule of the heart by living accord to loving God-like principles
for our own betterment, or continue to be possessed by our basic instincts
which will ultimately lead us to death and destruction. Death and destruction at the hands of the Anti-Christ are represented by Lucifer and his angels of death.

CHAPTER 6.

19TH CENTURY LEADERS AND ASSASSINS.

Assassinations are almost always as much about politics as they are about the individual concerned, the hope being that the death of a person will also result in the death of their ideas or principles, striking fear into the hearts of their contemporaries and shocking the wider world. The murder of prominent figures has historically sparked soul-searching, mass outpourings of grief and even conspiracy theories, as people struggle to come to terms with the consequences of assassinations.

Lord Frederick Charles Cavendish, was born at Compton House, Eastbourne in 1836, the second son of the 7th Duke of Devonshire, He was a typical second son of an English aristocratic family, constantly in the shadow of his elder brother, who would inherit the family title, and little was expected of Frederick except a sober industrious career in the public service. This he had duct delivered, and it is only in the dramatic manner of his assassination that he briefly eclipsed his elder brother's bright star. Frederick, as a politician, was murdered by Fenian extremists the day after his arrival in Dublin as chief secretary of Ireland and as a goodwill emissary from England, at the height of the Irish crisis in 1882.

The second son of the 7th Duke of Devonshire, Cavendish entered Parliament in 1865. The year before, he had married Mrs Gladstone's niece, Lucy, daughter of the 4th Baron Lyttelton. Gladstone came to admire and trust Cavendish, especially after taking him as private secretary in 1872, and looked to him as a future leader of the parliamentary Liberal Party. He was financial secretary to the Treasury from 1880 and, as such, was the right-hand man of Gladstone, as chancellor and later prime minister.

In 1882 Gladstone asked him to undertake the thankless and dangerous office of chief secretary for Ireland. Cavendish crossed to Dublin on the night of May 5. The following evening, he walked across Phoenix Park with Thomas H. Burke, the permanent undersecretary for Ireland. Burke was attacked by a Fenian splinter group armed with knives, Cavendish tried to defend him, and both were killed. Five of their assassins, members of a secret society called the Invincible, were betrayed and hanged in 1883; several others were sentenced to long prison terms.

Frederick Cavendish's father was the 8th Duke of Devonshire; his elder brother was the Marques of Harrington, who was a brilliant heir to the dukedom and was widely tipped to be Gladstone's successor at the helm of the Liberal party. Frederick with none of his brother's dash was always regarded as unexceptional and a plodder. However, with some influence of his brother's pre-eminence and his own, artfully married Gladstone's niece, Lucy, and found himself in a moderate position far away from Westminster, where he perhaps did some good and would likely come to little harm.

As he looked out of the lodge window that summer evening in 1882, Earl Spencer saw a park full of early evening activities- women with strollers, a young couple walking hand in hand cyclists crisscrossing over lawns and a polo match taking place beyond. What he later declared to be a group of scuffling drunks were, in fact, the assassin members of an extreme Irish nationalist sect calling themselves 'The Invincible'. Their target was not actually Cavendish who had arrived in Ireland only two days before, but his assistant, Permanent Under-Secretary Thomas Henry Burke. Burke of an old established catholic family, though only a civil servant, was considered a traitor to his country by the radical nationalists. Their anger at his alleged betrayal of Ireland was demonstrated by the savage way in which they performed the assassination: the two government officials were not merely stabbed to death, but we slashed across their bodies, their throats cut with surgical knives in final, horrifying *coup de grace*.

Spencer was naturally deeply shocked by the Phoenix Park murders. Gladstone, too, was extremely upset when he learned what happened. he had regarded the genial and un-treating Cavendish almost like a son and had often stayed with him and his wife when in London. Indeed, the whole nation seems devastated, with every national and regional newspaper demanding instant retribution. Five of the assassins- Thomas Caffrey, Daniel Curley, Joe Brady, Tim Kelly and Michael Fagan half died a year later, and other Invincible were then imprisoned.

The brutal assassinations of Cavendish and Burke had there effect of uniting British and much of Irish opinion against the more extreme soft Irish nationalism. For a time it seemed that the cause of Irish independence even Irish Home Rule, would be irredeemably lost. But Gladstone was adamant that his liberal policy towards Ireland would not be stopped in its tracks. He assured Cavefish's widow that her husband's death 'will not be in vain'. She subsequently wrote in her diary that ' there fell a bright ray of hope, and I saw a vision of Ireland at peace, and my darling's lifeblood accepted as a sacrifice for Christ's sake, to help bring this tom pass.'Cavendish was buried in the family tom at Chatsworth, Derbyshire, on 11th May 1883. Over 30,000 attended his funeral, including almost half of the House of Commons. How 'martyrdom' became something of a cult in later years, before the two tragic deaths of Cavendish and V Burke were eclipsed by the carriage of the First World War.

Lord Frederick Cavendish is barely remembered today, especially in an age in which Victorian history is as remote to most schoolchildren as the Assyrian Empire. He is not even remembered in Phoenix Park, the place of his assassination. Only his monument at Chatsworth survives to tell us of his family's great loss.

William McKinley was born January 29, 1843, Niles, Ohio, and died September 14, 1901, in Buffalo, New York), 25th president of the United States (1897–1901). Under McKinley's leadership, the United States went to war against Spain in 1898 and thereby acquired a global empire, which included Puerto Rico, Guam, and the Philippines.

McKinley was the son of William McKinley, a manager of a charcoal furnace and a small-scale iron founder, and Nancy Allison. Eighteen years old at the start of the Civil War, McKinley enlisted in an Ohio regiment under the command of Rutherford B. Hayes, later the 19th president of the United States (1877–81). Promoted second lieutenant for his bravery in the Battle of Antietam (1862), he was discharged a brevet major in 1865. Returning to Ohio, he studied law, was admitted to the bar in 1867, and opened a law office in Canton, where he resided—except for his years in Washington, D.C.—for the rest of his life.

Drawn immediately to politics in the Republican Party, McKinley supported Hayes for governor in 1867 and Ulysses S. Grant for president in 1868. The following year he was elected prosecuting attorney for Stark County, and in 1877 he began his long career in Congress as representative from Ohio's 17th district. McKinley served in the House of Representatives until 1891, failing reelection only twice—in 1882, when he was temporarily unseated in an extremely close election, and in 1890, when Democrats gerrymandered his district. An issue with which McKinley became most closely identified during his congressional years was the protective tariff, a high tax on imported goods that served to protect American manufacturers from foreign competition. While it was only natural for a Republican from a rapidly industrialising state to favour protection, McKinley's support reflected more than his party's pro-business bias. A genuinely compassionate man, McKinley cared about the well-being of American workers, and he always insisted that a high tariff was necessary to ensure high wages. As chairman of the House Ways and Means Committee, he was the principal sponsor of the McKinley Tariff of 1890, which raised duties higher than they had been at any previous time. Yet by the end of his presidency, McKinley had become a convert to commercial reciprocity among nations, recognising that Americans must buy products from other countries in order to sustain the sale of American goods abroad.

His loss in 1890 brought an end to McKinley's career in the House of Representatives, but, with the help of wealthy Ohio industrialist Mark Hanna, McKinley won two terms as governor of his home state (1892–96). During those years Hanna, a powerful figure in the Republican Party, laid plans to gain the party's presidential nomination for his good friend in 1896. McKinley went on to win the nomination easily.

The presidential campaign of 1896 was one of the most exciting in American history. The central issue was the nation's money supply. McKinley ran on a Republican platform emphasising maintenance of the gold standard, while his opponent—William Jennings Bryan, candidate of both the Democratic and Populist parties—called for a bimetallic standard of gold and silver. Bryan campaigned vigorously, travelling thousands of miles and delivering hundreds of speeches in support of an inflated currency that would help poor farmers and other debtors. McKinley remained at home in Canton, greeting visiting delegations of Republicans at his front porch and giving carefully prepared speeches promoting the benefits of a gold-backed currency. For his part, Hanna tapped big businesses for enormous campaign contributions while simultaneously directing a network of Republican speakers who portrayed Bryan as a dangerous radical and McKinley as "the advance agent of prosperity." McKinley won the election decisively, becoming the first president to achieve a popular majority since 1872 and bettering Bryan 271 to 176 in the electoral vote.

By the time McKinley took the oath of office as president, many Americans—influenced greatly by the sensationalistic yellow journalism of the Hearst and Pulitzer newspapers—were eager to see the United States intervene in Cuba, where Spain was engaged in the brutal repression of an independence movement. Initially, McKinley hoped to avoid American involvement, but in February 1898 two events stiffened his resolve to confront the Spanish. First, a letter written by the Spanish minister to Washington, Enrique Dupuy de Lôme, was intercepted, and on February 9 it was published in American newspapers; the letter described McKinley as weak and too eager for public adulation. Then, six days after the appearance of the Dupuy de Lôme letter, the American battleship USS *Maine* suddenly exploded and sank as it sat anchored in Havana harbour, carrying 266 enlisted men and officers to their deaths. Although a mid-20th century investigation proved conclusively that the *Maine* was destroyed by an internal explosion, the yellow press convinced Americans of Spanish responsibility. The public clamoured for armed intervention, and congressional leaders were eager to satisfy the public demand for action.

In March McKinley gave Spain an ultimatum, including demands for an end to the brutality inflicted upon Cubans and the start of negotiations leading toward independence for the island. Spain agreed to most of McKinley's demands but balked at giving up its last major New World colony. On April 20 Congress authorised the president to use armed force to secure the independence of Cuba, and five days later it passed a formal declaration of war.

In the brief Spanish-American War—"a splendid little war," in the words of Secretary of State John Hay—the United States easily defeated Spanish forces in the Philippines, Cuba, and Puerto Rico. Combat began early in May and ended with an armistice in mid-August. The subsequent Treaty of Paris, signed in December 1898 and ratified by the Senate in February 1899, ceded Puerto Rico, Guam, and the Philippines to the United States; Cuba became independent. The ratification vote was extremely close—just one vote more than the required two-thirds—reflecting opposition by many "anti-imperialists" to the United States acquiring overseas possessions, especially without the consent of the people who lived in them. Although McKinley had not entered the war for territorial aggrandisement, he sided with the "imperialists" in supporting ratification, convinced that the United States had an obligation to assume responsibility for "the welfare of an alien people."

This desire to care for the less fortunate was characteristic of McKinley and was nowhere better illustrated than in his marriage. McKinley married Ida Saxton (Ida McKinley) in 1871. Within two years, the future first lady witnessed the deaths of her mother and two daughters. She never recovered, and she spent the rest of her life as a chronic invalid, frequently suffering seizures and placing an enormous physical and emotional burden on her husband. Yet McKinley remained devoted to her, and his unflagging attentiveness earned him additional admiration from the public. Renominated for another term without opposition, McKinley again faced Democrat William Jennings Bryan in the presidential election of 1900. McKinley's margins of victory in both the popular and electoral votes were greater than they were four years before, no doubt reflecting satisfaction with the outcome of the war and with the widespread prosperity that the country enjoyed.

Following his inauguration in 1901, McKinley left Washington for a tour of the western states, to be concluded with a speech at the Pan-American Exposition in Buffalo, New York. Cheering crowds throughout the journey attested to McKinley's immense popularity. More than 50,000 admirers attended his exposition speech, in which the leader who had been so closely identified with protectionism now sounded the call for commercial reciprocity among nations. The following day, September 6, 1901, while McKinley was shaking hands with a crowd of well-wishers at the exposition, Leon Czolgosz, an anarchist, fired two shots into the president's chest and abdomen. Rushed to a hospital in Buffalo, McKinley lingered for a week before dying in the early morning hours of September 14. He was succeeded by his vice president, the man Mark Hanna sneeringly referred to as "that damned cowboy," Theodore Roosevelt.

For most of the 19th century, Spain was the sick man of Western Europe. In the days of colonial riches from the Spice trade, all-conquering armies were long gone. Instead, the 19th century threatened to err into a gleaming spark of full-scale civil war. The century ended disastrously for Spain, with the United States there year struggle to shake off the Spanish yoke ignorer to help itself to what remained of the Spanish Empire. The result was an utterly humiliating defeat for Spain in 1898, and the loss of the most remaining colonies of Puerto Rico, Guam the Philippines and of course Cuba.

José Canalejas, was born July 31, 1854, El Ferrol, Spain—died November 12, 1912, Madrid), Spanish statesman and prime minister whose anticlerical "Padlock Law" forbade the establishment of new religious orders and introduced obligatory military service. Canalejas's political career began with his election to the Cortes (parliament) in 1881 for the district of Soria. In the following years, Canalejas represented the districts of Agreda, Algeciras, Alcoy and Madrid. He was undersecretary to the presidency (1883), minister of public works and of justice (1888), minister of finance (1894–95), and co-minister of agriculture, industry, and commerce (1902). He became prime minister after the fall of the government of Segismundo Moret (February 1910). Although he presided over liberal governments under the monarchy, Canalejas always showed democratic tendencies, leaning toward radicalism on some issues. In 1906 he began an anticlerical campaign when he discovered that secret negotiations had been conducted with the Vatican. The campaign culminated with his anticlerical legislation when he became chief of the government.

After the French entry into Fès, Morocco, in 1910, Canalejas ordered (1911) the occupation of Larache, Alcázar, and Arcila by Spanish troops, but in 1912 he was forced to make an agreement that further reduced the Spanish Zone of Morocco. He presented a proposal for a law calling for a joint legislature for the four Catalan provinces with a small degree of autonomy, but he died before the law was passed. Canalejas tried to add a social-reform emphasis to Spanish liberalism, similar to that of Giovanni Giolitti in Italy and David Lloyd George in Britain. He was assassinated by an anarchist in 1912.

We have covered but few of the political assassinations of British history to give enough credence to the fact that Lucifer and these evil angels of death continue to run the show on the broad wide way of life on earth. Fast forwarding now to the memorable reign and assassinations of European and American history of the 19th century. Perhaps Paul of Russia opened best to open the curtain of the first major Assassination of the 19th century, for on the night of 23rd March 1801 a band of drunken aristocratic officers, recently dismissed because Russia as now called with napoleonic's France and supposedly at peace burst in time bedroom of the Tsar of Russia at the heart of St Petersburg's newly built St. Michael's Castle.

Paul I of Russia, also known as Tsar Paul, reigned as Emperor of Russia from 1796 to 1801. He succeeded his mother, Catherine the Great and immediately began a mission to undo her legacy. Paul had deep animosity towards his mother and her actions as empress. Catherine and her son and heir Paul maintained a distant relationship throughout her reign. The aunt of Catherine's husband, Empress Elizabeth, took up the child as a passing fancy. Elizabeth proved an obsessive but incapable caretaker, as she had raised no children of her own. Paul was supervised by a variety of caregivers. Roderick McGrew briefly relates the neglect to which the infant heir was sometimes subject: "On one occasion he fell out of his crib and slept the night away unnoticed on the floor." Even after Elizabeth's death, relations with Catherine hardly improved. Paul was often jealous of the favours she would shower upon her lovers. In one instance, the empress gave one of her favourites 50,000 rubles on her birthday, while Paul received a cheap watch. Paul's early isolation from his mother created a distance between them that later events would reinforce. She never considered inviting him to share her power in governing Russia.

Paul adamantly protested his mother's policies, writing a veiled criticism in his Reflections, a dissertation on military reform.[10] In it, he directly disparaged expansionist warfare in favour of a more defensive military policy. Unenthusiastically received by his mother, Reflections appeared a threat to her authority and added weight to her suspicion of an internal conspiracy with Paul at its centre. For a courtier to have openly supported or shown intimacy towards Paul, especially following this publication, would have meant political suicide. But once Paul's son Alexander was born, it appeared that she had found a more suitable heir.

This brief gives you the reader an introduction to the dysfunctional upbringing of Emperor Paul the chapter that follows gives the influence of the angels of Lucifer in the rise and ultimate assassination of a man of influence whose DNA characterised that of his father Peter 111 over that of the thorn in his side, mother Catherine the great whom he succeeded and immediately began a mission to undo her legacy. Paul had deep animosity towards his mother and her actions as empress.

CHAPTER 7.

ENTER THE MODERN AGE

Emperor Paul was idealistic and capable of great generosity, but he was also mercurial and capable of vindictiveness. In spite of doubts about his legitimacy, he greatly resembled his father, Peter III, and other Romanovs as well and shared the same character. During the first year of his reign, Paul emphatically reversed many of his mother's policies. Although he accused many of Jacobinism, he allowed Catherine's best-known critic, Radishchev, to return from Siberian exile. Besides Radishchev, he liberated Novikov from Schlüsselburg fortress, and also Tadeusz Kościuszko, yet after liberation both were confined to their own estates under police supervision. He viewed the Russian nobility as decadent and corrupt and was determined to transform them into a disciplined, principled, loyal caste resembling a medieval chivalric order. To those few who conformed to his view of a modern-day knight (e.g., his favourites Kutuzov, Arakcheyev, and Rostopchin) he granted more serfs during the five years of his reign than his mother had presented to her lovers during her thirty-four years. Those who did not share his chivalric views were dismissed or lost their places in court: seven field marshals and 333 generals fell into this category.

Paul's early foreign policy can largely be seen as a reaction against his mother's. In foreign policy, this meant that he opposed the many expansionary wars she fought and instead preferred to pursue a more peaceful, diplomatic path. Immediately upon taking the throne, he recalled all troops outside Russian borders, including the struggling expedition Catherine II had sent to conquer Iran through the Caucasus and the 60,000 men she had promised to Britain and Austria to help them defeat the French. Paul hated the French before their revolution, and afterwards, with their republican and anti-religious views, he detested them even more. In addition to this, he knew French expansion hurt Russian interests, but he recalled his mother's troops primarily because he firmly opposed wars of expansion. He also believed that Russia needed substantial governmental and military reforms to avoid an economic collapse and a revolution before Russia could wage war on foreign soil.

Paul offered to mediate between Austria and France through Prussia and pushed Austria to make peace, but the two countries made peace without his assistance, signing the Treaty of Campoformio in October 1797. This treaty, with its affirmation of French control over islands in the Mediterranean and the partitioning of the Republic of Venice, upset Paul, who saw it as creating more instability in the region and displaying France's ambitions in the Mediterranean. In response, he offered asylum to the Prince de Condé and his army, as well as the future Louis XVIII, both of whom had been forced out of Austria by the treaty.[9]:288–289 By this point, the French Republic had seized Italy, the Netherlands, and Switzerland, establishing republics with constitutions in each, and Paul felt that Russia now needed to play an active role in Europe in order to overthrow what the republic had created and restore traditional authorities. In this goal, he found a willing ally in the Austrian chancellor Baron Thugut who hated the French and loudly criticised revolutionary principles Britain and the Ottoman Empire joined Austria and Russia to stop French expansion, free territories under their control and re-establish the old monarchies.

The only major power in Europe that did not join Paul in his anti-French campaign was Prussia, whose distrust of Austria and the security they got from their current relationship with France prevented them from joining the coalition. Despite the Prussians' reluctance, Paul decided to move ahead with the war, promising 60,000 men to support Austria in Italy and 45,000 men to help England in North Germany and the Netherlands. Paul spent the following years away from the Imperial Court, content to remain at his private estates at Gatchina Palace with his growing family and perform Prussian drill exercises. As Catherine grew older, she became less concerned that her son attended court functions; her attention focused primarily on the future Emperor Alexander I.

After Alexander and his brother Constantine were born, she had them placed under her charge, just as Elizabeth had done with Paul. That Catherine grew to favour Alexander as sovereign of Russia rather than Paul is unsurprising. She met secretly with Alexander's tutor de La Harpe to discuss his pupil's ascension and attempted to convince Alexander's mother Maria to sign a proposal authorising her son's legitimacy. Both efforts proved fruitless, and though Alexander agreed to his grandmother's wishes, he remained respectful of his father's position as immediate successor to the Russian throne.

Catherine suffered a stroke on 17 November 1796 and died without regaining consciousness. Paul's first act as Emperor was to inquire about and, if possible, destroy her testament, as he feared it would exclude him from succession and leave the throne to Alexander. These fears may have contributed to Paul's promulgation of the Pauline Laws, which established the strict principle of primogeniture in the House of Romanov, leaving the throne to the next male heir. As emperor, Paul sought revenge for the deposition of his father, and the coup of his mother.

The army, then poised to attack Persia in accordance with Catherine's last design, was recalled to the capital within one month of Paul's accession. Upon his death in 1762, Peter had been buried without any honours in the Annunciation Church at the Alexander Nevsky Monastery in St. Petersburg. Immediately after the death of his mother, Paul ordered his father's remains transferred, first to the church in the Winter Palace and then to the Peter and Paul Cathedral in St. Petersburg, the burial site of the Romanovs. 60-year-old Count Alexei Orlov, who had played a role in deposing Peter III and possibly also in his death, was made to walk in the funeral cortege, holding the Imperial Crown of Russia as he walked in front of Peter's coffin. Peter III had never been crowned so at the time of his reburial, Paul personally performed the ritual of coronation on his remains. Paul responded to the rumour of his illegitimacy by parading his descent from Peter the Great. The inscription on the monument to the first Emperor of Russia near St. Michael's Castle reads in Russian "*To the Great-Grandfather from the Great-Grandson*". This is an allusion to the Latin *"Petro Primo Car therein Secunda"*, the dedication by Catherine on the 'Bronze Horseman' statue of Peter the Great.

The death of de Ribas in December 1800 delayed the assassination; but, on the night of 23 March 1801, a band of dismissed officers murdered Paul at the newly completed palace of Saint Michael's Castle. The assassins included General Bennigsen, a Hanoverian in the Russian service, and General Yashvil, a Georgian. They charged into Paul's bedroom, flushed with drink after dining together, and found the emperor hiding behind some drapes in the corner. The conspirators pulled him out, forced him to the table, and tried to compel him to sign his abdication. Paul offered some resistance, and Nikolay Zubov struck him with a sword, after which the assassins strangled and trampled him to death. Paul's successor on the Russian throne, his 23-year-old son Alexander, was actually in the palace at the time of the killing; he had "given his consent to the overthrow of Paul, but had not supposed that this would be carried out by means of assassination".[■] General Nikolay Zubov announced his accession to the heir, accompanied by the admonition, "Time to grow up! Go and rule!" Alexander I did not punish the assassins, and the court physician, James Wylie, declared apoplexy the official cause of death. There is some evidence that Paul I was venerated as a saint among the Russian Orthodox populace,[■] even though he was never officially canonised by any of the Orthodox Churches.

Paul's premonitions of assassination were well-founded. His attempts to force the nobility to adopt a code of chivalry alienated many of his trusted advisors. The Emperor also discovered outrageous machinations and corruption in the Russian treasury. As he had revoked Catherine's decree allowing corporal punishment of the free classes, and directed reforms that resulted in greater rights for the peasantry and provided for better treatment for serfs on agricultural estates, many of his policies greatly annoyed the nobility and induced his enemies to work out a plan of action.

Following Paul's death and the resumption of the war in 1804, Russia's record in combat was illustrious. In April 1805 Britain, Russia and Austria signed a treaty with the aim of removing the French from Holland and Switzerland. Yet the Austrians were crushed at the Battle of Ulm, and in December 1805, an Austro-Russian army nominally led by Alexander 1 was divided in combat at Austerlitz. Prussia entered the coalition in place of exhausted Austrians, and in October 1806, French troops entered Berlin. The French troops Rowen chased Russian forces out of Poland and forced Alexander to conclude a humiliating peace at Tilsit in July 180. Russia was now Napoleon's ally, and in return for Finland, stolen from neighbour Sweden, entered the lists against Britain and Austria.

In 1819 the French Empire reached its greatest extent. Franco-Russian relations had deteriorated to the extent that Alexander was now a very unwilling ally in the fight to eliminate British maritime power. Russia and Sweden signed a sect ret agreement directed against Napoleon's France. And later Napoleon committed some major errors that led to his downfall. His Grande Arm'ee of 650,000-men invaded Russia. His own health issues and delaying the winter. By November 1812, when its remnants crossed back into Poland and were peremptorily deserted by their emperor, only 27,000 fit soldiers remained. The great army of Ulm and Austerlitz was no more.

Tsar Alexander II was known as the 'Liberator', enacting wide-ranging liberal reforms across Russia. His policies included the emancipation of serfs (peasant labourers) in 1861, the abolition of corporal punishment, the promotion of self-government and the ending of some of the nobility's historic privileges. His reign coincided with an increasingly volatile political situation in Europe and Russia, and he survived several assassination attempts during his rule. These were mainly orchestrated by radical groups (anarchists and revolutionaries) who wanted to overthrow Russia's system of autocracy. He was assassinated by a group named *Narodnaya Volya* (The People's Will) in March 1881, bringing an end to an era that had promised ongoing liberalisation and reform. Alexander's successors, worried they would meet a similar fate, enacted much more conservative agendas.

The history of the Romanov Tsars of Russia did not have to end in a dark cellar in Ekaterinburg in July 1018. Om the second half of the 19th century, one ruler seized the chance to inaugurate genuine reform of Russia's rigid institutions. After Alexander 11 freed millions of surfs at the stroke of a pen and introduced genuine reforms. On the surface, it looked like Russia was liberated from it medieval shackles and embracing the modern era. Whilst many thought the pace of change was too slow, the agents of change promising reforms proposed by the Tzar still saw them as autocratic sovereign missions. The effect was that lifting the lid on Russia's long suppression of freedom prompted the contents to boil over. The assassination of Alexander 11 by a revolutionary suicide bomber, a savage means of execution, but bu no means peculiar to this 21st-century phenomenon, plunged Ri usia back into reaction, and laid the foundations for the tragic events of 1917-18.

Russian reform seemed impossible in 1855, the year Alexander came to the throne. How predecessor, Nicholas 1 had turned Russia into the policeman of Europe, and his own territories into little more than a police state. Personal and political censorship was rife, and criticism of authorities was regarded as a serious offence. Any semblance of protest was crushed with extreme vigour. Young Alexander soon showed he was very different from his reactionary father. To the horror of Nicholas, his eldest son showed no love of soldering. Instead preferred parties and patronage of the arts a far cry from frigid receptions to artistic innovation and achievements off his father's philistine regime.

Alexander's first reaction on ascending the throne in 1855 demonstrated his distal for military adventures. Russia was still mired in the Crimean War, which had reached a stalemate outside of the fortress city of Sebastopol. Alexander soon extricated his country from meaningful conflict, achieving peace with honour and ensuring that his exhausted opponents, Britain, France and Turkey, gained little worth with the war over.

 Alexander embarked on an astonishing sequence of social and political reforms. Firstly to apply Western standards of commercial development to the nations' backward approach to business. The Russian economy was liberalised and for the first time in its history private financing of companies and initiatives was achieved. Twenty years after Western Europe and North America had begun to build railway networks, Alexander commenced his own vast programs of railway construction, having no issue in borrowing from international; sources He then went into modernising his army and navy in 1874, using the British reforms of 1870s as his starting point. The judiciary was reformed in 1864. on the Napoleonic model. Local government was dramatically overhauled in the manner of Western European nations in the 1860s, with local elected assemblies gaining restrictive rights of taxation. police activity was curbed and centrally controlled, and capital punishment was abolished.

Alexander's ground-groundbreaking reforms inevitably met with protest from both the Left and Right. what is particularly impressive about his character is that repeated assignation attempts throughout his reign did not deter him from his reformist programme. Nor did the tsar shrink from military intervention where political advantage could be had. The 'Monument to the Tsar Liberator' in Sofia commemorates Alexander 11's decisive role in the part- liberation of Bulgaria from Ottoman rule during the brief, one-sided Russo-Turkish War 1877-78. However, Alexander's liberalism did not extend to all the territories in the Russian Empire. Poland and Lithuania were expressly excluded from reforms, and Alexander has made it clear that autonomous rule in these states was neatly a pipe dream. The Polish ' January Uprising' got 1863-4 was savagely repressed, with thousands of Poles executed, and tens of thousands deported to Siberia. Martial law was imposed in Lithuania, lasting from 1863 until the First World War, while native languages were banned in all western lands.

While dissent in Poland, Lithuania, Belarus and Ukraine was ruthlessly expunged. Then Alexander became strangely sympathetic to the nationalist cause of what is known as the Grand Duchy of Finland. In 1863 he reestablished the Diet of Finland, encouraging the use of Finnish as national language for all classes and permitted the reintroduction of Finland's currency, the *markka*. In 1864, while Poles were denouncing Alexander's ruthless attendance etc eradicated expressions of Polish nationhood, the Finns were etc erecting a monument to Alexander' The Liberator' in Helsinki.

The Finn's adulation was not, however, matched by the reactions to the reign of the many tsar's more disenchanted subjects. As his rule progressed, Alexander grew used to assassination attempts. On 4th April 1866, Dmitry Karakzov attempted to shoot him in St. Petersburg. On the morning of 20th April 1879, Alexander Solovjev shot at the fleeing tsar five times but missed. In December 1879, a radical group calling themselves 'Narodnaya Volya' ('The Peoples Will') blew up the railway line between Levadia and Moscow but missed the tsar's train. On the evening of 5th February 1880, the same revolutionaries set off an explosion that killed and injured some 67 of, the main guards, but Alexander himself was safe.

The last of Alexanders' nine lives expired on 13th March 1881. It seemed at first he had survived yet another attack when a bomb thrown in central St.Petersburg, hit the Tsar's bulletproof carriage, while several standing by were injured the Tsar was unharmed. This time though the assassin had backed up a plan, a suicide bomber carrying hand grades immediately assaulted the shaken tsar by

throwing the grenades in the carriage. The assassin was predictably, a Pole; Ignacy Hyrniewiecki from Bobrujsk. he died at the
scene whilst the Tsar lingered for a few hours. The assassin's assistants were rounded up, tried nat hanged. More seriously. the assassination dissolved and prospects of further reform. the Russian grip
on Poland tightened, and thousands of Jews were expelled from
red States for no good reason, other than that they pronounced
anti-Semitism of the tsar, Alexander 111. Almost all of Alexanders
'11 reforms except serfdom were reversed by this boorish, brusque
and innately conservative second son. Alexander 11's plan for a
genuinely representative assembly was completed before his assassination was thrown out. Such an assembly would not be con-
vened until 1917, and by then, it was already too late.

Abraham Lincoln is arguably America's most famous president: he led
America through the Civil War, preserved the Union, abolished slavery,
modernised the economy and bolstered the federal government. A champion of black rights, including voting rights, Lincoln was disliked by Confederate states. His assassin, John Wilkes Booth, was a Confederate spy whose
self-professed motive was to avenge the Southern states. Lincoln was shot
at point-blank range whilst he was at the theatre, dying the following morning.
It was in the middle of Act 11, Scene 2, that the character Asa Trenchard
played by actor Harry Hawk, uttered a line, that every night for sever
years, had provoked an enormous laugh. A fellow actor wan friend of the
theatre owner John.T.Ford, had intended to use this laughter to mask the
sound of gunfire. The ploy worked when the assassin slipped into Lincoln's
box and shot the president in the back of the head with his .44 Derringer
pistol. Lincoln's friend Major Henry Rathbone, also in the box, immediately tacked him but was stabbed and slashed by a dagger that the assassin had
brought with him for such an emergency and was forced to let the murderer
go.

The assassin John Wilkes Booth, a southern sympathiser, then jousted from
the box to the sr tag, reputedly breaking his leg after it snagged in the patri-
otic butting use as stage decoration. Some witnessed v later claimed he
shouted sic temper tyrannies- thus always to tyrants. He then staggered to
his waiting horse and rode to a nearby sympathetic doctor to have his injured leg treated.

The assassin, John Wilkes Booth, was born in Maryland in 1838, from his earliest childhood he was steeped in the classics, and in particular, he developed his skill as a Shakespearian actor,. Strikingly handsome, a proficient athlete and an excellent swordsman, he was the Oliver of his day. Booth was a fervent supporter of the Confederate cause from the very beginning of the war despite living in upstate Maryland, lying north of the national capital, was predominantly Southern in allegiance. Nevertheless, he promised his pro-Union mother that he would not enlist in the Confederate army, and he lived out the war performing as an actor- and behind the sevens, a Confer derate spy-in Washington, D.C.

President Lincoln was an avid theatre-goer, Indeed, he had actually seen a play at the Ford Theatre with Booth as the main character. Lincoln had asked to meet Booth after a performance who huffily refused. Soon after this event, Booth planned to kidnap the president, allegedly in order to secure the release of 10,000 Southern soldiers held in Northern prisons. Approaches to the Confederate Secret Service come to nothing. However, fired up by the Southern military collapse he began to plot his revenge. Booth's final scene involved not only the assassination of the president, his assistants were supposed to murder Secret of State William Seward and Vice-President Andrew Johnson, while Booth himself was to subsequently kill celebrated army commander-in-chief, General Grant. In the ensuing chaos, Booth hoped that the Confederate government could recognise and then take the initiative to recommence the war. Booth did not evade capture for long. he was eventually cornered been Union troops in a barn near Bowling Green, Virginia, on 26 April. The barn was set on fire, and Booth was fatally wounded by gunfire and died on the farmhouse pouch. Lincoln did not die immediately, though doctors had declared the wound fatal. He lay in a coma for nine hours before he was officially pronounced dead at 7.20 a.m. on 15th April 1865. Abraham Lincoln's legacy as the 16th President of the United States is immense. he is judged by many to have been the most skilled. and successfully won overall American Heads of State. His adherence, even in the darkest days of civil war, to the cause of American nationhood, and have helped inspire succeeding generations. As a right-wing member of the US House he founded the Republican party, anchoring his policies firmly to the abolition of slavery. Thus it was not surprising t he won the republican nomination from the Northern supporters of slave free States. In the ensuing contest, he split the vote in the South and won over many democratic voters, enabling Lincoln to win.

The Confederate act of belligerence in attacking Fort Sumter, South Carolina, in April 1861 made civil war inevitable. But in the next four years, Lincoln constantly insisted that the fighting was to preserve the Union and to abolish slavery. he saw his Emancipation Proclamation of 22 September 1862, freeing slaves in territories not under Union control from 1 January 1863, largely as a way of weakening the economic base of the South rather than as an anti-slavery measure. That came later when the 13th Amendment to the US Constitution permanently abolished slavery throughout the nation. Lincoln's leadership was vital in his ultimate victory. He dismissed those senior generals who failed; beginning with Commander-in-Chief George B. McLellan, who was standing against him in the 1864 election. But when he found a military leader who emerged to have the right answers, in the person of Ulysses S. Grant, he defended him from vicious internal criticism. Lincoln was an outstanding diplomat and successful defuser of a war with Britain in 1861. Lincoln's memorable Gettysburg Address of 19th November 1863, although a little ahead of its time, brilliantly articulated the rationale behind the Union effort. At the same time, Lincoln managed his own landslide victory, an astonishing achievement at the time of a bitterly divisive civil conflict.

Lincoln's assassination was immediately recognised as an irreparable loss, He became the first president to lie in state, and thousands lined the route as his body was carried by train in a grand funeral procession through several states on the way back to Illinois, where he was buried in Oak Ridge cemetery, Springfield.

CHAPTER 8.

DECADES OF ASSASSINATIONS

Just before 10 a.m. on Sunday 28h June 1914. **Archduke Franz Ferdinand**, the heir to the Austro-Hungarian throne, arrived by train in Sarajevo, the capital of Bosnia-Herzegovina. The aim of the visit was a goodwill tour of a dangerous treatise province, which began with a motorised cavalcade through the streets of the city. Franz Ferdinand and his wife, Sophie, were placed in the second car of the public procession, behind the commissioner of police and the Major of Sarajevo. The top of the royal vehicle was rolled back in order to allow the crowds a good view of its occupants.

Bosnia-Herzegovina was then the Austro-Hungarian Empire's most south-easterly outpost. Serbian nationalists, who wished to unite the Serbian parts of Bosnia with the independent Serbia, had taken advantage of the turbulent state of Balkan politics- with two local wars in the past three years- to form a nationalist group, known as the Black Hand, devoted to the attaining of Serbian independence by violent means. Had they been able to communicate with Franz Ferdinand before their fate-filled assignation, they would have been privy to the fact that he was already planning their independence to unite Serbia in any cast. But the plot was greater than their intentions, for not gave a secret society of One World Order the excuse to ignite the First World War as a result of the assignation. The black hand had previously unsuccessfully attempted to assassinate Emperor Franz Josef himself in 1911. Now with Franz Ferdinand heir to the throne, they saw the chance to throw the torrenting Austrian Empire into disarray. With the tangled web of countries ill at ease with their lot under one kingdom or another in the European world, the mind of the bloody black hand of assassins could not see the bigger picture through their actions. Franz Ferdinand's death was the catalyst for bringing on the bloodiest war to date.

The target arch duel had grown up a poor little rich boy, in the kingdom of his father Karl Ludwig of Austria. Franz was the younger brother of Emperor Franz Josef and became heir to the dukedom of Modena when he was age 12 and thereby one of the richest individuals typical of a healthy young man of his time, seemingly removed from the imperial throne, he indulged himself in the passion of hunting and travel. However, his life lost its balance somewhat with the suicide of his cousin in 1889, Crown Prince Rudolf with his mistress at his hunting lodge in Mayerling. So Franz's father, Archduke Karl Ludwig became heir to the throne of Austria-Hungary. However, he was an old man and all eyes were on the young Franz Ferdinand, his eldest son, to invigorate the hardened arteries of Austria's shaky multiple-speaking states under the empire.

In his treatment of his newly appointed nephew, Emperor Franz Josef showed he had learnt nothing from the tragic death of his son by his own hand. History appears to repeat itself when, in 1895, Franz Ferdinand met a minor aristocrat Countess Sophie von Chatek, a lady in waiting for the Duchess of Teschen, at the ball in Prague. They quickly fell in love, keeping the affair secret for two years. However, Habsburg marriages were traditionally conducted with the reigning families of Europe. The Chatek was emphatically not one of these, and when the affair was discovered in 1889, Sofie was dismissed from her position, and the emperor forbade the wedding.

Whilst Franz Josef was oblivious of recent history,, other European sovereigns were not, and those like Tsar Nicholas 11 of Russia and Kaiser Wilhelm 11 of Germany begged him to reconsider. Finally, in 1899, Emperor Franz Joseph agreed to permit Franz Ferdinand to marry Sophie, on the condition that the marriage would restrict her from the throne and that their descendants would not have succession rights to the throne. Sophie would not share her husband's rank, title, precedence, or privileges; as such, she would not normally appear in public beside him. She would not be allowed to ride in the royal carriage or sit in the royal box in theatres. The wedding took place on 1 July 1900, at Reichstadt (now Zákupy) in Bohemia; Franz Joseph did not attend the affair, nor did any archduke including Franz Ferdinand's brothers.[5] The only members of the imperial family who were present were Franz Ferdinand's stepmother, Princess Maria Theresa of Braganza; and her two daughters. Upon the marriage, Sophie was given the title "Princess of Hohenberg" (*Fürstin von Hohenberg*) with the style "Her Serene Highness" (*Ihre Durchlaucht*). In 1909, she was given the more senior title "Duchess of Hohenberg" (*Herzogin von Hohenberg*) with the style "Her Highness" (*Ihre Hoheit*). This raised her status considerably, but she was still required to yield precedence at court to all the archduchesses. Whenever a function required the couple to assemble with the other members of the imperial family, Sophie was forced to stand far down the line, separated from her husband.

Franz Ferdinand, like most males in the ruling Habsburg line, entered the Austro-Hungarian Army at a young age. He was frequently and rapidly promoted, given the rank of lieutenant at age fourteen, captain at twenty-two, colonel at twenty-seven, and major general at thirty-one.[17] While never receiving formal staff training, he was considered eligible for command and at one point briefly led the primarily Hungarian 9th Hussar Regiment. In 1898 he was given a commission "at the special disposition of His Majesty" to make inquiries into all aspects of the military services and military agencies were commanded to share their papers with him.

He also held honorary ranks in the Austro-Hungarian Navy, and received the rank of Admiral at the close of the Austro-Hungarian naval manoeuvres in September 1902. Franz Ferdinand exerted influence on the armed forces even when he did not hold a specific command through a military chancery that produced and received documents and papers on military affairs. This was headed by Alexander Brosch von Aarenau and eventually employed a staff of sixteen. His authority was reinforced in 1907 when he secured the retirement of the Emperor's confidant Friedrich von Beck-Rzikowsky as Chief of the General Staff. Beck's successor, Franz Conrad von Hötzendorf, was personally selected by Franz Ferdinand.

On Sunday, 28 June 1914, at about 10:45 a.m., Franz Ferdinand and his wife were assassinated in Sarajevo.of The perpetrator was 19-year-old Gavrilo Princip, a member of Young Bosnia and one of a group of assassins organised and armed by the Black Hand. Earlier in the day, the couple had been attacked by Nedeljko Čabrinović, also a Young Bosnia conspirator, who had thrown a grenade at their car. However, the bomb detonated behind them, injuring the occupants in the following car. On arriving at the Governor's residence, Franz asked "So you welcome your guests with bombs!"

After a short rest at the Governor's residence, the royal couple insisted on seeing all those who had been injured by the bomb at the local hospital. However, no one told the drivers that the itinerary had been changed. When the error was discovered, the drivers had to turn around. As the cars backed down the street and onto a side street, the line of cars stalled. At this time, Princip was sitting at a cafe across the street. He instantly seized his opportunity and walked across the street and shot the royal couple. He first shot Sophie in the abdomen and then shot Franz Ferdinand in the neck. Franz leaned over his crying wife. He was still alive when witnesses arrived to render aid. His dying words too Sophie were, "Don't die, darling, live for our children." Princip's weapon was the pocket-sized FN Model 1910 pistol chambered for the .380 ACP cartridge provided him by Serbian Army Military Intelligence Lieutenant-Colonel and Black Hand leader Dragutin Dimitrijević. Franz Ferdinand's aides attempted to undo his coat but realised they needed scissors to cut it open: the outer lapel had been sewn to the inner front of the jacket for a smoother fit to improve his appearance to the public. Whether or not as a result of this obstacle, his wound could not be attended to in time to save him, and he died within minutes. Sophie also died en route to the hospital.

Serbia was delighted with the assassination, whilst Austria held Serbs responsible for the tragic event. An Australia ultimatum which demanded control of the newly independent count try's affairs, was presented to the Serbian government on 23 July and Austria declared war and assured of support of Germany. Supported by German followers, slavs in Russia, and Serbia resisted., and on 28th July Austria declared war on the Balkan state. This prompted Russia to mobilise its armed forces; which in turn encouraged Germany to do likewise. This way the First World War began.

The assassin Gavrilo Princip, after the assassination, tried to kill himself by poison. The poison was past its use-by date and did not work, whilst his pistol was wrestled from his hand before he had a chance to shoot himself. Astonishingly he was not executed according to Austria's custom of the time, as he was under 20 years of age. Thus, the young man was given the death penalty and sentenced to 20 years in prison. He died in his cell of tuberculosis on 28 April 1918.

Grigory Yefimovich Novykh-'Rasputin may not have been single-handedly responsible for the 1917 Russian Revolution, but his assassination in 1916 did nothing to stem the tide of nationwide protest. To some extent, a direct correlation can be made between the ascendancy of the mystical Siberian monk in the years immedi-

ately preceding the 1917 Revolution and the exception of the Romanovs in the damp Siberian cellar, barely 18 months after
Rasputin's own untimely and excessively violent death.

Word of Rasputin's spirituality and charisma spread through Siberia in the
early 1900s. At some point in 1905, he travelled to the city of Kazan, where
he was admired as a holy man who could help people resolve their spiritual
crises and anxieties. Despite rumours that Rasputin was having sex with
female followers, he made a favourable impression on the Father Superior
of the Seven Lakes Ministry outside Kazan as well as the local church officials. They recommended to Bishop Sergei, the rector of St. Petersburg
Theological Seminary at Alexander Nevsky Monastery, for Rasputin to
travel to St.Petersburg. Sergei had introduced Archimandrite Theofan, in-
spector of the theological seminary, who was well connected in St. Petersburg society and later served as confessor to the Tzar and his wife. Theofan
was so impressed with Rasputin that he invited him to stay at his house and
introduced him to influential friends in St. Petersburg, thus gaining him entry into salons and aristocratic gatherings for religious discussions. It was
through these meetings that Rasputin attracted some of his early influential
followers though many would ultimately turn away from him.

So in brief I now recall the life and tales told of Rasputin He was born of
peasant stock in the village of Pokrovskoye, along the Tura River in the
Tobolsk Governate, Siberia on 21st January 1869. The day after his birth
was the feast day of Orthodox Saint Gregory (Grigori) of Nysa, he was thus
named Grigori Yefimovich Rasputin. Yefim, his father juggled a peasant
farm and duties as a church elder, government courier and ferryman of
goods and people across the Tura River. All of Rasputin's seven siblings
died in infancy or early childhood except for a ninth child Feodosiya whom
Rasputin was very close to and was Godfather to her children. Historians
agree that he was not formally educated and remained illiterate well into his
adulthood. There are archival records suggesting that he was a somewhat
unruly youth possibly involved in heavy drinking, small episodes of theft
and showed total disrespect for the local authorities. There is no evidence to
prove the truth of his horse stealing, blasphemy and bearing false witness,
of which he was accused. In 1886 as a young man he made his way, probably on foot to Tyumen, some 250 km to the east by northeast, then headed
due east for another 2,800 km to Moscow. There he met Praskovya

Dubrovina, a peasant girl. After a brief courtship, he married her in 1887 and returned to his native village. Praskovya remained there for the rest of her life, raising three children, one boy born Dmitri (1895) and two girls. Maria (1898) and Varvara (1900). Rasputin continued his wanderings and from time to time returned to the village to be with his devoted wife Praskovya and their family. In 1897 Rasputin left his pregnant wife on the family farm and went on a pilgrimage as he had developed a renewed interest in religion.

It is suggested but not proven that he had a vision of the Virgin Mary and set out on a spiritual quest. But it has also been suggested that he left the village to escape charges for his role in a horse theft. It was after this time of his initial pilgrimage that a theological student Melty Zaborosky may have influenced him. Whatever the reasons for Rasputin's continuing pilgrimages, he cast off his old life at the ripe old age of twenty-eight and despite having been married ten years, left his wife with an infant son and another on the way. It was apparent that he was occasioned some sort of emotional conflict or spiritual crisis in his life. On shorter pilgrimages, he had stayed at the Holy Znamensky Monastery and also on another at the Tobolsky's Cathedral. It was the visit to the St. Nicholas Cathedral in 1897 that he was transformed. There he met and was profoundly humbled by an elder known as Makary. He apparently spent several months there and learned to read and write. He later complained of some monks being engaged in homosexual acts and criticised the monastic life as being to coercive. Returning to the farm and his wife, looking dishevelled and behaving differently, he became a vegetarian, swore off alcohol, and was often seen praying and singing out much more reverently than he had ever done in the past.

He would leave his wife and family often on pilgrimages for months and even years at a time, wandering the country and visiting holy sites. It is believed he wandered as far as Mount Athos, the centre of Eastern Orthodox monastic life in 1900 and where the gifts of the Magi, wise men are still housed. The three gifts to the infant Jesus at his birth; are gifts of spiritual meaning: gold as a symbol of kinship on earth, frankincense as a symbol of deity, and myrrh, an embalming oil as a symbol of death,. Like all Prophet's seem to do, by the early 1900s he had developed a small circle of followers, primarily family members and other local peasants, who prayed with him on Sundays and on holy days. He returned to his home and village church from time to time and eventually built a small chapel in g his father's root cellar where his family household group and followers met in secret from the local villagers and the priest who considered his activities with some suspicion and hostility. It was rumoured that female followers were ceremoniously washing him before each meeting, that the group sang strange songs and that Rasputin had joined a religious sect whose ecstatic rituals were rumoured to include self-flagellation and sexual orgies. However, repeated investigations failed to establish that Rasputin was ever a member of a sect, and rumours of self-flagellation and sexual orgies have been unfounded.

Alternative religious, spiritual and theosophy movements were popularised among city aristocracy, so Rasputin's ideas and strange behaviours made him the subject of intense curiosity. His appeal may have been enhanced by the fact that he was a native Russian unlike other self-described 'holy men' before him. He formed friendships with several members of the aristocracy, including the " Black Princesses," Militsa and Anastasia of Montenegro, who married the Tsar's cousin, Grand Duke Peter Nikolaevich and Prince George Maximilianovich Romanowsky, and were instrumental in introducing Rasputin to the Tsar and his family. They met at Peter's Palace on 1st November 1905 and the Tsar wrote in his diary: "…made an acquaintance of a man of God- Grigori, from Tobosky Province." Rasputin returned home after that meeting and after six months returned to St Petersburg sending Nicholas a telegram asking to be presented to the Tsar. He met the royal family again in July 1906 and in November was introduced to their children. At some point, the Royal family became convinced that Rasputin possessed miraculous power to heal the son's affliction. Due to the fact Alexei's hereditary condition caused painful internal bleeding, Rasputin was initially asked to pray for the child. Much of Rasputin's influence over the Royal family and others was the fact that on several occasions the pain eased and the bleeding stopped. Princess Alexandra had a "passionate attachment" to Rasputin, believing he could cure her son's affliction. The fact that son Alexia's bleeding condition ceased immediately after Rasputin prayed for him in the spring of 1907, Rasputin was then hailed as 'an indispensable member of the Royal entourage.' The Tsarina's good friend, Anna Vyrubova became convinced as a faithful follower of Rasputin, that he had miraculous powers. She became his most convinced and devoted influential advocate. It is thought that Rasputin controlled the bleeding of Alexis by disallowing the administering of Aspirin and other psychic abilities.

During the summer of 1912, Alexei developed a haemorrhage in his thigh and groin after a jolting in a carriage he was riding at the royal hunting grounds at Spara. He was in severe pain and delirious with a fever and appeared close to death. Alexandra asked Anna her friend, to send Rasputin a telegram in Siberia where he was staying, asking him to pray. Rasputin quickly replied: "God has seen your tears and heard our prayers. Do not grieve. The little One will not die, Do not allow the doctors to bother him too much." The next morning Alexei's condition had not changed, but Alexandra was encouraged by the message and regained some hope that her child would not die. Alexei's bleeding stopped the next day. The attending Dr. Fedrov later admitted: "The recovery was wholly inexplicable from a medical viewpoint." He understood how the press had faith in Rasputin as a miracle man. "On another occasion, when Alexie's bleeding occurred, Rasputin would come, walk up to the patient, look at him and spit. The bleeding would stop in no time. How could the Empress not trust Rasputin after that?" History has it recorded that Rasputin stopped the bleeding by calming both mother and child, through hypnosis. Of course, his healing powers gained him considerable status and power at the court, The tsar appointed him ' lamplighter,' charging him with keeping the lamps lit before religious icons in the palace, and gained him regular access to the palace and the royal family. He becomes close enough to ask a special favour of the Tsar, to change his name to Rasputin-Noviy (New). Rasputin used his influence to gain sexual favours from admirers and worked diligently to expand his influence.

Rasputin became a controversial figure. He was accused by his enemies of religious heresy and rape, was suspected of exerting undue political influence on the Tsar, and was rumoured to be having an affair with the Tsarina. Opposition to Rasputin's influence grew in the church and he was soon denounced as a heretic; the local Bishop accusing him of spreading false doctrines. In St.Petersburg, Rasputin faced opposition from prominent critics, including Prime Minister Peter Stolypin and the Tsar's secret police force. Stolypin on ordering an investigation about Rasputin's activities, approached the Tsar with his report. However, he did not succeed in reigning in Rasputin's influence nor exiling him from St.Petersburg. One of his former followers, a Kehioniya Berlatskaya accused him of rape.

Rumours multiplied that Rasputin had assaulted female followers and behaved inappropriately on visits to the royal family. Particularly with the teenage daughters Olga and Tatyana, which was reported widely in the press in 1910. Whilst World War 1, the dissolution of feudalism, and a meddling government bureaucracy all contributed to Russia's economic decline, many laid the blame on Alexandra and her evil advisor Rasputin. In November 2016, an outspoken member of the Duma Vladimir Purishkevick stated that the Tsar's ministers had "been turned into marionettes slating him as 'the evil genius of Russia and the Tsarina'- who has remained a German on the Russian throne and alien to the country and its people." The die had been cast and it was not long before the Royals would be exiled in a revolution and Rasputin would be brought to death.

In July 2014 Rasputin had survived an assassination attempt by a peasant woman back in his home at Pokrovskoye. He had been seriously wounded but somehow survived after a long recovery in hospital Another earlier attempt on his life in 1911 was by Guseva, who was a follower of Iliodor, one of a group of established figures who attempted to drive a wedge between the Royal family and Rasputin and failed. Iliodorr was banished from St.Petersburg and ultimately defrocked. Guseva the former priest who had supported Rasputin before denouncing his sexual escapades and self-aggrandisement, claimed to have acted alone having read in the newspapers and believing "the false prophet was an Antichrist." Both the Police and Rasputin believed that Iliodor had instigated the attempt on Rasputin's life...he thus fled the country before he could be questioned and Guseva was not found to be responsible for reasons of insanity.

Rasputin was murdered in a plot organised by a group of noted leaders led by Prince Felix Yusupov, Grand Duke, and right-wing politician Vladimir Purishkevich, who decided that Rasputin's influence over the Tsarina and the whole Royal family threatened the empire. They concocted a plan to kill him in December 1916, by inviting him to a dinner engagement on 30th December 1916 at the home of Felix Yusupov. On arrival, Rasputin was usurped into the basement dining area and was offered tea and cakes laced with cyanide. However, after eating his fill of cake and drinking the tea he appeared unaffected by the poison. Rasputin then asked for Madeira wine which was also laced with poison. He drank three full glasses but still showed no sign of distress. At around 2.30 am Yusupov excused himself to go upstairs where his fellow conspirators were waiting. He took a revolver from Dmitry Pavlovich and returned to the basement, pointed the gun at Rasputin and declared: "You better look at the crucifix on the wall and say a prayer, then shot him in the chest. The conspirator then took Rasputin's coat and in disguise drove to Rasputin's apartment in an attempt to make it look like he had returned home. They then returned to the Monika Palace, wherein Yusupov returned to the basement to ensure Rasputin was dead. Suddenly Rasputin leapt up and attacked Yusupov, grabbing him by the throat. Yusupov freed himself with great effort and raced upstairs. Rasputin followed and made it to the Palace's courtyard before being shot at point-blank range by Purishkevich in the forehead. The conspirators then wrapped his body in cloth, tied him in chains and weighed down his body with rocks, then drove to the Petrovsky Bridge and dropped his body in the ice-cold waters of the Malaya Nevka River. It was later reported by the two workmen who noticed blood on the bridge and Rasputin's boot on the ice, that his body had been found 200 meters downstream from the bridge. Once retrieved, it appeared Rasputin had broken the chains and crawled along the bottom of the river before his death.

Dr. Dmitry Kosorotov, the city's senior autopsy surgeon, reported that Rasputin's body had shown signs of severe trauma, including three gunshot wounds, one at close range to the forehead, a slice wound on his left side many of which he felt he had sustained post-mortem. He found no water in Rasputin's lungs. He found only one bullet in Rasputin's body but found it too difficult to identify the type to be traced. Rasputin's funeral and burial on January 2nd 1917 was attended by the Royal family and a few friends and he was buried in the grounds of the Royal palace. Rasputin's wife, mistress and children weren't invited, His body was exhumed and burned by a detachment of soldiers shortly after the Tsar abdicated the throne in March 1917, so that the grave would not become a rallying point for supporters of the old regime. The royal family were ultimately captured by revolutionary forces, denied asylum to Britain, and then brutally shot at Ekaterinburg on the 16th of July 1918.

CHAPTER 9.

THOSE THAT PLAN AND KILL

There is a theory that the British Secret Intelligence Service were involved in Rasputin's assassination, as the British agents were concerned that Rasputin would urge the Tsar to make peace with Germany, which would allow Germany to concentrate its military efforts on the Western front. The planned assassination was carried out under the command of Samuel Hoare and Oswald Rayner, who had attended Oxford University with Yusopov. Another theory exposed that Rayner had personally shot Rasputin. The British Intelligence archives state: "There is no convincing evidence that places any British agents at the murder scene. If British agents had been involved we would have expected to find some trace of that." The British archives on Rasputin are well buried now as is the smoking gun, reportedly a British revolver that fired a Webley 455-inch bullet found in the courtyard where Rasputin fell. British agent Rayner's chauffeur later wrote: "it is a little known fact that Rasputin was shot, not by a Russian but an English-man,'" and implied that his former boss was centrally involved. On his re-turn to England, Oswald Rayner not only confided to his cousin that he had been present at Rasputin's murder but also showed family members a bullet which he claimed he had acquired at the murder scene. Sadly, Rayner burnt all his papers before he died in 1961.

It is thus difficult to conclude whether Rasputin's death was indeed the result of the machinations of the British government or the plot of a group of conservative aristocrats and Romanov relatives. No one was ever charged for the assassination of Rasputin. The mystic and holy man died as he had lived with a powerful fight and much passion to live until his un-timely death. Rasputin knew of the power of words, of the political influ-ence he swayed over Russia and the Royal family, of his own powers to heal. He believed in the power of prayer of speaking in tongues and the in-fluence of his own nature had been granted to him by God from his birth.

Engelbert Dollfuss, (born October 4, 1892, Texing, Austro-Hungarian Empire—died July 25, 1934, Vienna, Austria), an Austrian statesman and, from 1932 to 1934, chancellor of Austria who destroyed the Austrian Republic and established an authoritarian regime based on conservative Roman Catholic and Italian Fascist principles.

After studying law and economics in Vienna and Berlin, Dollfuss became secretary to the Farmers' Association of Lower Austria province (Niederösterreichischer Bauernbund) and, in 1927, director of the Lower Austrian Chamber of agriculture. He was a member of the conservative and clerically oriented Christian Social Party, the core of whose constituency came from Austria's conservative peasantry. Dollfuss rose rapidly in Austrian politics, serving as president of the federal railways in 1930 and as minister of agriculture from 1931. In May 1932 he became chancellor, heading a conservative coalition led by the Christian Social Party. Faced with a severe economic crisis caused by the Great Depression, Dollfuss decided against joining Germany in a customs union, a course advocated by many Austrians. He was in part dissuaded by a League of Nations loan of $9,000,000 and by the fear of Allied countermeasures. Severely criticised by Social Democrats, Pan-German nationalists, and Austrian Nazis, he countered by drifting toward an increasingly authoritarian regime. The Italian leader Benito Mussolini became his principal foreign ally. Italy guaranteed Austrian independence at Riccione (August 1933), but in return, Austria had to abolish all political parties and reform its constitution on the Fascist model. Dollfuss' attacks on Parliament, begun in March 1933, culminated that September in the permanent abolition of the legislature and the formation of a corporate state based on his Vaterländische Front ("Fatherland Front"), with which he expected to replace Austria's political parties. In foreign affairs, he steered a course that converted Austria virtually into an Italian satellite state. Hoping therewith to prevent Austria's incorporation into Nazi Germany, he fought his domestic political opponents along fascist-authoritarian lines. In February 1934 paramilitary formations loyal to the chancellor crushed Austria's Social Democrats in bloody encounters. With a new constitution of May 1934, his regime became completely dictatorial. In June, however, Germany incited the Austrian Nazis to civil war. Dollfuss was assassinated by the Nazis in a raid on the chancellery.

Alexander I of Yugoslavia (16 December 1888– 9 October 1934), also known as Alexander the Unifier, was King of the Serbs, Croats and Slovenes from 16 August 1921 to 3 October 1929 and King of Yugoslavia from 3 October 1929 until his assassination in 1934. His reign of 13 years is the longest of any monarch of the Kingdom of Yugoslavia. Born in Cetinje, Montenegro, Alexander was the second son of Peter and Zorka Karađorđević. The Karađorđević dynasty had been removed from power in Serbia 30 years prior, and Alexander spent his early life in exile with his father in Montenegro and then Switzerland. Afterwards, he moved to Russia and enrolled in the Imperial Page Corps. Following a coup d'état and the murder of King Alexander I Obrenović in 1903, his father became king of Serbia. In 1909, Alexander's elder brother, George, renounced his claim to the throne, making Alexander heir apparent. Alexander distinguished himself as a commander during the Balkan Wars, leading the Serbian army to victory over the Ottomans and the Bulgarians. In 1914, he became prince regent of Serbia. During the First World War, he held nominal command of the Royal Serbian Army.

In 1918, Alexander oversaw the unification of Serbia and the former Austrian provinces of Bosnia, Croatia and Slovenia into the Kingdom of Serbs, Croats and Slovenes. He ascended to the throne upon his father's death in 1921. An extended period of political crisis followed, culminating in the assassination of Croat leader Stjepan Radić. In response, Alexander abrogated the Vidovdan Constitution in 1929, prorogued the parliament, changed the name of the country to the Kingdom of Yugoslavia and established a royal dictatorship. The 1931 Constitution formalised Alexander's personal rule and confirmed Yugoslavia's status as a unitary state, further aggravating the non-Serb population. Political and economic tensions escalated on the outbreak of the Great Depression, which devastated the predominantly rural country. In foreign affairs, Alexander supported the Balkan Pact with Greece, Romania and Turkey, and sought to improve relations with Bulgaria.   In 1934, Alexander embarked on a state visit to France in order to secure support for the Little Entente against Hungarian revanchism and Italy's imperialist designs. During a stop in Marseille, he was assassinated by Vlado Chernozemski, a member of the pro-Bulgarian Internal Macedonian Revolutionary Organization, which received assistance from the Croatian Ustaše led by Ante Pavelić. French Foreign Minister Louis Barthou also died in the attack. Alexander was succeeded by his eleven-year-old son, Peter II, under the regency of his first cousin Prince Paul. Alexander's maternal grandfather was Nicholas I, Prince of Montenegro. Despite enjoying support from the Russian Empire, at the time of Alexander's birth and early childhood, the House of Karađorđević was in political exile, with family members scattered all over Europe, unable to return to Serbia.

Serbia had recently been transformed from a principality into a kingdom under the Obrenovićs, who ruled with strong support from Austria-Hungary. The antagonism between the two rival royal houses was such, that, after the assassination of Prince Mihailo Obrenović in 1868 (an event Karađorđevićs were suspected of taking part in), the Obrenovićs resorted to making constitutional changes, specifically proclaiming the Karađorđevićs banned from entering Serbia and stripping them f their civic rights.

Alexander was two when his mother, Princess Zorka, died in 1890 from complications while giving birth to his younger brother, Andrew, who died 23 days later. Alexander spent his childhood in Montenegro. In 1894, his widower father took the four children, including Alexander, to Geneva where the young man completed his elementary education. Alongside his older brother George, he continued his schooling at the imperial Page Corps in St Petersburg, Russian Empire. The British historian Robert Seton-Watson described Alexander as becoming a Russophile during his time in St. Petersburg, feeling much gratitude for the willingness of Emperor Nicholas II to give him a refuge, where he was treated with much honour and respect. As a page, Alexander was described as hardworking and determined while also being a "loner" who kept to himself and rarely showed his feelings.[6] Being a Karađorđević led to Alexander being invited by Nicholas II to dinner at the Winter Palace, where he was the guest of honour at meals hosted by the Russian imperial family, which was a great honour for a prince from Serbia's deposed princely family.

During his time in St. Petersburg, Alexander visited the Alexander Nevsky Monastery, where the abbot gave Alexander an icon of Prince Alexander Nevsky and guided him to the grave of Marshal Alexander Suvorov.[7] After his visit to the monastery, Alexander expressed the wish to be a great general like Marshal Suvorov or Prince Alexander Nevsky, saying he wanted to command either a great army or a great armada when he was a man. In 1903, while young George and Alexander were in school, conspirators pulled off a bloody coup d'état in the Kingdom of Serbia known as the May

Overthrow in which King Alexander and Queen Draga were murdered and dismembered. The House of Karađorđević thus retook the Serbian throne after forty-five years and Alexander's 58-year-old father became king of Serbia, prompting George's and Alexander's return to Serbia to continue their studies. After Alexander's 15th birthday, King Peter had Alexander enlisted into the Royal Serbian Army as a private with instructions to his officers to only promote his son if he proved worthy.[6] On 25 March 1909, Alexander was suddenly recalled to Belgrade by his father with no explanation offered other than that he had an important announcement for his son. A key event for Prince Alexander occurred on 27 March 1909 when his older brother, Crown Prince George, publicly renounced his claim to the throne after strong pressure from political circles in Serbia. Many in Serbia, including powerful political and military figures such as Prime Minister Nikola Pašić, as well as high-ranking officers Dragutin "Apis" Dimitrijević and Petar Živković, did not appreciate the young man's impulsive nature and unstable, incident-prone personality, had long regarded George as unfit to rule. They believed that Prince Alexander had the makings of a fine sovereign. Prince Alexander donated a large sum of money to the Black Hand-oriented journal *Pijemont* (*Piedmont*) (founded in August 1911).

George killed his servant Kolaković by kicking him in the stomach, which served as the final straw. The death caused a huge scandal amongst the Serbian public as well as in the Austro-Hungarian press, which reported extensively on it, and 21-year-old Prince George was forced into renouncing his claim to the throne.

In 1910, Crown Prince Alexander nearly died from stomach typhus and was left with stomach problems for the rest of his life. In the run-up to the First Balkan War of 1912–1913, Alexander played the role of a diplomat, visiting Sofia to meet Tsar Ferdinand of Bulgaria for secret talks for a Balkan League, which was intended to drive the Ottomans out of the Balkans. Both Bulgaria and Serbia had rival claims to the Ottoman region of Macedonia, and the talks with Ferdinand were difficult. Together with Tsar Ferdinand's son, Crown Prince Boris (the future Tsar Boris III of Bulgaria), Alexander travelled to Saint Petersburg to see the Russian Emperor Nicholas II to ask for Russian mediation on certain points that were dividing the Serbs and Bulgarians.[11] In March 1912, Serbia and Bulgaria signed a defensive alliance that was later (May 1912) joined by Greece. In March 1912, Alexander had a meeting with ten senior military commanders. They all agreed to end all internal conflicts in the army and fully commit to realising national goals, which allowed space for consolidation before the two successive Balkan wars.

In the First Balkan War in 1912, as commander of the First Army, Crown Prince Alexander fought victorious battles in Kumanovo and Bitola. One of Alexander's most cherished moments came when he drove the Ottomans out of Kosovo and on 28 October 1912 led the Serb Army on a review of the Field of Blackbirds.[8] The Field of Blackbirds was where the Serbs under Prince Lazar had been defeated in a legendary battle by the Ottoman Sultan Murad I on 28 June 1389 and is regarded by the Serbs as holy ground. It was a great honour for him to pay his respects to the Serbs who had fallen in that earlier battle.[8] In the aftermath of the First Balkan War, disputes emerged among the victors over control of Macedonia, and Serbia and Greece signed an alliance against Bulgaria. Later in 1913, during the Second Balkan War, Alexander commanded the Serb Army at the Battle of Bregalnica against the Bulgarians.

After the Ottoman withdrawal from Skopje (most of whom had left after the Albanian revolt of 1912), Prince Alexander was met with flowers by the local people. He stopped and asked a seven-year-old girl, Vaska Zoicheva, "What are you?" (*Pa šta si ti?*) When she replied "Bulgarian!" (*Bugarka!*), the prince slapped her. This news of the event spread quickly around Bulgaria. In 1920 and 1921, Serbian authorities searched for the girl's father, Danail Zoichev, and offered him money to renounce the event as fictional, but he refused.

In the aftermath of the Second Balkan War, Prince Alexander took sides in the complicated power struggle over how Macedonia should be administered. In this, Alexander bested Colonel Dragutin Dimitrijević "Apis" and in the wake of this, Alexander's father, King Peter, agreed to hand over royal powers to his son. Though Colonel Dimitrijević was the mastermind of the 1903 coup that had restored the House of Karađorđević to the Serbian throne, Alexander distrusted him, regarding his attempts to set himself up as a "king-maker" and to have the Serbian Army be a "state within the state" existing outside of civilian control as a major threat.

Additionally, Alexander saw Dimitrijević as an irresponsible intriguer who having betrayed one king might always betray another. In January 1914, the Serbian prime minister Nikola Pašić sent a letter toEmperor Nicholas II in which King Peter expressed a desire for his son to marry one of the daughters of Nicholas.[19][20] Nicholas in his reply stated that his daughters would not be forced into arranged marriages, but noted Alexander on his most recent trips to St. Petersburg had during dinners at the Winter Palace kept giving loving looks at the Grand Duchess Tatiana, leading him to guess that it was her whom Alexander wanted to marry. On 24 June 1914, Alexander became the regent of Serbia.

On 24 July 1914, Alexander was one of the first Serbian officials to see the Austrian ultimatum containing terms deliberately written to inspire rejection.[21] Turning to Russia for help, Alexander was advised to help the ultimatum as much as he could. Alexander was late to say he "went as far as an independent could" to accept the ultimatum, as Serbia accepted all of the terms except for the one demanding that Austrian police officers investigating the assassination of Archduke Franz Ferdinand could operate on Serbian soil with the powers of arrest, which would have been the effective end of Serbia as an independent state.[22] As expected, the Austrians declared war on Serbia, and Alexander threw himself into preparing his nation's defence.[22] In a letter to King Nicholas of Montenegro, Alexander wrote: "God has willed yet again that the Serbian people should give their lives for Serbs everywhere ... I pray for the support of my dear and wise forefathers".

At the outbreak of World War I he was the nominal supreme commander of the Serbian army; true command was in the hands of the Chief of Staff of Supreme Headquarters, a position held by Stepa Stepanović (during the mobilisation), Radomir Putnik (1914–1915), Petar Bojović (1916–1917) and Živojin Mišić (1918). The Serbian army distinguished itself in the battles at Cer and at the Drina (the Battle of Kolubara) in 1914, scoring victories against the invading Austro-Hungarian forces and evicting them from the country.

The British historian Max Hastings described the Royal Serbian Army in 1914 as the toughest army in Europe and also the most egalitarian with none of the distinctions of rank that characterised the other European armies, exemplified by how the Serb Army was the only army in Europe where officers would shake hands with the other ranks.[24] However, the Serbian Army suffered major shortages of equipment with a third of the men called up in August 1914 having no rifles or ammunition and new recruits being advised to bring their own boots and clothing as there were no uniforms for them.[24] Alexander ordered the Serbian police to conduct searches of houses all over Serbia to see if there were any rifles and ammunition to be seized for the army.

In 1915, the Serbian army was attacked on several fronts by the allied forces of Germany and Austria-Hungary, suffering heavy losses. On 7 October 1915 an Austro-German army group under the command of Field Marshal August von Mackensen invaded Serbia and after encountering fierce resistance took Belgrade on 9 October.[25] On 14 October 1915, Bulgaria invaded Serbia and on 16 October the Bulgarians took Niš, severing the railroad that linked Serbia to Salonika in Greece.[25] Being attacked from the north by the Austrians and the Germans and from the south by the Bulgarians, the Serbs by 25 November 1915 had been forced into the Kosovo region.

The massacres committed by the Austrians in 1914 when they invaded Serbia twice caused enormous panic and hundreds of thousands of Serbs fled their homes to escape the Austrians, which greatly delayed the movement of the Serb Army.[25] Field Marshal Radomir Putnik persuaded Crown Prince Alexander and King Peter that it was better to keep the Serb Army intact to one day liberate Serbia rather than to stand and fight in Kosovo as many Serb officers wanted.

The Serbian Army withdrew through the gorges of Montenegro and northern Albania to the Greek island of Corfu, where it was reorganised. The march across the Prokletije ("accursed") mountains was a harrowing one as the Serb Army together with a mass of refugees had to cross mountains that rose to 3,000 feet high in the middle of winter with the average daily temperature being −20° while battling the hostile Albanian tribes with the armies of Austria, Germany and

Bulgaria in pursuit.[26] Many Serbs died along the way as one Serb soldier wrote in his diary how the refugees rested by the side of the road were: "Immobilised by the snow their heads rest to their breasts. The white snowflakes dance around them while the alpine winds whistle their songs of death. The heads of horses and oxen which have fallen protrude from the snow"

As the Serbs braved the icy winds and snowdrifts, the only consolation for Alexander was that the winter weather was also delaying the German, Austrian and Bulgarian armies under the command of von Mackensen that were pursuing his army.[25] Alexander repeatedly exposed himself to danger during the march to the sea while his health declined.[23] Upon reaching the sea, the surviving Serbs who numbered about 140,000 were rescued by British and French ships, which took them to Corfu.

In September 1915, the Royal Serbian Army was estimated to have the strength of about 420,000 men, of whom 94,000 had been killed or wounded while another 174,000 had been captured or were missing during the fall campaign in 1915 and the subsequent retreat to the sea.[26] The losses taken by Serb civilians during the autumn campaign in 1915 together with the retreat to the sea have never been calculated, but are estimated to be massive. [26] The situation was further worsened by the which ravaged the country in 1915. Serb losses as a percentage of the population were the greatest of any belligerent in the war. The surviving Serb soldiers were ultimately taken to Thessaloniki to join the *Armées alliées en Orient*. In the fall of 1916, Alexander's long-standing dispute with the Black Hand group came to a head, when Colonel Dimitrijević began to criticise his leadership.[18] Suspecting a threat to the throne, Alexander promptly had officers who were members of the Black Hand arrested in December 1916 and tried for insubordination; after their convictions, Dimitrijević and several other Back Hand leaders were executed by firing squad on 23 June 1917.At the same time, the Serbian government-in-exile led by Prime Minister Nikola Pašić was in contact with the Yugoslav Committee, a group of anti-Habsburg Croats and Slovenes led by Ante Trumbić who talked about creating a new nation to be called Yugoslavia which would unite all of the South Slav peoples into one state.[27] In June 1917, the Corfu Declaration was signed by Pašić and Trumbić promising Yugoslavia after the war.

Alexander seems to have been dubious about the plans for Yugoslavia, as, throughout the war, he spoke in terms of liberating Serbia.[28] The introduction of the 14 Points by American President Woodrow Wilson in January 1918 increased Alexander's doubts about Yugoslavia as Point 10 spoke of "substantial autonomy" in the Austrian Empire after the war, not breaking it up.[29] Not willing to antagonise Wilson, Alexander favoured a "greater Serbia" that saw the Serbs annex certain provinces of the Austrian Empire.[28] Though the Crown Prince declared in a speech during a visit to Britain that he was "fighting for Yugoslav unity in a Yugoslav state", when he addressed his own soldiers he stated he was fighting for "the reestablishment of Serbia, our dear homeland"

In a sign of the trouble to come, Trumbić demanded to have the right to speak for the South Slavs living under Austrian rule, a demand that Alexander rejected under the grounds that the Serb government represented the South Slavs.[29] After the army was regrouped and reinforced, it achieved a decisive victory on the Macedonian Front, at Kajmakcalan. The Serbian army carried out a major part in the final Allied breakthrough on the Macedonian Front in the autumn of 1918. The debate whether the Serbian Army was fighting for Yugoslavia or Serbia resolved itself in October–November 1918 as the Austrian Empire collapsed, leaving the Royal Serbian Army to move into the vacuum.

On 1 December 1918, the National Council asked Alexander to declare Serbia united with the former Austrian provinces of Bosnia, Croatia and Slovenia on the basis of the Corfu declaration Serbia had been devastated by the war, and 1 out of every 5 Serbs who were alive in 1914 were dead by 1918. Much of Alexander's time in the immediate post-war years was to be taken up with reconstruction.

CHAPTER 10.

THE NEW WORLD FOR THE OLD

On 1 December 1918, in a prearranged set piece, Alexander, as Prince Regent, received a delegation of the People's Council of Slovenes, Croats and Serbs, an address was read out by one of the delegations, and Alexander made an address in acceptance. This was considered to be the birth of the Kingdom of Serbs, Croats and Slovenes. One of Alexander's first acts as Prince Regent of the new kingdom was to declare his support for the widespread demand for land reform, stating: "In our free state there can and will be only free landowners"

On 25 February 1919, Alexander signed a land reform decree breaking up all feudal estates over the size of 100 cadastral *yokes* with compensation to be paid for the former landowners except for those who belonged to the House of Habsburg and the other ruling families of enemy states in the Great War.[33] Under the land reform decree, some two million hectares of land were handed over to a half million peasant households, though the implementation was very slow, taking 15 years before land reform was complete.

In both Macedonia and Bosnia-Herzegovina, the majority of the landlords who lost land were Muslims while the majority of their former tenants who received the land were Christians, and in both places, land reform was seen as an attack on the political and economic power of the Muslim gentry.[33] In Croatia, Slovenia, and Vojvodina, the majority of the landlords who lost their land were Austrian or Hungarian nobility who usually did not reside in those places, meaning that however much they might have resented the loss of their land it did not have the sort of political repercussions it did in Macedonia and in Bosnia where the Albanian and Bosnian Muslim landlords lived.

On August 16, 1921, upon the death of his father, Alexander ascended to the throne of the *Kingdom of Serbs, Croats and Slovenes*, which from its inception was colloquially known both in the Kingdom and the rest of Europe alike as *Yugoslavia*. The historian Brigit Farley described Alexander as something of a cipher to historians as he was a taciturn and reserved man who loathed to express his feelings either in person or in writing. As Alexander kept no diary or wrote no memoirs, Farley wrote that any biography of Alexander could easily be titled "In Search of King Alexander" as he remains an elusive and enigmatic figure.

The British historian R.W. Seton-Watson, who knew Alexander well, called him a soldiery man most comfortable in a military milieu who was very quiet and surprisingly modest for a king.[35] Seton-Watson described Alexander as having an "autocratic" personality, a man who was first and foremost a soldier who spent "six of his formative years" in the Serbian Army, which left him with a "military outlook which unfitted him to deal with the delicate problems of constitutional government and which made compromise hard for him". Seton-Watson wrote that Alexander "...was very courageous, though not ever a man of strong physique or robust health. He had a strong fixity of purpose, great devotion to duty, and powers of sustained work. He had great charm and simplicity of manner. He was accessible and very open to opinions he rarely acted on them, and though occasionally he reacted with positive violence, as in the case of the Slovene Zerjav who fainted in his presence."

One of the things that historians can be certain about Alexander was his belief in keeping Yugoslavia as a unitary state and his consistent opposition to federalism, which he believed would lead to the break-up of Yugoslavia and perhaps his own assassination.[38] In turn, Alexander's opposition to federalism related to his belief that in a federalised Yugoslavia, the *prečani* Serbs would be discriminated against by the Croats and Bosnian Muslims, once telling a Serb Orthodox priest that federalism would be "stabbing the Serbs in the back".

On 8 June 1922, he married Princess Maria of Romania, who was a daughter of Ferdinand I of Romania. They had three sons: Crown Prince Peter, and Princes Tomislav and Andrej. He was said to have wished to marry Grand Duchess Tatiana Nikolaevna of Russia, a cousin of his wife and the second daughter of Tsar Nicholas II, and was distraught by her untimely death in the Russian Civil War. The Russophile Alexander was horrified by the murders of the House of Romanov-including the Grand Duchess Tatiana-and during his reign was very hostile towards the Soviet Union, welcoming Russian emigres to Belgrade.

The lavish royal wedding to Princess Maria of Romania was intended to cement the alliance with Romania, a fellow "victor nation" in World War I which like Yugoslavia had territorial disputes with the defeated nations like Hungary and Bulgaria.[42] For Alexander, the royal wedding was especially satisfactory as most of the royal families of Europe attended, which showed that the House of Karađorđević, a family of peasant origins who were disliked for slaughtering the rival House of Obrenović in 1903, was finally accepted by the rest of European royalty.

In foreign policy, Alexander favoured maintaining the international system created in 1918–19, and in 1921 Yugoslavia joined the Little Entente with Czechoslovakia and Romania to guard against Hungary. Hungary refused to accept the Treaty of Trianon and made territorial claims against all three states of the Little Entente. In 1921, a war veteran and communist Spasoje Stejić Baćo attempted to assassinate King Alexander by throwing a bomb at his carriage. The bomb was thrown from a balcony and it got stuck in the telephone wires and it ended up wounding several bystanders.

The principal enemy of Yugoslavia in the 1920s was Fascist Italy, which wanted much of what is now modern Slovenia and Croatia. [43] The origins of the Italo-Yugoslav dispute concerned the Italian contention that they had been "cheated" out of what they had been promised in the secret Treaty of London in 1915 at the Paris Peace Conference in 1919. It was largely out of the fear of Italy that Alexander in 1927 signed a treaty of alliance with France, which therefore became Yugoslavia's principal ally.[45] In fact, Alexander I and Benito Mussolini were arch-rivals.

Starting in 1926, an alliance of the Serb Democrats led by Svetozar Pribićević and the Croat Peasant Party led by Stjepan Radić had systematically obstructed the *skupština* to press for federalism for Yugoslavia, filibustering and filing nonsensical motions to prevent the government from passing any bills.[46] In response to obstructionism from the opposition parties, in June 1928, one frustrated deputy from Montenegro took out his handgun and shot Radić on the floor of the *skupština*.[46] The charismatic Radić, the "uncrowned king of Croatia", had inspired intense devotion in Croatia and his assassination was seen as a sort of Serb declaration of war.[47] The assassination pushed Yugoslavia to the brink of civil war and led Alexander to consider the "amputation" of Croatia as preferable to federalism.

Alexander mused to Pribićević: "We cannot stay together with the Croats. Since we cannot, it would be better to separate. The best way to be to effect a peaceful separation like Sweden and Norway did".When Pribićević protested that this would be an act of "treason", Alexander told him he would think some more about what to do.[46] Alexander appointed the Slovene Catholic priest, Father Anton Korošec prime minister with one mandate, namely to stop the slide towards civil war.[47] On 1 December 1928, the lavish celebrations of the 10th anniversary of the founding of the triune Kingdom of Serbs, Croats and Slovenes that the government organised led to rioting that left 10 dead in Zagreb.

In response to the political crisis triggered by the assassination of Stjepan Radić, King Alexander abolished the Constitution on 6 January 1929, prorogued the Parliament and introduced a personal dictatorship (the so-called "January 6th Dictatorship", *Šestojanuarska diktatura*). One of the first acts of the new regime was to carry out a purge of the civil service with one-third of the civil service being fired by May 1929 in an attempt to address popular complaints about rampant corruption in the bureaucracy.[47] He also changed the name of the country to the Kingdom of Yugoslavia and changed the internal divisions from the 33 oblasts to nine new *banovinas* on 3 October. Of the *banovinas*, only one had a Slovene majority, two had Croat majorities and the rest had Serb majorities, which especially angered the Bosnian Muslims who were in a minority in every *banovine*.

The way in which the *banovinas* were based on new borders that did not correspond to the historical regional borders led to much resentment, especially in Bosnia and Croatia.[48] The *banovinas* were named after the topography of Yugoslavia rather than the historical names in a bid to weaken regional loyalties, being governed by *bans* appointed by the King.[47] In the same month, he tried to banish by decree the use of Serbian Cyrillic to promote the exclusive use of the Latin alphabet in Yugoslavia.

Alexander replaced the three regional flags for the triune Kingdom of Serbs, Croats and Slovenes with a single flag for the entire country, brought in a single legal code for his realm, imposed a single fiscal code so all of his subjects would pay the same tax rate, and a Yugoslav Agrarian Bank was created by merging all of the regional agrarian banks into one.[47] Alexander tried to promote a sense of Yugoslav identity by always taking his vacations in Slovenia, naming his second son after a Croat king, and being a godfather to a Bosnian Muslim child.[50] Alexander had once fraternised frequently with ordinary people, being known for his habit of making unannounced visits to various villages all over Yugoslavia to chat with ordinary people but after the proclamation of the royal dictatorship, his social circle consisted of a few generals and courtiers, causing the King to lose touch with his subjects.

Within Serbia, the royal dictatorship for the first time made Alexander an unpopular figure.[52] The British historian Richard Crampton wrote many Serbs "...were alienated by the attempt, albeit unsuccessful, to lessen the Serbian domination on which, to add insult to injury, many of the faults of the previous system were blamed. Alexander had implicitly made the Serbs, the most reliable proponents of centralism, the villains of the Vidovdan piece".[52] The royal dictatorship was seen in Croatia as merely a form of Serbian domination, and one result was a marked upswing in support for fascistic *Ustashe*, which advocated winning Croat independence via violence.

By 1931, the *Ustashe* was waging a terrorist campaign of bombings, assassinations and sabotage, which at least in part explained Alexander's reluctance to engage with ordinary people as he had done in the past out of the fear of assassination.[53] On 14 February 1931, Alexander visited Zagreb, and the men of the Turnopolje district, who for centuries always provided a mounted honour guard for any royal visitor to Zagreb, failed to show up, a snub that showed how unpopular Alexander had become in Croatia.[53] On 19 February 1931, the Croat historian Milan Šufflay was murdered by police agents, becoming an international *cause célèbre* with Albert Einstein and Heinrich Mann leading a campaign to pressure Alexander to prosecute Šufflay's killers.

The Great Depression was especially severe in predominantly rural Yugoslavia as it caused deflation leading to a collapse in the price of agricultural products.[53] The Croat politician Ante Trumbić summed up the feelings of many when he gave a speech in early 1931 stating: "We are in a crisis, an economic, financial and moral crisis. There is no material or moral credit in the country. Nobody believes anything anymore!"[53] However, Alexander remained unperturbed, stating in an interview with the press: "Yugoslav politics will never again be driven by narrow religious, regional or national interests".[54] In response to pressure from Yugoslavia's allies, especially France and Czechoslovakia, Alexander decided to lessen the royal dictatorship by bringing in a new constitution that allowed the *skupština* to meet again.

In 1931, Alexander decreed a new Constitution which transferred executive power to the King. Elections were to be by universal male suffrage. The provision for a secret ballot was dropped and pressure on public employees to vote for the governing party was to be a feature of all elections held under Alexander's constitution. Furthermore, the King would appoint half of the upper house directly, and legislation could become law with the approval of one of the houses alone if it were also approved by the King. The 1931 constitution kept Yugoslavia as a unitary state, which enraged the non-Serbian peoples who demanded a federation and saw Alexander's royal dictatorship as thinly disguised Serbian domination.[54] In the elections for the *skupština* in December 1931 – January 1932, the call of the opposition parties to boycott the vote was widely heeded, a sign of popular dissatisfaction with the new constitution.

In response to the impoverishment of the countryside caused by the Great Depression, Alexander reaffirmed in a speech the right of every peasant family to a minimum amount of land that could not be seized by a bank in the event of a debt default. In 1932 he issued a decree suspending all debt payments by farmers to the banks for six months and forbade any more foreclosures by the banks against farmers.[55] Alexander's measures preventing the banks from foreclosing on farmers who were unable to pay their loans saved many peasants from being ruined and prevented economic distress in the countryside from turning political, but in the long run, his policies did not solve the economic problems of the rural areas.

The losses taken by the banks and their inability to foreclose on farmers who had delinquent loans made the banks unwilling to make new loans to the farmers.[55] As Yugoslav agriculture, especially in the southern parts of the country was backward, the farmers needed loans to modernise their farms, but the unwillingness of the banks to lend to the farmers made modernisation of the farms impossible in the 1930s.

In September 1932, Alexander's friend, the Croat politician Ante Trumbić gave an interview with *The Manchester Guardian* newspaper, where he stated that life for ordinary Croats was better when they were part of the Austrian empire and stated that perhaps the Croats would be better off if they broke away from Yugoslavia to form their own state.[56] For Alexander, who always respected and liked Trumbić to see his former friend come very close to embracing Croat separatism was a painful blow.[56] On 7 November 1932, Trumbić and Vladko Maček of the Croat Peasant Party issued the so-called Zagreb Points, which demanded a new constitution that would turn Yugoslavia into a federation, and stated that the Croats would otherwise demand independence. Alexander had Maček imprisoned without charges, but the issuing of the Zagreb Points inspired the other peoples to issue similar declarations with the Slovenes issuing the Ljubljana Points, the Bosnian Muslims issuing the Sarajevo Points and the Magyars issuing the Novi Sad points.[56] The emergence of a multi-ethnic opposition movement embracing the non-Serb peoples threatened to break the country apart and forced Alexander to ease the level of repression as his ministers warned him that he could not imprison the entire country.

In Macedonia, the Internal Macedonian Revolutionary Organisation was continuing its long-running guerrilla struggle while in Croatia the security situation had further deteriorated by 1932.[57] By the end of 1932, the *Ustashe* had blown up hundreds of trains and assassinated hundreds of government officials.[57] The often violent response of the mainly Serb gendarmes to *Ustashe* terrorism fuelled more support for the *Ustashe*.[57] To many, it appeared that Yugoslavia was sliding into the civil war that Alexander's "self-coup" of January 1929 was supposed to prevent.

Starting in 1933, Alexander had become worried about Nazi Germany. In March 1933, the French minister in Belgrade, Paul-Émile Naggiar, told Alexander that France was seriously worried about the stability of Yugoslavia and warned that the King could not continue to rule in the face of opposition from the majority of his subjects and that Paris viewed that Alexander was starting to become a liability for France.[58] Naggiar predicted the new regime in Germany was going to challenge the international order created by the Treaty of Versailles sooner or later and that France needed Yugoslavia to be stable and strong, which led Naggiar to advise the King to adopt federalism for his realm.

However, one point of agreement of Alexander with Mussolini was his fear of *Anschluss* which would make Germany a direct neighbour of Yugoslavia. Alexander had no desire to have Germany as a neighbour, which led him to support the continuation of Austrian independence.[59] Despite his distaste for communism, the King gave support, albeit in a very cautious and hesitant way, to the plans of French Foreign Minister Louis Barthou to bring the Soviet Union into a front meant to contain Germany.[59] In 1933–34, Alexander became the proponent of a Balkan Pact, which would unite Yugoslavia, Greece, Romania and Turkey.

Although the Balkan Pact was directed primarily against Italy and its allies (Hungary, Albania and Bulgaria), Alexander hoped the pact might provide some protection against Germany.[45] After the coup d'état in May 1934 in Sofia, King Alexander also hoped that Bulgaria would join the Balkan Entente. The new Bulgarian government had started repression against IMRO. In September 1934, Alexander visited Sofia to improve relations with Bulgaria. A Bulgarian military organisation, Zveno, supported the unification of Bulgaria and Albania into Yugoslavia, which agreed with Alexander's policy *Balkans for the Balkan peoples*. After the Ustaše's Velebit uprising in November 1932, Alexander said through an intermediary to the Italian government, "If you want to have serious riots in Yugoslavia or cause a regime change, you need to kill me. Shoot at me and be sure you have finished me off because that's the only way to make changes in Yugoslavia."

The French Foreign Minister Louis Barthou had attempted in 1934 to build an alliance meant to contain Germany, consisting of France's allies in Eastern Europe like Yugoslavia, together with Italy and the Soviet Union.[61] The long-standing rivalry between Benito Mussolini and King Alexander had complicated Barthou's work as

Alexander complained about Italian claims against his country together with Italian support for Hungarian revisionism and the Croat *Ustaše*.

As long as the French ally Yugoslavia continued to have disputes with Italy, Barthou's plans for an Italian-French rapprochement would be stillborn. During a visit to Belgrade in June 1934, Barthou promised the King that France would pressure Mussolini into signing a treaty under which he would renounce his claims against Yugoslavia.[63] Alexander was sceptical of Barthou's plan, noting that there were hundreds of *Ustašhi* being sheltered in Italy and it was rumoured that Mussolini had financed an unsuccessful attempt by the *Ustaše* to assassinate him in December 1933.

Mussolini had come to believe that it was only the personality of Alexander that was holding Yugoslavia together and that if the King were assassinated, Yugoslavia would descend into civil war, which would allow Italy to annex certain regions of Yugoslavia without the fear of France.[64] However, France was Yugoslavia's closest ally, and Barthou invited Alexander for a visit to France to sign a Franco-Yugoslav agreement that would allow Barthou to "go to Rome with the certainty of success".[64] As a result of the previous deaths of three family members on Tuesdays, Alexander refused to undertake any public functions on that day of the week. On Tuesday, 9 October 1934, however, he had no choice, as he was arriving in Marseille to start a state visit to France to strengthen both countries' alliance in the Little Entente.

While Alexander was being slowly driven in a car through the streets along with French Foreign Minister Barthou, a gunman, the Bulgarian Vlado Chernozemski, stepped from the street and shot the King twice and the chauffeur with a Mauser C96 semiautomatic pistol. Alexander died in the car and was slumped backwards in the seat with his eyes open.[67] Barthou was also killed by a stray bullet fired by French police during the scuffle following the attack.[68] Lieutenant-Colonel Piollet, having finally managed to turn his horse, struck the assailant with his sword. Ten people in the procession were wounded, including General Alphonse Georges was hit by two bullets as he tried to intervene, and nine people in the crowd who came to see the king, four of them fatally, among them Yolande Farris, barely 20 years old, on Place Castellane, who came to the Palais de la Bourse to see the king. She was hit by a stray bullet and died at the Hôtel-Dieu on October

11, 1934. Mrs Dumazet and Durbec, who also came to see the king, also died.

It was one of the first assassinations to be captured on film; the shooting occurred in front of the newsreel cameraman,[69] who was only metres away at the time. While the exact moment of the shooting was not captured on film, the events leading to the assassination and the immediate aftermath were. The body of the chauffeur Foissac, who had been mortally wounded, slumped and jammed against the brakes of the car, which allowed the cameraman to continue filming from within inches of the King for a number of minutes afterwards. The film record of Alexander I's assassination remains one of the most notable pieces of newsreel in existence,[70][71] alongside the film of Emperor Nicholas II of Russia's coronation, the funerals of Queen Victoria of the United Kingdom and Emperor Franz Joseph I of Austria, and the assassination of John F. Kennedy. A 20th Century Fox newsreel presented by Graham McNamee was manipulated to give the audience the impression that the assassination had been captured on film. Three identical gunshot sounds were added to the film afterwards, but in reality, Chernozemski fired his handgun over ten times and killed or wounded a total of 15 people. A straw hat is shown on the ground, as if it had belonged to the assassin, unlike in reality. A Mauser C96 semi-automatic pistol with a 10-round magazine is shown as the assassination weapon, but the actual one had a 20-round magazine. The exact moment of the assassination was never filmed.[72] Just hours later, Chernozemski died in police custody.

The assassin was a member of the pro-Bulgarian Internal Macedonian Revolutionary Organization (IMRO or VMRO) and an experienced marksman.[74] Immediately after assassinating King Alexander, Chernozemski was cut down by the sword of a mounted French policeman, and then beaten by the crowd. By the time he was removed from the scene, the King was already dead. The IMRO was a political organisation that fought for the liberation of the occupied region of Macedonia and its independence, initially as some form of second Bulgarian state, followed by a later unification with the Kingdom of Bulgaria.

The IMRO worked in alliance with the Croatian Ustaše group, led by Ante Pavelić.[69][76] Chernozemski and three Croatian accomplices had travelled to France from Hungary via Switzerland. After the assassination, Chernozemski's accomplices were arrested by French police.[69] A prominent diplomat with the Palazzo Chigi, Baron Pompeo Aloisi, expressed fears that the *Ustashi* based in Italy had killed the King and sought reassurances from another diplomat, Paolo Cortese, that Italy had not been involved.[64] Aloisi was not reassured when Cortese told him that with Alexander being dead, Yugoslavia was about to break up.

Public opinion and the press in Yugoslavia held that Italy had been crucial in the planning and directing of the assassination.[77] Demonstrators outside of the Italian embassy in Belgrade and the Italian consulates in Zagreb and Ljubljana blamed Mussolini for Alexander's assassination.[78] An investigation by the French police quickly established that the assassins had been trained and armed in Hungary; had travelled to France on forged Czechoslovak passports; and frequently telephoned *Ustaše* leader Ante Pavelić, who was living in Italy.

The incident was later used by Yugoslavia as an argument to counter the Croatian attempts at secession and Italian and Hungarian revisionism.[69] The participants in the assassination were Ivan Rajić, Mijo Kralj, Zvonimir Pospišil and Antun Godina. They were sentenced to life in prison although the Yugoslav authorities had expected that they would be sentenced to death. In 1940, after the fall of France, they were released from prison by Germany.

Pierre Laval, who succeeded Barthou as foreign minister, wished to continue the rapprochement with Rome and saw the assassinations in Marseille as an inconvenience that was best forgotten.[Both London and Paris made it clear that they regarded Mussolini as a responsible European statesman and in private told Belgrade that under no circumstances would they allow *Il Duce* to be blamed.[81] In a speech in Northampton, England, on 19 October 1934, British Foreign Secretary Sir John Simon expressed his sympathy to the people of Yugoslavia over the king's assassination and stated that he was convinced by Mussolini's speech in Milan that denied being involved in the assassination.

When Yugoslavia made an extradition request to Italy for Pavelić on charges of regicide, the Quai d'Orsay expressed concern that if Pavelić were extradited, he might incriminate Mussolini and were greatly reassured when its counterparts at the Palazzo Chigi stated there was no possibility of Pavelić being extradited.[83] Laval cynically told a French journalist off the record that the French press should stop going on about the assassinations in Marseille because France would never go to war to defend the honour of a weak country like Yugoslavia.

The following day, the body of King Alexander I was transported back to the port of Split in Yugoslavia by the destroyer JRM *Dubrovnik*. After a huge funeral in Belgrade that was attended by about 500,000 people and many leading European statesmen, Alexander was interred in the Oplenac Church in Topola, which had been built by his father. The Holy See gave special permission to bishops Aloysius Stepinac, Antun Akšamović, Dionisije Njaradi, and Gregorij Rožman to attend the funeral in an Orthodox church.[84] As his son King Peter II was still a minor, Alexander's first cousin Prince Paul took the regency of the Kingdom of Yugoslavia.

A ballistic report on the bullets found in the car was made in 1935, but its results were not made available to the public until 1974. It revealed that Barthou was hit by an 8 mm Modèle 1892 revolver round commonly used in weapons, carried by French police.

After the assassination, relations between Yugoslavia and France became colder and never returned to the previous level. Also, the Little Entente and the Balkan Pact lost their importance. The Yugoslav public considered it shocking that the assassination had happened on French soil. In the coming years, Prince Paul (as regent) attempted to keep a neutral balance between London and Berlin until 1941, when he yielded to heavy pressure to join the Tripartite Pact.

CHAPTER 11.

MOVERS AND SHAKERS

Huey Pierce Long Jr. (August 30, 1893–September 10, 1935), by the name "The Kingfish", was an American politician who served as the 40th governor of Louisiana from 1928 to 1932 and as a United States senator from 1932 until his assassination in 1935.

In spite of an impoverished background, young Long managed to obtain enough formal schooling to pass the bar examination in 1915. He was politically ambitious and won election to the state railroad commission at age 25. In this post, his calls for the equitable regulation of the state utility companies and his attacks on Standard Oil earned him widespread popularity. He ran for the Louisiana governorship in 1924 and was defeated, but in 1928 he won the governorship through the heavy support of the discontented rural districts. His picturesque if irreverent speech, fiery oratory, and unconventional buffoonery soon made him nationally famous, and he was widely known by his nickname, "Kingfish." Long made a genuine contribution with an ambitious program of public works and welfare legislation in a state whose road system and social services had been sadly neglected by the wealthy elite that had long controlled the state government. Always the champion of poor whites, he effected a free-textbook law, launched a massive and very useful program of road and bridge building, expanded state university facilities, and erected a state hospital where free treatment for all was intended. He was opposed to excessive privileges for the rich, and he financed his improvements with increased inheritance and income taxes as well as a severance tax on oil—earning him the bitter enmity of the wealthy and of the oil interests.

Long's folksy manner and sympathy for the underprivileged diverted attention from his ruthless autocratic methods. Surrounding himself with gangster-like bodyguards, he dictated outright to members of the legislature, using intimidation if necessary. When he was about to leave office to serve in the U.S. Senate (1932), he fired the legally elected lieutenant governor and replaced him with two designated successors who would obey him from Washington. In order to fend off local challenges to his control in 1934, he effected radical changes in the Louisiana government, abolishing local government and taking personal control of all educational, police, and fire job appointments throughout the state. He achieved absolute control of the state militia, judiciary, and election and tax-assessing apparatus while denying citizens any legal or electoral redress.

In the Senate (1932–35) he sought national power with a "Share-the-Wealth" program ("every man a king"), which was tempting to the Great Depression-shocked public. In 1934 he transformed his proposed program into a national crusade by establishing the Share-Our-Wealth Society, inviting Americans everywhere to organise local branches. Had Long been able to unite the various nationwide radical movements, a private poll taken in the spring of 1935 estimated that he would have won up to four million votes in the next presidential election, wielding a balance of power between the two major parties. Long was at the height of his power when assassinated 8th September 1935 by Carl Austin Weiss, the son of a man whom he had vilified. The Long political dynasty was carried on by his brother Earl K. Long, who served as governor (1939–40, 1948–52, and 1956–60), and his son, Russell B. Long, who served in the U.S. Senate from 1948 to 1987.

Leon Trotsky (/ˈtrɒtski/) was actually Lev Davidovich Bronstein born on 7 November 1879, was a Russian revolutionary, politician, journalist and political theorist. He was a central figure in the establishment of Soviet Russia and the Soviet Union. Leon Trotsky was a leading Marxist revolutionary of the first half of the 20th century. He is famous for playing leading roles in the Russian Revolutions of 1905 and 1917, and for organising the Red Army during the ensuing Russian Civil War.

In the 1920–30s, Trotsky was an important figure in the Marxist opposition against Joseph Stalin. He critiqued what he saw as the degeneration of the Soviet regime, and inspired many socialists who continued working for an international working-class revolution in opposition to the model of 'socialism in one country'. He was expelled from the USSR in 1929 and was assassinated in 1940. Trotsky is also well-known as a theoretician, cultural commentator and historical chronicler. His body of work informs the movement known as Trotskyism.

After escaping from Siberia in 1902, Bronstein adopted the pseudonym Trotsky, according to legend, the name of one of his jailers. He became involved with London's community of exiled revolutionaries, establishing a friendship with Lenin and writing for *Iskra,* the newspaper of the Russian Social Democratic Labour Party (RSDLP). This friendship broke down, however. Trotsky criticised the centralised 'vanguard party' model advocated by Lenin, seeing it as an authoritarian approach. In the years up to 1917, Trotsky maintained independence from both the Bolshevik and Menshevik factions, hoping for their reconciliation.

In 1905, Trotsky returned to Russia, intending to take part in the revolutionary movement more directly and proved that he had a talent for practical mass politics, writing for various revolutionary newspapers, making stirring speeches and pushing for the end of the Tsarist regime. He soon became a leading figure of the St. Petersburg Soviet of Workers' Deputies, which had been organised by workers to coordinate demonstrations and strike action. Trotsky was arrested in December 1905 as the autocracy reasserted its grip. For the second time, he was exiled to Siberia and escaped, settling in Vienna in 1. Trotsky formulated the theory of 'permanent revolution' in the aftermath of 1905, seeking to develop the Marxist theory of revolution.

Before 1917, most Marxists believed that society would progress through a series of ordered stages. They interpreted the previous great revolutions as marking the leap from feudalism to capitalism. Only once capitalism had been firmly established could there follow a further revolution – a working-class, socialist revolution.

By the early 20th century Russia had yet to achieve its 'bourgeois' revolution, with the majority of its peasant population barely integrated into the capitalist system. Russian Marxists, therefore, commonly sought an alliance with the liberal bourgeoisie to remove the remnants of feudalism and Tsarist absolutism which impeded the full development of capitalism. Like Lenin, Trotsky was dissatisfied with this alliance between socialists and liberals. He thought the Russian bourgeoisie was incapable of leading a successful revolution. According to Trotsky, the 'bourgeois-democratic' revolution would have to be accomplished by the working class movement itself, which would then pass directly into the struggle for socialism.

He argued that the victory of Russian socialists might be the spark to rouse the working class to revolution in the industrialised capitalist nations. Revolutionary Russia could become part of a fraternal network of European socialist states which would aid its economic development. The fate of

Russia would depend on the fate of the world revolution. Trotsky felt vindicated by news of the Revolution in 1917, and returned to Russia, plunging once more into practical revolutionary politics. Trotsky made common cause with the Bolsheviks, seeking to radicalise the revolution further. He was arrested after the July Days, though and then released as part of Kerensky's effort to mobilise revolutionary workers against the Kornilov revolt.

In September Trotsky was again elected Chairman of the revived Petrograd Soviet. In this position he moved quickly to organise a Military Revolutionary Committee, preparing armed insurrection against the Provisional Government. He was the principal organiser of the Bolshevik uprising in October 1917. The period after the end of the Civil War saw heated debates within the Bolshevik leadership about all aspects of Soviet policy, including the shift to the New Economic Policy (NEP), foreign relations and the prospects for international revolution, and the potential sources of instability facing the government.

With Lenin's death in 1924, the Communist Party (as the Bolsheviks now called themselves) lost its unifying figurehead, and the party began to split into opposing factions. As a leading figure of the so-called Left Opposition in the mid-1920s, Trotsky warned against the bureaucratisation of the Soviet regime and feared that the Stalinist policy of 'socialism in one country' would mean abandoning the attempt to support world revolution.

Many leading Communists distrusted Trotsky, who had joined the party relatively late after being critical of the Bolsheviks for many years. Trotsky was marked out by his personal arrogance and disdained to act decisively to secure his power base until it was too late. By 1926 Stalin's hold on the Communist Party had become unassailable and in 1927 Trotsky was expelled. Trotsky was exiled to Soviet Central Asia, and then to Turkey in early 1929. Like Nicholas II a decade before, Trotsky sought refuge in Britain and was also rejected. After being hounded out of France and Norway, Trotsky was granted asylum in Mexico in 1936. Trotsky's political agitation did not cease with his exile from the USSR. He sharpened his attacks on Stalin and sought to organise an international Left Opposition to continue the struggle.

In the 1930s Stalin's Great Purges claimed the lives of many 'Old Bolsheviks' who had led the party in Lenin's time. During the Moscow Trials (1936–38), many of the defendants spuriously confessed to being part of a joint Trotskyist-Nazi plot against the USSR and were executed. After surviving previous assassination attempts, Trotsky himself was killed by a Stalinist agent in August 1940. Trotsky played an important part in preserving Soviet power during its precarious first years, though he was also in part responsible for the centralised, authoritarian apparatus which would later be taken over by Stalin.

The 20th century is the most violent century in history. While this century witnessed many great leaders, such as Franklin D. Roosevelt, Dr. Martin Luther King, Winston Churchill, Mahatma Gandhi, and Nelson Mandela, it had more than its "fair" share of utterly evil leaders. We have seen throughout history the rise and fall of many a tyrant, but the 20th century is hard to match in the number of dictators of evil that have arisen during this century.

One needs to consider what Lucifer found in the defects of the character of each of the dictators that followed that allowed their egocentricity and evil actions to tyranny, mass murder and chaos to get so far out of hand. It seems crucial for the dictator to have the man up and character of Lucifer himself- a pathological narcissistic ego-driven belief in their vision of greatness. It is the ultimate vision of immortality, the fount of all wisdom; a god-like religious zeal of infallibility. Theirs is the hope that their dream put into reality is a divine favour. To do this they appear to be a man of the people, fusing their personalities and promises between leadership and their right to rule as they think fit. They turn the myth into a lie- a brand of manufacturing the collective and eventually complying masses under an icon symbolism making after much killing and compromise a leadership of evil conformity, and worst of all the masses want to be led like this. The masses of people in their quiet desperation capitulate to the mob mentality of the bison of the madman. Like all missions built on death and destruction, somewhere along the line, the bison fades because there is no permanent stability in either the tyrant or his vision. Ultimately good outstays evil as light rules over darkness, but in the meantime, millions of people die in the fulfilment of the narcissistic vision of one man.

Any list of evilness invariably is topped by German Chancellor and **Führer Adolf Hitler** who came to power (democratically!) in January 1933. His mad quest for revenge, conquest, and ethnic cleansing nearly succeeded. In

December 1941, nearly all of Europe was under his heel. After Stalingrad though, the Third Reich lost battle after battle, and in May 1945, after Hitler committed suicide, Germany unconditionally surrendered. The country lay in ruins, six million Jews were murdered, and in World War II in total, some 55 million died. Hate, racism, xenophobia, and megalomania are but a few words to describe this man..

The number 2 man on the list of mass murderers was **Mao Zefdong**. Mao was a successful guerrilla fighter against the Japanese invaders and the corrupt Kuomintang government of Generalissimo Chiang Kai-shek. In 1949, he had overcome them all and the People's Republic of China was proclaimed. It went downhill ever after. In the purges of the early 1950s, millions of "wealthy" peasants, intellectuals, and "saboteurs" were killed. Then came the "Great Leap Forward" (1958-1962) one of the most insane experiments in social engineering ever. Private plots were abolished and communal kitchens were introduced. It was a disaster. Production plummeted and the ensuing "Great Chinese Famine" cost the lives of up to 45 million people. Not having had enough, a few years later, the dictator launched the "Great Proletarian Cultural Revolution" in 1966. Millions of people were persecuted and suffered public humiliation, arbitrary imprisonment, torture, hard labour, and execution. When Mao died in 1976, the country's per capita income was lower than Congo's, and China had lost over 55 million lives. Not that Mao cared. Purity above everything else--his purity.

In any list of evil men, Soviet dictator Joseph Stalin ranks high. He rose to power in the 1920s, after the death of Lenin. A succession of Five-Year programs industrialised the country but at unimaginable human costs. This, and the forced collectivisation of agriculture, led to widespread famine, which cost the lives of countless millions. Then came the "Great Terror" involving purge after purge of the party apparatus and society. Millions were sent to forced labour camps, their death, or both, the death rate in the Gulags was horrific. Almost all senior Red Army officers were purged shortly before Hitler attacked, ensuring the dismal performance and the horrific losses in the early stages of World War II. In the early 1950s, he was planning another bloody terror but thankfully he died before he could unleash it upon the harried nation.

Pol Pot (1925-1998) was the leader of the Communist Khmer Rouge. He grabbed power in Cambodia in 1975 and set about to create a communist paradise on earth. Not surprisingly, it was worse than Dante's Seventh Circle of Hell (violence). To fulfil his vision of an agricultural society, the urban population was forcibly relocated to the countryside to work in collective farms. Money was abolished and all citizens were made to wear the same drab black clothing, which made Mao costumes look fashionable. Intellectuals were summarily murdered—this included people who wore glasses. This experiment in social engineering cost the lives of about 25 % of the population and was immortalised in the Hollywood movie *Killing Fields*. His evil government was toppled after four years by invading Vietnamese forces.

The Belgian **king Leopold II** was a nasty piece of work. He deserves inclusion in this list because of what happened in Congo, which he acquired as his private property in 1885 in the Berlin Conference when much of Africa was divided among European powers. From the beginning, he was in it for the money, extracting the maximum amount of wealth from this huge colony. Millions of Congolese inhabitants, including children, were mutilated, killed, or died from disease during his rule. Failure to meet rubber collection quotas was punishable by death. Forced labour was instituted to increase production. Around 10 million people died during his brutal regime in Congo. Not that he cared. Things got so bad that in 1908, he was forced to hand over the colony to the Belgian state.

Kim Il-Sung was the dictator of North Korea from 1949 till his death in 1994. The official name of North Korea is the "Democratic People's Republic of Korea." All of it is a lie. There is nothing democratic about North Korea. The people are treated as slaves, and it is not a republic but a de facto kingdom with leadership going from father to son. Kim invaded South Korea in 1950, and in this war, some 3 million people perished, including 12-15% of North Korea's population. Subsequent Stalinist economic policies and widespread repression led to poverty and famine in which hundreds of thousands if not millions, died. Sadly, the country has not improved much under his son and grandson, both of whom are utterly ruthless, evil leaders in their own right. What a family.

Saddam Hussein was president of Iraq from 1979 to 2003. The common thread in his life was his morbid thirst for power, absolute power, no matter how high the cost in human blood. Saddam was notable for using terror against his own people, including mustard and nerve gas to subdue the Kurds. He attacked Iran in 1980. The war ended in a stalemate and one million dead. Having learned nothing, he invaded Kuwait in 1990, leading to the First Gulf War, and another 85,000 dead. Uprisings after the war led to the death of some 150,000 civilians. The list goes on until he was toppled in 2003 by American and Allied forces, and hanged in 2006. Good riddance.

Idi Amin ruled as dictator of Uganda after launching a military coup in 1971. His nickname is "Butcher of Uganda." Amin's behaviour steadily worsened during the 1970s. He expelled all Asians and handed over their businesses to his cronies, which led to a collapse of the economy. Yet, the Asians were "lucky" compared to his violent persecution of rival Uganda tribes, who were killed by the tens of thousands. The total death toll of his regime amounted to half a million out of a population of 10 million. He was feared for feeding victims alive to crocodiles. He boasted that he kept the decapitated heads of political enemies in his freezer, although he said that human flesh was generally "too salty" for his taste. His megalomania knew no limits. Among his titles were "Lord of All the Beasts of the Earth and Fishes of the Seas" and "Conqueror of the British Empire in Africa." He was deposed in 1979 and fled to Saudi Arabia. He never expressed any remorse for his brutal deeds. He, too, was the subject of a Hollywood movie, *Last King of Scotland*.

Mengistu Haile Mariam rose to power in 1977 as a member of the murderous Derg regime in Ethiopia, which had toppled and murdered Emperor Haile Selassie in 1974. His policies were to modernise Ethiopia's economy along Leninist-Stalinist-Maoist lines. Land, companies, banks, etc., were all nationalised. Farmers were compelled to join collectives. The free market was abolished. Not surprisingly, it was a disaster. People resisted, famine ensued, and economic destitution was widespread. This did not stop Mengiest. Widespread resistance was met with brutal force. Between 1.2 and 2 million people were killed during his regime. According to the *Times*, it was not uncommon to see students, suspected government critics or rebel sympathisers hanging from lampposts each morning. Mengistu himself is alleged to have murdered opponents by garrotting or shooting them, saying that he was leading by example. Yes, we really need such examples Human Rights Watch describes his regime as "one of the most systematic uses of mass murder by a state ever witnessed in Africa." After the collapse of the Soviet Union, his position became untenable and he fled the country.

No list of 20th-century evil leaders is complete without **Josef Mengele's,** whose nickname *Todesengel* ("Angel of Death") says enough. He was the most prominent medical doctor at the Auschwitz death camp (concentration camp seems too friendly a term). He selected victims to be killed in the gas chambers, and happily administered the gas himself. That is bad enough, but what earned him his place in this top ten of infamy is his experimentation on humans. Mengele used Auschwitz as an opportunity to continue his research into genetics and heredity. He was fascinated by twins. The experiments he performed on twins included amputation of limbs, intentionally infecting one twin with typhus or some other disease, and transfusing the blood of that twin into the other. He experimented to change the eye colour including injecting chemicals into the eyes of living subjects. And so on. Mendele has become the stereotype of the mad scientist for whom ethical boundaries were a nuisance, who would do anything to satisfy their lust for knowledge. Unfortunately, he was never captured.

It may at first glance seem obtuse and even grotesque to document an assassination of one individual within the context of worldwide violent turmoil in which millions lost their lives. However, the killing of Nazi SS Obergruppenfuhrer Reinhard Heydrich, known as the ' Hangman, ' proved to be a momentous vent in the history of WW11. Heydrick was no ordinary Nazi and the angel of death in Lucifer's team were entrenched in his soul if he had one in the first place. As a senior officer in the Reich Security Head office, he was responsible for the running of the Gestapo and additionally the Reich's Governor of territories of Bohemia an Moravia. He was tipped to be Hitler's successor and, most importantly, one of the principal architects o the Holocaust. he was the chair of the Wannsee conference of 1942 where leading Nazis agreed on plans for the extermination of European Jews.

Reinhard Heydrich was born the son of a composer with exceptional talent as a skilled violinist and developed into an accomplished athlete. He was destined for a great career in the German Navy when in 1931, he was dismissed on the order of Great Admiral Raeder on matters that were not publicised. This may well have been the trigger for his defect of character to eventually evolve into a mass murderer. Reinhard's own version of events is that he refused to marry a woman he had been sleeping with who had a close friendship to Raeder.

Whilst Raeder survived the war he refused to disclose his reasons for sacking Heydrich. There was also a report that he was spying on naval personnel; for the nazis. It was not long after his dismissal that SS leader Heinrich Himmler appointed him to expand the SD and the SS" 's new ' security service.' Hendrick rise within the ranks of the Nazi party e was rapid. He took care to build an elaborate card file system recording potential threats, including other Nazi officers, to the security service regime. He demonstrated a talent for dispassionate cruelty which was lacking in his superior Himmler, who was apparently afraid of his subordinate officer. In 1934 Heydrich gained not only control of the Gestapo but the civil police force. Two years later he merged the criminal investigative police into the security police and ran the whole show himself.

Whilst Hendricks's ability left no doubt, he proved extremely competitive and aggressive, advising Hermann Goring and his council of ministers that he would expertise limitless power be it granted them or not. In time his scrupulous records within the Reich unleashed his talent for muckraking and espionage, proving invaluable to both Himmler and Hitler himself. It was his careful plan that provide the pretext for the nazi invasion of Poland. in 1939. he was given the task as head of the euphemistically named Central Office of Jewish Emigration, and the fate of Jews in Nazi-occupied Europe. The 'Final solution' or complete extermination was officially recommended by Heydrich on half of a conference of delegates and rubber-stamped by both Goeing and Hitler. The reign of terror on Jewish extermination resulted in The Holocaust and between 1941 and 1945, Nazi Germany and its collaborators systematically murdered some six million Jews across German-occupied Europe, around two-thirds of Europe's Jewish population. The murders were carried out primarily through mass shootings and poison gas in extermination camps, chiefly Auschwitz-Birkenau, Treblinka, Belzec, Sobibor, and Chełmno in occupied Poland.

British Intelligence was privy to Heydrick's part in the Jewish extermination where over six million Jews died. In 1942 the British parachuted two former Special operatives into Czechoslovakia to assassinate him, and on 27th May 1942 they staged their assassination. Wounded in his car by the trained assassins he died one week later on 4th June from septicaemia.

CHAPTER 12.

ATOMIC MAN

We must not forget the devastation caused by wars be they considered mass murder, killing fields for the ultimate welfare of the world or repeated assassins as has happened repeatedly in history. Case in point is the abrupt end of WWW11 with the atomic bombing of Hiroshima and Nagasaki in 1945. Hiroshima was bombed on the morning of August 6, 1945. The city, flat and surrounded by hills, was in many ways an ideal target for the atomic bomb, at least from the perspective of its creators. Their goal was destruction and spectacle, to show the Japanese, the Soviets, and the whole world, what the potential of this new weapon was. The geography of Hiroshima meant that a bomb with the explosive yield of "Little Boy" (the equivalent of 15,000 tons of TNT), detonated at the ideal altitude, could destroy nearly the entirety of the city. On August 8, news reports from Japan, plus a damage report created by the United States, began to paint a picture of the destruction. Aerial surveys revealed at least 60% of the city's "built-up areas" were destroyed, leading to the conclusion that perhaps "as many as 200,000 of Hiroshima's 340,000 residents perished or were injured," as one United Press story put it.

A cold war peace was the aftermath of the remainder of the 20th century but many political leaders, civil rights workers and peacemakers of international action were assassinated in their efforts to ensure WWW111 does not follow, a nuclear war of Armageddon proportions is the fear and justification for the killing of the few for the sake of the many. Just for the sake of recall, however, let us consider what happened on those fate-filled three days when the A-bombs were dropped on Nagasaki.

Chuck' Sweeney had made three runs over the hopelessly clouded Japanese city. Now he was over their primary target of Kokura, loaded with a 4.5-ton A bomb, Fat Man. He shockingly discovered the auxiliary gasoline pipe of his B-29 was blocked and unless they dropped the bomb soon they were never going to get home. He turned his plane southwest for his secondary target, 'Nagasaki, urban area.' A radio announcer saw the B-29 over Shimabara just before 11 a.m. and excitedly broadcasted a warning and Nagasaki people who heard him ran for shelter. Moments later Sweeney and his crew saw Nagasaki right below through a cloud break, immediately recognising the Urakami River and the Matsuyama Sports Ground. That put them 3 kilometres northwest of the planned drop on the industrial area of the city, but time had run out. It was just 11. a.m. 'Fat-man' went plummeting down onto the city of 200,000 souls of whom 70,000 would die, many without a trace.

The moment she heard the plane, the schoolmistress at the Yamazato schoolyard ran with two children from the playground to the air raid shelter. As they entered they were picked up and hurled to the far wall as she blacked out. Coming too, she heard the children whimpering at her feet and wondered why it was so dark. As light penetrated the darkness she was paralysed with fear. At the shelter entrance, two hideous monsters appeared making croaking noises and trying to crawl in. As the darkness lifted further she saw they were human beings who had been outside when the bomb exploded. They were but 750 metres from the epicentre and their raw bodies had been picked up and smashed against the shelter. Three kilometres away Farmer San was working on his rice Paddy on Mt. Kawabira. He heard a noise, looked up and saw the B-29 emerging from the clouds. It degorged a huge black bomb and he threw himself to the ground. He waited a minute, then came an awful penetrating light, this was followed by an eerie stillness.

He looked up and gaped at a huge pillar of smoke, swelling grotesquely as it rose. Suddenly he realised a hurricane was rushing towards him with houses, buildings and trees cut down before his startled eyes. Then came a hush and deafening roar and he was hurled like a twig into a stone wall three metres away. Shaken to the core he gaped at the pines, chestnuts and camphor laurels torn from the ground or broken at the trunk. Even the grass was gone! Within 1000 metres of the epicentre, near the school, four children stood transfixed without clothing or skin. Their hands had been torn away at the wrists and skin hung from their fingernails looking like gloves turned inside out. The two surviving monsters off the shelter lay groaning calling for water. A cry that would and could be heard throughout Nagasaki. Many, many thousands nearby were pinned under the roofs of their homes, the epicentre, following the lightning flash and horrific roar. The blast caused air rushing at 2 kilometres per second, 60 times the velocity of a major cyclone and was followed by a violent wind that sucked back like a vacuum left at the epicentre.

People staggered the streets naked and swollen like pumpkins. A babel of croaking voices piteously calling for water. There was a puddle of dirty water outside a shelter and crawling victims lowering their lips drank from that puddle. One by one they came forward to drink the slime water, all crumbling up afterwards, motionless. What terrible thirst would drive men to act like demented lemmings? Kato-San was walking his cow on a hillside outside Oyama, 8 km south of the epicentre. Startled by the flash, he watched, rooted to the spot, as a huge white cloud like a grotesque organism fattened itself with some magic wand. The cloud was white but fired by some hideous red energy within. Then came flashes of red, yellow and purple as the cloud went into a mushroom shape and a black stain grew on its stem. When the cloud reached its zenith it collapsed like an obscene grub that had gouged on more than its stomach could hold. The mountains all around were lit by the sun; below the peaks all was darkness.

The Plutonium 239 bomb exploded over Nagasaki that day with the equivalent force of 22,000 tons of conventional explosives but with a vast difference. Setting aside the lethal radiation and the poisonous black rain that was to follow for days, the A-bombs intense heat reached several million degrees centigrade at the explosive point. The whole mass of the huge bomb was ionised and a fireball was created, making the air around it all luminous emitting near ultraviolet rays and infra-red rays and blistering roof tiles up to a kilometre from the epicentre. Exposed human skin was scorched up to 4 kilometres away. Electric light poles, trees and houses chard on the surface facing the blast. Acres of dust, debris and smoke hung in the air for an eternity. At the end of the war, the Allied nations became the basis of the United Nations. It is hard to say with exact certainty how many people were killed during World War 11, but estimates vary between 50 million and over 80 million. One thing that everybody agrees with is that it has been the deadliest war ever, wiping out around 3 per cent of the world population at the time. It is estimated that around 15,000,000 soldiers died during the war. Military deaths, which include soldiers missing in action as well as fatalities due to disease,

accidents and prisoners of war deaths along with battle deaths, are
estimated to be between 22,000,000 and 30,000,000. Civilians killed
by war-related disease and famine counted between 19,000,000 and
25,000,000. The madness of the men, I mused. The events and tragic
death toll of WW11 could easily be repeated in today's world but it
would more likely be a Nuclear War. I shuddered at the thought as
presidents and dictators played their games of cat and mouse, continuing to send up experimental nuclear warheads to show off their mus-
cle continually out-manoeuvring one another with hurtful egotistical
barbs, using weapons of mass destruction here say- mythical commentary that could easily start WW 111. Another feather for the cap
of the Prince of Darkness; is that great Destroyer who gets his kicks
from sickness and ultimately death.

I was thinking about my first experience with a gun. In the far New
England Ranges, I was camping with my Uncle Fred. he was a timber
getter and a crack shot with rise. He later became the New South
Wales small bore champion. We camped out mostly but this day we
were back sitting on the veranda of his bush hut and he handed me his
rifle, cocked the trigger and showed me how to aim at a rather large
bird sitting in a not-too-distant tree. He just said 'Aim, breathe, hold
your breath and pull the trigger.' The bird fell silently to the
ground below. I was not yet five years old. Goodness knows why my
parents let me go stay with him in the midst of the bush many moons
from my home. I learnt a lot about shooting in my military cadets at
boarding school. I did not take too kindly to the discipline though. I
was always on detention parades, an opportune time to learn the art of
dissembling and reassembling guns. Later I owned a gun shop for a
short time. I handed in my licence as I got to know too many locals
who eventually suicide using a gun. I taught my boys how to shoot
and the need for safety when out hunting kangaroos, foxes and rabbits
with mates. Always on friends' properties, they had their outings
helping on the land to kill the beasts who destroyed pasture! My second youngest then was not all that keen to shoot but the day he shot
his first rabbit, he cried out 'I got him.' I looked at him and the tears

flowed down his cheeks. The tragedy of his young suicide still haunts me now but it was not with a gun.

As I walked I recalled thoughts of another Uncle, Frank. He was a sniper during WW2 and was left alone on an Island near New Guinea after the Japanese invasion. It was 'infested' with a large number of Japanese soldiers. His mission by the armed forces was to stay there until he had killed them all. He lived off berries, nuts and wildlife in the jungle and he was there for most of the war but he successfully completed his mission. Never talked about it much and, in fact, didn't speak much at all really. He always gave me a friendly smile when I had the privilege of being in his company. I liked him but he was a strange one. Walking the Way, the question crossed my mind, could I assassinate someone? I was thinking about two mates who had both been sexually abused as children and a cousin who was raped by a Marist brother.. If someone gave me a rifle, cocked the trigger, and said 'Just aim it, breath, hold your breath and pull the trigger.' Yes, I would still drop the bastards just like I did that bird when I was a child. Yes. I could be an assassin given the right cause. The mental devices of my brain rule over a Golden rule for living. How could I overcome my defects except through the power of prayer which seemed logically to be an answer?

I noted that in the 20th century, there was hardly a year gone by that there was an assassination or an attempt a one. Much was made of CIA involvement with political killings, but equally the KGB or M16 could well have been involved. And of you the Russians who It seemed historically get up close 6o kill with poison, dagger or small bore hand gun. This all changed for both allied forces and the East with he introduction of the standard U.S. military rifle, the M-16 which was substantially more destructive than the Russian counterpart, the AK-47, despite the fact that the AK-47 is of larger calibre and fires a much heavier bullet with a genetic energy(m muzzle) 25% greater thank the M-16. It is considerably cheaper and more dependable. Armed with a laser light, it will ensure a kill at a greater distance than most and even an untrained assassin can hit the mark more often than not. These rifles are used by military assassins and the police in siege situations.

The CIA has been implicated for their involvement in several high-level assassinations and assassination attempts throughout history. Most notably, the U.S. Senate found that there were at least eight attempts on Fidel Castro's life. Statistics concerning the prevalence of CIA assassins and their work are hard to find as the CIA is extremely tight-lipped about this and most other areas of its operations. Few details are known about their training programs as well, as leaks in this information could compromise both agent and national security.

Assassin training requires discipline, loyalty, secrecy and courage. Applicants must be willing to put the CIA and the mission above all personal relationships and duties. The life of an assassin in training is very strenuous. Students are put through rigorous training exercises to cultivate discipline and a "killer instinct." Training typically lasts between six months and two years, depending on the acumen of the student and his skill level. However, training as an assassin is a lifelong process, where experience is the real teacher. Students who graduate from CIA assassination training are part of an elite class of soldiers. Their work is only ever acknowledged by their superiors. They live a life of secrecy and they risk their lives regularly. CIA assassins in training should know that their actions may be scrutinised by future administrations, and total knowledge of their involvement in assassinations may be disavowed.

The function of a CIA assassin is to kill those who pose a threat to U.S. national security. CIA assassins have allegedly been responsible for some of the most recognised assassinations and assassination attempts in the past century. They may also be responsible for "black ops," operations that are strictly off the books--operations that governments can deny they had any involvement in. Agents killed during a black op are never recognised publicly by the government. CIA assassination training and a career as an assassin is not an advisable career for anyone who wishes to lead a normal life. Total commitment to the mission and the job are required above all else. Agents routinely risk their lives, and there is a strong possibility of death on the job. Agents must also deal with the psychological ramifications that result from killing another person.

In the King James version and the World English Bible, the text is near the same: "You have heard that it was said, an eye for an eye and a tooth for a tooth." This verse begins in the same style as earlier references to the Old Testament. This is an ancient statement that dates back to the code of Hammurabi. This phrasing appears several times in the Old Testament in Exodus 21:24, Leviticus 24:20 and Deuteronomy 19:21. This was a moderate rule compared with the blood feuds described in Genesis 4:23-24. There were 282 Hammurabi's code of laws. There are no less than 27 codes of death for murder, incorrect accusations, sorcery, stealing, break-and-enter deception, and adultery. All were tried and put to death under the code. Other codes related to the plucking out of eyes, cutting off limbs and drowning as punishments. In Jesus' era, such punishments were no longer in practice, rather they had been replaced by fines judged to be equal to the damage caused. Thus, Jesus was not here condemning the violence or brutality of such punishment in his Sermon on the Mount lesson, but rather, the very idea of retribution. "You have heard it said ' Eye for eye and tooth for tooth.' "But I tell you, do not resist an evil person. If anyone slaps you on the right cheek, turn to them the other cheek also. And if anyone wants to sue you and take your shirt, hand him over your coat as well. If anyone forces you to go one mile, go with them two miles. Give to the one who asks you, and do not turn away from one who wants to borrow from you."

The Port Arthur massacre of 28 April 1996 was a mass shooting in which 35 people were killed and 23 wounded. It occurred mainly at the Port Arthur former prison colony, a popular tourist sight in southeastern Tasmania, Australia. It was the deadliest mass shooting in Australian history and amongst the most notable in history. Martin Bryant, then 28 years of age, from Hobart Tasmania carried out the shootings and was given 35 years life sentence without the possibility of parole. Bryan inherited $570,000 from a friend Helen Harvey, who left her estate to him. Bryant befriended her on one of his many rounds searching for clients for his lawn mowing business. Helen Harvey died in a car accident with Bryant as the sole passenger. He had been seen on previous occasions taking the wheel from Helen Harvey whilst she was driving and doing erratic turns off the steering wheel. Bryant was not suspected of killing her and was never charged with any offence and never held a driving licence at that time.

Bryant used part of the money he inherited to take many trips around the world from 1993 onward. He used at least some of the money in late 1993 to purchase an AK 10 semi-automatic rifle through a newspaper advertisement in Tasmania. In March 1996, he had his AK-10 repaired at a gun shop and made enquiries about AR1-15 rifles in other gun shops. It was also unofficially reported after the shootings at Port Arthur, though never proven, that Bryan had returned from overseas and on a recent visit often sat in the back corner of a restaurant taking photos. He cased out potential targets for his killing spree and his very precision accuracy with the killings of innocent people at Port Arthur smacked of something more than a disarranged mind but had the marks of a skilled and well-trained Assassin.

Just six weeks into the job, Prime Minister John Howard was at Kirribilli House, the Sydney-based residence off the P.M., when he received a call alerting him to the tragedy unfolding at Port Arthur. He turned on the T.V. And within minutes others from his office and the Federal police Commissioner rang him to explain what was happening. Later that day the Premier of Tasmania, Tony Rundle, phoned and they talked about the possibility of tightening gun laws. The tragedy would be both a tremendous challenge and a moment that defined Howard's leadership and his Prime Ministership as strong, determined, and practical. John Howard flew with then Labor leader, Beazley and the DemocratsCheryl Kernot flew to Tasmania to attend services for victims and lay a wreath at Port Arthur. He also met with the traumatised emergency workers who had to deal with the shattered bodies of the 23 wounded. But forefront in his mind was how to prevent this from ever happening again. What followed was a concerted effort led from the top to stop the importation and sale of automatic and semi-automatic weapons in Australia. Gun laws were then primarily a state matter. The Federal Government having control over importation meant Mr Howard had to convince all the states and territories to embrace consistent laws which he would propose. The Government worked with the states to buy back banned weapons and any weapons people no longer wanted, with nearly 700,000 handed in. New consistent laws on licensing and storage of legal weapons were introduced by all the states and territories. People who needed guns for their own livelihood had to be licensed and their weapons registered and guns to be stored in locked cupboards, unloaded.

Following the spree, the Prime Minister formulated the National Firearms Programme Implementation Act 1996, restricting private ownership of semi-automatic rifles, semi-automatic shotguns and pump-action shotguns as well as introducing uniform firearms licensing. It was implemented with bipartisan support from all states and territories. This massacre happened just six weeks after the Dunblane massacre, in Scotland, with U.K. Prime Minister John Major passing their own changes to gun laws in 1997. On December 15-16, 2014, the Sydney hostage crisis at the Lindt Cafe, Martin Place Sydney occurred. Lone gunman Haron Monas held ten customers and eight employees of the Lindt chocolate cafe hostage. The police treated the event as a terrorist attack at the time, but Monas' motives have subsequently been debated. The Sydney siege led to a sixteen-hour standoff, after which gunshots were heard, a Tactical Operations Unit stormed the cafe. Hostage Tori Johnson was killed by Monas and hostage Katrina Dawson was killed by a police bullet that ricochet in the raid. Monas was also killed. Three other hostages and a police officer were injured by police gunfire.

Earlier on, hostages were seen holding an Islamic black flag up against the window of the cafe, featuring the Shahadah creed. Monas later demanded that the ISIL flag be brought to him. Prime Minister Tony Abbott described on radio that the hostage crisis was politically motivated. The eventual assessment was that Monas was a mix of extremists with mental issues and plain criminals. In the aftermath of the siege, Muslim groups issued a joint statement which condemned the incident and memorial services were held in nearby St. Mary's Cathedral and St. James Church. Condolence books were set up in other Lindt cafes and the community turned Martin Place into a 'field of flowers.' In 1996, at the time of the Port Arthur massacre, there were an estimated 3,200,000 licit and illicit, guns held by civilians in Australia. At the end of 2016, despite the new gun laws that were implemented by the Howard Government and the change in the Firearms Act of 1996, the number has risen back to the 3,200,000 number again.

Whilst the Port Arthur massacre and the Lindt cafe siege are the most recent assassinations by a lone gunman in Australia, they are by no means the least of public concerns. The 1984 Milperra Massacre was a major incident in a series of conflicts between various outlaw motorcycle gangs. In 1987, the Hoddle Street Massacre and the Queen Street Massacre took place in Melbourne. In the Strathfield massacre in 1991, two public victims were killed by knife and five more with a firearm. The use of firearms and the killing sprees still go on, not only in Australia but throughout the world. The proud claim that Australia may have 'solved the gun problem' might only be a temporary illusion. For the first time in 20 years, this year Australia's national arsenal of private guns is larger than what it was before the Port Arthur massacre. Although Australia hasn't seen a public mass shooting since 1996, we have no shortage of firearm-related crime. Gun owners know only too well, be they family members or gang members, have always been the ones to kill each other most frequently.

Then there is the killer in the room. About 80% of gun deaths in Australia have nothing to do with crime. Instead, they're suicides and unintentional shootings. In 1996, immediately following the buy-back spree, rapid-fire rifles were replaced by freshly imported single-shot firearms. In the years that followed, gun buying climbed steadily to new heights. By 2015 the arms trade had broken all previous records. Last financial year Australia imported 104,000 firearms and the gun surge is now showing an upward momentum. When guns found in crime are traced back to their origin, experts agree that most are found to have leaked from licensed gun owners and rogue firearm dealers. This is usually the way of the 'grey market,' a large pool of illicit firearms created by Australian gun owners who did not register their firearms after the law changed in 1996. Whilst Australia has placed the most comprehensive and perhaps the most effective mesh of gun control measures on the planet, no law is effective until taken seriously.

CHAPTER 13.

ASSASSINATION OF THE GOOD ONES

These days dedicated gun-crime task forces target armed career criminals, firearm-related prosecutions have soared since police launched a 'national blitzes' on gun owners' homes and seized thousands of firearms and lethal weapons from violence-prone or suicide risk households: and actual sanctions imposed on shooters who ignore safe storage regulations. But perhaps the most profound change since the Port Arthur massacre, seen in media coverage, is a resurgence of public scepticism about the motives of self-interest groups seeking to wind back gun laws. Dedicated single-issue political potency remains with the pro-gun lobbyists. We seem to be the only country in the world with two state political parties built and run by the gun lobby. On an international scale, the arms dealers are slowly being reined in, but ever so slowly.

In 2010 the notorious arms smuggler, Viktor Bout, was extradited from Thailand to America following a five-year operation by the DEA. The Russian national stands accused of illegally arming the Revolutionary Armed Forces of Colombia in their operations against US forces and may remain in jail for life. A millionaire by 25, Bout had an entire aviation empire by 30, even earning a gift from the Sheikh of Sharjah for 'developing the Emirates airport infrastructure.' Bout dismissed claims made against him by the UN. He said 'I am a businessman. I have lots of planes and don't care what I transport because that is not my responsibility.' Victor Bout of Central African Airways was described in the House of Commons as a 'Merchant of Death.' In the wake of 9/11, scrutiny of illegal arms trading increased. Bowing to American pressure, Bout's friends in the governments of Rwanda and the Central African Republic cut their ties with him. At Britain's request, his Emirates firms were shut down. Eventually, he moved back to Russia – which does not extradite its citizens abroad- where he tried and failed to make a living selling reindeer and kitchen tiles. Soon he was mired in debt and giving interviews on Russian radio claimed he was 'a scapegoat for the war on terrorism.' He added "If there is a Russian entrepreneur abroad, they always attach some labels, followed by 'mafia', followed by 'weapons'. I should go around smelling of vodka and garlic, the Russian bear scaring the West."

In 2007, a South African associate, was approached by a friend secretly working for the American Drug Enforcement Agency (DEA) and asked to broker an arms deal between Bout and men he was told were Columbian Fare revolutionaries. Bout agreed to a rendezvous to discuss a deal in a hotel in Thailand. The meeting was recorded on videotape, only this time it was a secret camera planted by the agents, who recorded Bout offering to sell them anti-aircraft missiles.

In a Thai jail, getting to his feet to protest his innocence after hearing his sentence Bout protested. "If you're going to apply the same standards to me, you should hail all the arms dealers in America too." Bout had never actually committed a crime chargeable in an American court, and a charge of 'conspiring to kill Americans' was only brought about because the agent posing as a Farc soldier told Bout that's what he wanted to do. He is a dealer from within the jail system as a procurer of arms and an agent of Death' again. The dark angel could rise again with a justifiable innocence - 'Guns don't kill people, people do.'

In seeking a way out of Lucifer's grasp let us look now at the lives of men of good intent for humanity at the expense of their own suffering and ultimate assassination.

Mohandas Karamchand Gandhi was born of a wealthy political family in the princely state of Porbandar, Gujarat, West India. At the time of his birth in 1869, his father, Karamchand was Chief Minister for the area and had taught Gandhi from childhood political astuteness that would serve him well in life. Gandhi's lifetime pursuit of the perfect mental, physical and spiritual diet for his being was from the indoctrination of his devout mother, an adherent of the Jain religion. She taught him the tenets of her faith: the sanctity of life, vegetarianism, abstinence from alcohol, fasting for self-purification, and mutual tolerance across creeds and sects. These principles were the framework to help guide his adult political life. At the age of nineteen, he was sent to University College in London where he studied law and graduated in 1891 and trained as a barrister of the Inner Temple. He failed to find a job in India as a barrister, so he took a post in 1893 for a one-year appointment in Natal in South Africa but he remained there for the next twenty years championing the legal rights of the Indian community and there he adopted his strategy of non-cooperation.

An incident in the early 1890s one day in South Africa was revealing. As was expected in those days two Indians walking along a pavement were expected to walk in the gutter when approached by white folk. On this occasion, as they passed Gandhi reportedly remarked to his Indian companion: " It has always been a mystery to me' he stated without anger: " how men can feel honoured by the humiliation of their fellow beings." He was twenty-two at the time and such audacity in the face of any white South African was a sign of things to come when he would shake the world with his advocacy and belief in 'Satyagraha,' the name he later gave to non-passive resistance to British rule in India.

Gandhi returned to India in 1914, at the beginning of World War 1. He joined the Indian National Congress, campaigning for civil rights and Indian self-government. It was in that first year that he initiated protests against social injustice, which continued for the rest of his life. Soon appointed leader of the Congress, he introduced non-violent boycotts of British Institutions. He was tried for sedition and imprisoned until 1924. On release, he withdrew from politics to travel around India for the next three years promoting his crafts and the plight of the 'Untouchables' (Dalits), the lowest rank of India's caste system. He married and continued on his passive-aggressive campaign cumulating in his 1930's ' Salt March.,' where he called thousands of followers to march to the ocean to make salt, to campaign against the tax on salt that the British had imposed on India. To those followers who feared being jailed by the British for this unlawful march, he simply stated: "There are only 40,000 British in India and we are over 400,000,000 at this time. They can't jail us all." He did ultimately land himself back in jail but not over the " Salt March.'

It was his resolve not to support British India's wartime role when he launched in 1939 a "Quit India" Campaign against British domination. He was jailed in 1942 with other Congress leaders after negotiations for Independence failed. When Independence finally came, he was opposed to the Mountbatten plan of dividing the country on religious grounds, thus forming two states, one of India and the other of Pakistan. This of course suited British political influences after World War, as they sought to checkmate Stalin's Russia from taking over oil-rich areas surrounding India and Pakistan which the West ultimately controlled. Gandhi's lifestyle and beliefs ultimately were the cause of his assassination by an extremist Hindu in 1948.

John F. Kennedy was the 35th President of the United States (1961-1963), the youngest man elected to the office. On November 22, 1963, when he was hardly past his first thousand days in office, JFK was assassinated in Dallas, Texas, becoming also the youngest President to die. On November 22, 1963, when he was hardly past his first thousand days in office, John Fitzgerald Kennedy was killed by an assassin's bullets as his motorcade wound through Dallas, Texas. Kennedy was the youngest man elected President; he was the youngest to die. Of Irish descent, he was born in Brookline, Massachusetts, on May 29, 1917. After graduating from Harvard in 1940, he entered the Navy. In 1943, when his PT boat was rammed and sunk by a Japanese destroyer, Kennedy, despite grave injuries, led the survivors through perilous waters to safety.

Back from the war, he became a Democratic Congressman from the Boston area, advancing in 1953 to the Senate. He married Jacqueline Bouvier on September 12, 1953. In 1955, while recuperating from a back operation, he wrote Profiles in Courage, which won the Pulitzer Prize in history. In 1956 Kennedy almost gained the Democratic nomination for Vice President, and four years later was a first-ballot nominee for President. Millions watched his television debates with the Republican candidate, Richard M. Nixon. Winning by a narrow margin in the popular vote, Kennedy became the first Roman Catholic President.

His Inaugural Address offered the memorable injunction: "Ask not what your country can do for you–ask what you can do for your country." As President, he set out to redeem his campaign pledge to get America moving again. His economic programs launched the country on its longest sustained expansion since World War II; before his death, he laid plans for a massive assault on persisting pockets of privation and poverty. Responding to ever more urgent demands, he took vigorous action for the cause of equal rights, calling for new civil rights legislation. His vision of America extended to the quality of the national culture and the central role of the arts in a vital society. He wished America to resume its old mission as the first nation dedicated to the revolution of human rights. With the Alliance for Progress and the Peace Corps, he brought American idealism to the aid of

developing nations. But the hard reality of the Communist challenge remained.

Shortly after his inauguration, Kennedy permitted a band of Cuban exiles,
already armed and trained, to invade their homeland. The attempt to overthrow the regime of Fidel Castro was a failure. Soon thereafter, the Soviet
Union renewed its campaign against West Berlin. Kennedy replied by rein-
forcing the Berlin garrison and increasing the Nation's military strength,
including new efforts in outer space. Confronted by this reaction, Moscow,
after the erection of the Berlin Wall, relaxed its pressure in central Europe.
Instead, the Russians now sought to install nuclear missiles in Cuba. When
this was discovered by air reconnaissance in October 1962, Kennedy imposed a quarantine on all offensive weapons bound for Cuba. While the
world trembled on the brink of nuclear war, the Russians backed down and
agreed to take the missiles away. The American response to the Cuban crisis evidently persuaded Moscow of the futility of nuclear blackmail.

Kennedy now contended that both sides had a vital interest in stopping the
spread of nuclear weapons and slowing the arms race–a contention that led
to the test ban treaty of 1963. The months after the Cuban crisis showed
significant progress toward his goal of "a world of law and free choice, ban-
ishing the world of war and coercion." His administration thus saw the beginning of new hope for both the equal rights of Americans and a world of
peace.

In the modern age, the events that register as shattering to the nation and
international psyche that characterise an age. In the 21st century, the collapse of the Twin Towers of the World Trade Centre on 11th September
2001 has reconfigured the world in ways that are still unfolding. In 1963 it
was at the assassination of President John F Kennedy. The first of many
assassinations to follow appear on the television camera and is replayed
many times since it was a moment in time that symbolises the reaction of
the old and outworn against the promise of the new.

In his time he established the Peace Corps, authorised the CIA to support
the invasion of Cuba by anti-communist exiles in the Bay of Pig fiasco, Introduced a   Civil rights bill in Congress, succeeded in forcing a Soviet
climbdown during the Cuba Missile Crisis, signed a   Nuclear Test Band

treaty, the first disarmament agreement of the nuclear age and ask economic advisers to prepare " War on Poverty programme.

By 1968, **Martin Luther King** could easily have begun to take it easy had he wished d to do so. He had in the year of President Kennedy's assassination addressed 250,000 people and uttered one of the most remarkable speeches of the 20th century. he had seen the passing of the 1964 Civil Rights Act and won the Noble Peace Prize, but five years later he was not ready to retire. For he had unmarked on a new campaign to combat poverty and was in Memphis, Tennessee in support of striking African Americans.

In early April, Martin Luther King returned to Memphis as part of his ' Poor People's Campaign' at the beginning ion the year. It was common knowledge that he generally stayed at a very modest Lorraine Motel in his favourite room, 306. On April 4, 1968, as he stood on the second-floor balcony of the Lorraine Motel in Memphis, Tennessee, where he had come to lead a march by striking sanitation workers. In response to King's death, more than 100 American inner cities exploded in rioting, looting, and violence. James Earl Ray, a career small-time criminal who became the object of a more than two-month manhunt before he was captured in England pled guilty to the shooting and received a 99-year prison sentence. He quickly recanted his plea and spent the rest of his life claiming that he had been framed by a conspiracy that was really responsible for King's assassination. The Martin Luther King, Jr., assassination was one of the earthshaking events of 1968 that made it among the most tumultuous and momentous years in American history. The civil rights movement, the Vietnam War and the antiwar movement all were in full swing as the year began. King's opposition to the Vietnam War had been building steadily since 1965 though initially, he was reluctant to prominently criticise the conduct of the war by Pres. Lyndon B. Johnson, who had been a key ally in the effort to pass the Civil Rights Act of 1964 and the Voting Rights Act of 1965. When the war effort began to rob funding from Johnson's Great Society plan however, King became a more vocal critic, and his opposition to the war grew to embrace a more radical critique of what he saw as U.S. militarism and imperialism. King also took American capitalism to task and began portraying inequality in economic as well as racial terms. "Beyond Viet nam," the address that he gave at Riverside Church in New York City on

April 4, 1967, exactly one year before his death, brought all of these elements together in a speech that made manifest his opposition to the war.

A number of mainstream publications, including *The New York Times* and *The Washington Post*, thought King had gone too far with the speech. He had already begun to find himself betwixt and between. Many whites saw him as a dangerous radical. On the other hand, despite his increasingly radical message, a growing number of militant African Americans had become impatient with his nonviolent methods and what they saw as a lack of success in his civil rights efforts in northern cities. It had been several years since his southern triumphs in the Montgomery bus boycott, the Birmingham campaign, and the Selma March.

When news broke of King's assassination, outrage among African-American communities prompted a nationwide wave of riots in more than sixty American cities. President Johnson declared a national day of mourning for the civil rights leader. That same day, King 'spoke' at his own funeral which took place at the Ebenezer Baptist Church in Atlanta, Georgia, where he had his father had both been pastor. A record riding of the ' Drum Major' sermon, given 4 February 2 1968, was played at the ceremony. King had asked that no mention st his generals be made of his many awards and honours, but requested that he merely be remembered for ' trying to feed the hungry;, clothe the naked' and ' love and serve humanity.'

On 5 April 1967, the day after the assassination of Martin Luther L King, US Attorney-General Robert Kennedy delivered a speech in Cleveland, Ohio. it was a sharply critical attack on hatred and prejudices that seemed to be tearing America apart. ' What has violence ever accomplished?' he asked/ 'What has it ever created? No martyr's cause has ever been stilled by an assassin's bullet...No one, no matter where he lives or what he does, can be certain who next will suffer from such a senseless act of bloodshed.' It was exactly a month later, that Robert Kennedy himself fell victim y an assassin's bullet. It seemed as if no political leader was safe in modern America.

Robert Fitzgerald' Bobby' Kennedy was surely destined to be President of the United States. In March 1968 the incumbent, President Lyndon K Johnson, had finally announced that he was not standing for the election, bowing out to make way for his vice-president, Hubert Humphrey. By then

Kennedy had already established a clear lead over his principal Democrat-
ic Party rival, Eugene McCarthy, in the early primaries, and his exciting,
reformist ideas and comparative youth made Humphreys look leaden, old
and very much a creature of the Establishment. The Republican front run-
*ner, Richard M. Nixon, who had na*rrowly lost to Kohn F. Kennedy in 1960,
now seemed a tarnished and apparently broken figure from the past. In
June 1968, Kennedy defatted McCarthy in the critical Democratic primary.
The way seemed open to Kennedy now or the Democratic nomination and
the Presidency. The exhilarating expectation that Brother John had raised
on his election in 1960, prematurely dashed his assassination in 1963, could
now be fully realised, yet. moments after claiming victory, shortly after
midnight on 5 June, the man destined to be the next president of the United
States was shot and killed.

Robert Francis Kennedy was born on November 20, 1925, in Brookline,
Massachusetts, the seventh child in the closely-knit and competitive family
of Rose and Joseph P. Kennedy. "I was the seventh of nine children," he
later recalled, "and when you come from that far down you have to struggle
to survive." He attended Milton Academy and, after wartime service in the
Navy, received his degree in government from Harvard University in 1948.
He earned his law degree from the University of Virginia Law School three
years later. Perhaps more important for his education was the Kennedy
family dinner table, where his parents involved their children in discussions
of history and current affairs. "I can hardly remember a mealtime," Robert
Kennedy said, "when the conversation was not dominated by what Franklin
D. Roosevelt was doing or what was happening in the world."In 1950,
Robert Kennedy married Ethel Skakel of Greenwich, Connecticut, daughter
of Ann Brannack Skakel and George Skakel, founder of Great Lakes Car-
bon Corporation. Robert and Ethel Kennedy later had eleven children. In
1952, he made his political debut as manager of his older brother John's
successful campaign for the US Senate from Massachusetts.

The following year, he served briefly on the staff of the Senate Subcommittee on Investigations, chaired by Senator Joseph McCarthy. Disturbed by
McCarthy's controversial tactics, Kennedy resigned from the staff after six
months. He later returned to the Senate Subcommittee on Investigations as
chief counsel for the Democratic minority, in which capacity he wrote a
report condemning McCarthy's investigation of alleged Communists in the

Army. His later work as Chief Counsel for the Senate Rackets Committee investigating corruption in trade unions won him national recognition for exposing Teamsters' Union leaders Jimmy Hoffa and David Beck.

In 1960, he was the tireless and effective manager of John F. Kennedy's presidential campaign. After the election, he was appointed Attorney General in President Kennedy's cabinet. While Attorney General, he won respect for his diligent, effective and nonpartisan administration of the Department of Justice. Attorney General Kennedy launched a successful drive against organised crime, and convictions against organised crime figures rose by 800% during his tenure. He also became increasingly committed to helping African Americans win the right to vote, attend integrated schools and use public accommodations. He demonstrated his commitment to civil rights during a 1961 speech at the University of Georgia Law School: "We will not stand by or be aloof. We will move. I happen to believe that the 1954 [Supreme Court school desegregation] decision was right. But my belief does not matter. It is the law. Some of you may believe the decision was wrong. That does not matter. It is the law."

In September 1962, Attorney General Kennedy sent US Marshals and troops to Oxford, Mississippi to enforce a federal court order admitting the first African American student - James Meredith - to the University of Mississippi. The riot that had followed Meredith's registration at "Ole Miss" had left two dead and hundreds injured. Robert Kennedy believed that voting was the key to achieving racial justice and collaborated with President Kennedy in proposing the most far-reaching civil rights statute since Reconstruction, the Civil Rights Act of 1964, which passed eight months after President Kennedy's death.

Robert Kennedy was not only President Kennedy's Attorney General, he was also his closest advisor and confidant. As a result of this unique relationship, the Attorney General played a key role in several critical foreign policy decisions. During the 1962 Cuban Missile Crisis, for instance, he helped develop the Kennedy administration's strategy to blockade Cuba instead of taking military action that could have led to nuclear war. He then negotiated with the Soviet Union on the removal of the weapons. Soon after President Kennedy's death, Robert Kennedy resigned as Attorney General and, in 1964, ran successfully for the United States Senate from New York. His opponent, incumbent Republican Senator Kenneth Keating, labelled Kennedy a "carpetbagger" during the closely contested campaign. Kennedy responded to the attacks with humour. "I have [had] really two choices over the period of the last ten months," he said at Columbia University. "I could have stayed in I could have retired. [Laughter.] And my father has done very well and I could have lived off him. [Laughter and applause.] ... I tell you frankly I don't need this title because I [could] be called General, I understand, for the rest of my life. [Laughter and applause.] And I don't need the money and I don't need the office space... [Laughter.] . Frank as it is - and maybe it's difficult to believe in the state of New York - I'd like to just be a good United States Senator. I'd like to serve." Kennedy waged an effective statewide campaign and, aided by President Lyndon Johnson's landslide, won the November election by 719,000 votes. As New York's Senator, he initiated a number of projects in the state, including assistance to underprivileged children and students with disabilities and the establishment of the Bedford-Stuyvesant Restoration Corporation to improve living conditions and employment opportunities in depressed areas of Brooklyn. Since 1967, the program has been a model for communities all across the nation.

These programs were part of a larger effort to address the needs of the dispossessed and powerless in America - the poor, the young, racial minorities and Native Americans. He sought to bring the facts about poverty to the conscience of the American people, journeying into urban ghettos, Appalachia, the Mississippi Delta and migrant workers' camps. "There are children in the Mississippi Delta," he said, "whose bellies are swollen with hunger... Many of them cannot go to school because they have no clothes or shoes. These conditions are not confined to rural Mississippi. They exist in dark tenements in Washington, DC, within sight of the Capitol, in Harlem, in South Side Chicago, in Watts. There are children in each of these areas who have never been to school, never seen a doctor or a dentist. There are children who have never heard conversation in their homes, never read or even seen a book." He sought to remedy the problems of poverty through legislation to encourage private industry to locate in poverty-stricken areas, thus creating jobs for the unemployed and stressing the importance of work over welfare.

Robert Kennedy was also committed to the advancement of human rights abroad. He travelled to Eastern Europe, Latin America and South Africa to share his belief that all people have a basic human right to participate in the political decisions that affect their lives and to criticise their government without fear of reprisal. He also believed that those who strike out against injustice show the highest form of courage. "Each time a man stands up for an ideal," he said in a 1966 speech to South African students, "or acts to improve the lot of others, or strikes out against injustice, he sends forth a tiny ripple of hope, and crossing each other from a million different centres of energy and daring, those ripples build a current that can sweep down the mightiest walls of oppression and resistance."

Kennedy was also absorbed during his Senate years by a quest to end the war in Vietnam. As a new Senator, Kennedy had originally supported the Johnson administration's policies in Vietnam but also called for a greater commitment to a negotiated settlement and a renewed emphasis on economic and political reform within South Vietnam. As the war continued to widen and America's involvement deepened, Senator Kennedy came to have serious misgivings about President Johnson's conduct in the war. Kennedy publicly broke with the Johnson administration for the first time in February 1966, proposing participation by all sides (including the Viet Cong's political arm, the National Liberation Front) in the political life of South Vietnam. The following year, he took responsibility for his role in the Kennedy administration's policy in Southeast Asia and urged President Johnson to cease the bombing of North Vietnam and reduce, rather than enlarge, the war effort. In his final Senate speech on Vietnam, Kennedy said, "Are we like the God of the Old Testament that we can decide, in Washington, DC, what cities, what towns, what hamlets in Vietnam are going to be destroyed?... Do we have to accept that?... I do not think we have to. I think we can do something about it."

Robert Kennedy, like his brother before him, attracted popular support in their primaries-appealing to the people over the heads of the Establishment. Kennedy's ticket was unapologetically liberal. he called for racial and economic justice, a non-aggressive stance in foreign policy, the decentralisation of government and an ambitious programme of social improvements. he particularly praised and targeted the young, whom he publicly identified as representing the future of a reinvigorated American society based on partnership and equality. Kennedy's victory in the Californian primary effectively knocked McCarthy out of the race. The same day, his victory over Humphreys in the letters's home state of South Dakota suggested Humphrey's too, would prove no obstacle. All seemed set for the party's nomination at the August National Democratic Convention, which he hoped would witness his peaceful coronation as Johnson's heir-apparent.

Around midnight on 4/5 June, Kennedy addressed his eutrophic supporters in the ballroom at the Los Angeles Ambassador Hotel. he left the stage after his victory speech r taking a shortcut through the hotel kitchen whilst talking to reporters. It was there a 24-year-old Palestinian, Sirhan Sirhan, opened fire with a .22 calibre revolver shooting Kennedy in the head at close range. Sirhan was apprehended by security operatives. Kennedy, meanwhile was rushed to Good Samaritan Hospital, where he died the next day. Kennedy was not the only one who died that night, For thousands of Americans, hope in a brighter, wonder and peaceful future died too, Many continue to ponder what might have happened if the best candidate America has ever had had gone on to run for the presidency.

CHAPTER 14.

TO TAME THE SAVAGE MAN

The day of the 7h September 1978 was the birthday of the Bulgarian Communist party; leader and soviet stooge Todor Zhivkov. The Bulgarian A Secret police assisted by the notorious Soviet secret service the KGB, had already undertaken two failed attempts to assassinate the expatriate Bulgarian dissident Georgi Markov. Now they chose the occasion of Zhivkov's birthday to attempt once more, in possibly the most bizarrely conceived political murders ever conducted. It was a most unusual birthday present for the most ill-mannered and boorish of dictators.

As he stood on a London bridge on a cloudy afternoon in September 1978, Georgi Markov didn't know he was being watched. He didn't know that in four days he'd be dead. The 49-year-old Bulgarian dissident was waiting to catch a bus to the BBC, where he worked as a broadcaster. Nearby, a man was holding what appeared to be an everyday object an umbrella. "Markov feels a very sharp pain in the back of his thigh and turns around to see someone who is picking up an umbrella," Kyle Wilson, a visiting fellow at ANU's Centre for European Studies, says. "This someone murmurs excuses in a very foreign accent, dashes across Waterloo Bridge to the other side of the road, jumps in a taxi and disappears." Markov boarded the bus and went to work. His fate was sealed. Markov had been on edge. He had received veiled threats and told a colleague at the BBC that the Bulgarian authorities were "gunning for him". Bulgarian freelance journalist Dimiter Kenarov says Markov became "a little bit paranoid", and would sometimes lock himself in his office. "Sometimes he would go to visit friends and he would refuse to touch the food, things like that, the sort of precautions that a lot of emigres at the time were taking," he says.

Markov had good reason to be cautious. A famous playwright and author in Bulgaria, by the late 1960s his writing was pushing the boundaries of what was acceptable to the dictatorship. Kelly Hignett, a senior lecturer in history at Leeds Beckett University, says Joseph Stalin once referred to writers and artists as "engineers of the human soul". "He thought the cultural elite had a very important role to play in shaping popular opinion," Dr Hignett says. "Used positively they could ... reinforce and promote the values of the regime. But any independent thought, any criticism, was seen as very dangerous." She says Markov became concerned that his criticism of the government was about to get him imprisoned.

"It was during a performance of his play that was taking place in Bulgaria, where a member of the intelligence services stood up in the audience and declared that the play was anti-communist and kind of criticised Markov," she says. He escaped to London in the summer of 1970, where his life changed dramatically. "He went from being a celebrity who was driving a BMW in Bulgaria, to somebody who was down and out in London for quite some time. He didn't speak the language at first," Kenarov says.

By the late 1970s, Markov began working for the BBC as a journalist. He also presented a program on Radio Free Europe, which could be heard throughout the Soviet Union and cast light on the cracks beginning to appear in the regimes behind the Iron Curtain. It also put him in the spotlight. Markov became a target after he insulted the Bulgarian prime minister Todor Zhivkov. According to Mr Wilson, there's credible evidence that the Bulgarians sought the assistance of the KGB to "physically liquidate Markov". He says the Soviet Union had possessed a highly secret poison laboratory since 1921.

Kyle Wilson was in Moscow at the time of Markov's death.*(ABC: Ian Cutmore)*. "It had very rich experience in using poisons and other methods to assassinate people who were perceived as threats to the Soviet Union, its political culture, its government or its regime," Mr Wilson says. "It was the KGB, according to KGB General Kalugin, who designed and manufactured the umbrella which would shoot and inject the tiny, microscopic sphere into Markov's thigh," he says. A microscopic sphere filled with poison was injected into Markov's leg.*(Supplied: VISNEWS)*. The projectile would be laced with the poison ricin. On the day of the umbrella incident, Markov left work at the BBC with a high fever. "At first he thought that it was just some kind of flu," Mr Kenarov says. "But Markov started suspecting that the little jab during the day that he had received in his thigh had something to do with his condition."Within 24 hours his situation had deteriorated so much that an ambulance took him to hospital. Three days later he was dead."Markov's assassination was not mentioned in state media, there was complete silence about it. Nobody ever talked about it, although it was the hugest scandal in the UK, around the world," Kenarov says.

Mr Wilson was a postgraduate student on exchange in Moscow at the time of Markov's death. "There was a great deal of ... what you might call 'suppressed subversion'. People were really careful of what they said. We used to leave the university building if we wanted to have a conversation around a sensitive topic," he recalls. Mr Wilson's study was focussed on state control and censorship of the arts."I was fascinated by the question about why the Soviet Russian authorities paid culture, literature, theatre and film the great compliment of seeking to control it very strictly," he says."Quite clearly they did that because they perceived it as a potential threat."Georgi Markov was a writer, and he was perceived in Bulgaria — what he wrote and said on the BBC — as a serious threat to the Bulgarian state." Mr Wilson says the use of assassinations for political reasons runs through Russia's history, and that a 2006 law even legalised the "extra-judicial killing" of those Moscow accuses of extremism. "If you look at the history of these assassinations by the Russian Secret Service, either by poisoning or by pistol, revolver, from the years 1921 until now ... we have well-documented evidence that about 70–75 such assassinations have been carried out."Those are just the assassinations we know of, he adds.

In August last year, Russian opposition leader **Alexei Navalny** was flown to Germany for treatment after collapsing on a plane in Russia. Germany has said that he was poisoned with a Soviet-style Novichok nerve agent, an assertion many Western nations accept. To this day, no one has been charged over Markov's death. "It's still an open case. The case has not been closed either by Scotland Yard or by Bulgaria. Here we are nearly half a century later," Mr Wilson says.

On 20 August 2020, Russian opposition figure and anti-corruption activist **Alexei Navalny** was poisoned with a Novichok nerve agent and was hospitalised in serious condition. During a flight from Tomsk to Moscow, he became ill and was taken to a hospital in Omsk after an emergency landing there, and put in a coma. He was evacuated to the Charité hospital in Berlin, Germany, two days later. The use of the nerve agent was confirmed by five Organisation for the Prohibition of Chemical Weapons (OPCW) certified laboratories. On 7 September, doctors announced that they had taken Navalny out of the induced Coma and that his condition had improved. He was discharged from the hospital on 22 September hospital on 22 September 2020.

The OPCW said that a cholinesterase inhibitor from the Novichok group was found in Navalny's blood, urine, skin samples and his water bottle.[At the same time, the OPCW report clarified that Navalny was poisoned with a new type of chemical reopened was not included in the Chemical Weapons Convention. Other prominent Russians, especially those critical of the Kremlin, have suffered poisoning attacks in the last two decades. Navalny accused President Vladimir Putin of being responsible for his poisoning.

George Moscone was a San Franciscan who rose to be major in his city, and one of the ablest, most tolerant and feral leaders of the city own San Francisco has ever boasted. His story is an impressive and typical American tale of rags-to-riches success. Tragically, today he is remembered largely for the fact that he met his death along with his city official Harvey Milk, who was a victim of the world's first anti-gay assassination. On November 27, 1978, San Francisco Mayor George Moscone and San Francisco Supervisor **Harvey Milk** were shot and killed in San Francisco City Hall by former Supervisor Dan White. On the morning of that day, Moscone intended to announce that the Supervisor position White resigned from would be given to someone else. White, angered, entered City Hall before the scheduled announcement time and first shot Moscone in the Mayor's office, then Harvey Milk in White's former office space, before escaping the building. Board of Supervisors President Dianne Feinstein first announced Moscone and Milk's deaths to the media, and because of Moscone's death, succeeded him as Acting Mayor of San Francisco.

Dan White was charged with first-degree murder with circumstances that made him eligible for the death penalty. However, in a trial verdict reached on May 21, 1979, White was convicted of the lesser crime of voluntary manslaughter. The verdict sparked the "White Night riots" in San Francisco that evening and led to the state of California abolishing the diminished capacity criminal defence. It also led to the urban legend of the "defence", as many media reports had incorrectly described the defence as having attributed White's diminished capacity to the effects of sugar-laden junk food.

White committed suicide in 1985, a year and a half after his release from prison.

Feinstein was elected by the Board of Supervisors to become the first female Mayor of San Francisco on December 4, 1978, a title she would hold for the next ten years. She eventually became a **United States Senator** for California. In the mid-1970s, the San Francisco Bay Area and the City of San Francisco in particular faced a series of bomb threats and actual bombings directed against government targets, largely attributed to the leftist militant New World Liberation Front.[4][5] These bombings began in the fall of 1975 and continued into 1977. The Mayor of San Francisco and several City Supervisors had had bombs mailed to them and/or had bomb threats made against them, and City Hall itself received threats.[6] On February 9, 1977, new tighter security began at City Hall to protect the Mayor and City Supervisors, including locking most entrances, and providing guards and metal detectors at public entrances,[6] measures which had remained through 1978.

Dan White had been a **San Francisco police officer**, and then later became a firefighter. He and Milk were each elected to the **Board of Supervisors** in the November 1977 elections, which introduced district-based seats. The election ushered in "a range of legislators perhaps unmatched in San Francisco history in their diversity", including its first Chinese-American, first unwed mother, first black woman, first homosexual (Milk) and first former firefighter (White). All supervisors were sworn in on January 9, 1978, with Dianne Feinstein as the president of the board. The city charter prohibited anyone from retaining two city jobs simultaneously, so White resigned from his higher-paying job with the fire department. In 1978, White would try to supplement his $9,600 a-year Supervisor salary with a food concession stand on **Pier 39**.

With regard to business development issues, the 11-member board was split roughly 6–5 in favour of pro-growth advocates including White, over those who advocated the more neighbourhood-oriented approach favoured by Mayor Moscone. Debate among the board members was sometimes acrimonious and saw White verbally sparring with other supervisors, including Milk and **Carol Ruth Silver**. Much of Moscone's agenda of neighbourhood revitalisation and increased city support programs was thwarted or modified in favour of the business-oriented agenda supported by the pro-growth majority on the Board. Further tension between White and Milk arose with Milk's vote in favour of placing a group home within White's district. Subsequently, White would cast the only vote in opposition to San Francisco's landmark gay rights ordinance, passed by the Board on April 3, 1978 and signed by Moscone soon after.

The city charter amendment to raise the salaries of City Supervisors was proposed in the Summer of 1978, and a committee White was on stopped the amendment from going forward, in the context of the then-recent passage of California Proposition 13 in June 1978. The low salary of the Supervisor position took its toll on White, and he finally tendered his resignation to Mayor Moscone on November 10. White stated that he couldn't support his family on only the $9,600 Supervisor salary, and that being forced to work two jobs was preventing him from adequately serving his constituents. His resignation quickly renewed a call to amend the city charter to raise Supervisor salaries, this time proposed in White's name by Carol Ruth Silver. White's resignation would leave an open seat on the Board of Supervisors, a vacancy which would be filled by appointment by Mayor Moscone. This alarmed some of the city's business interests and White's constituents, as it indicated Moscone could tip the balance of power on the Board and appoint a liberal representative for the more conservative district.

On the morning of November 15, five days after resigning, White asked Mayor Moscone to return his letter of resignation (a letter that had already been accepted and filed by the Board of Supervisors) and expressed his intent to continue serving as a Supervisor after receiving loans from family and receiving encouragement from his district's constituents to stay on. [Moscone returned the letter, but on November 16, City Attorney George Agnost ruled that White had in fact resigned and was no longer on the Board, pending legal review, and whether White could be appointed back to the position from which he had just resigned was also an open question. Moscone stated that if "legal problems" in the finality of White's resignation arose, he would appoint White back to the seat, but in any case, some of the more liberal city Supervisors and leaders, most notably Milk and Silver, lobbied Moscone not to reappoint him. On November 17, Moscone stated that White's resignation was final, and gave no indication that White was guaranteed to be re-appointed.

On November 18, news broke of the mass deaths of members of the Peoples Temple in Jonestown. Prior to the group's move to Guyana, Peoples Temple had been based in San Francisco, so most of the dead were recent Bay Area residents, including Leo Ryan, the United States Congressman who was murdered in the incident. The city was plunged into mourning, and the issue of White's vacant Board of Supervisors seat was pushed aside for several days.

On the 21st, Moscone confirmed that the city's legal position on White was that he had resigned, and further, that filling White's vacancy was one week away. He again made no guarantee of re-appointing White unless he was legally obligated to. White appeared to interpret Moscone's statements to mean that he would be re-appointed to his former position. San Francisco Mayor Moscone decided to appoint Don Horanzy, a more liberal federal housing official, to the position of District 8 Supervisor, rather than re-appoint Dan White. He scheduled a press conference to make this announcement on November 27, 1978, at 11:30 a.m.; advance copy had been sent to newspapers with late editions so they could begin preparing their stories. [White had a former aide drive him to San Francisco City Hall that morning.[He was carrying a five-round .38-caliber Smith & Wesson Model 36 Chief's Special loaded with hollow-point bullets, his service revolver from his work as a police officer, with ten extra rounds of ammunition in his coat pocket. White rapped on a basement] lab window, and told a building engineer inside that he had misplaced his keys and needed access to City Hall. White climbed into the window at about 10:25 a.m., thereby avoiding metal detectors and guards at public entrances. White proceeded to the mayor's office, where Moscone was conferring with California State Assemblyman Willie Brown. White requested a meeting with the mayor and was permitted to meet with him after Moscone's meeting with Brown ended.

As White entered Moscone's outer office, Brown exited through another door. Moscone met White in the outer office, where White requested again to be reappointed to his former seat on the Board of Supervisors. Moscone refused, and their conversation turned into a heated argument over Horanzy's pending appointment. Wishing to avoid a public scene, Moscone suggested they retreat to a private lounge adjacent to the mayor's office, so they would not be overheard by those waiting outside. At approximately 10:45 a.m., as Moscone lit a cigarette and proceeded to pour two drinks, White pulled out his revolver. He then fired shots at the mayor's shoulder and chest, tearing his lung. Moscone fell to the floor and White approached Moscone, pointed his gun 6 inches (150 mm) from the mayor's head, and fired two additional bullets into Moscone's ear lobes, killing him instantly. While standing over the slain mayor, White reloaded his revolver. Witnesses later reported that they heard Moscone and White arguing, later followed by gunshots that sounded like a car backfiring.

White left the Mayor's office and hurried across City Hall, toward the shared office space of the Board of Supervisors, inside which Supervisors each had an enclosed cubicle and desk. Dianne Feinstein, who was then President of the San Francisco Board of Supervisors, saw White run past her office door and called after him. White responded with "I have something to do first." He intercepted Harvey Milk at his office, who was speaking to a radio reporter and friend of his. White interrupted the conversation with a knock and asked Milk to step inside his former office for a moment. Milk agreed to join him. Once the door to White's office was closed, he positioned himself between the doorway and Milk, and after a brief conversation, opened fire on Milk at 10:55 a.m.. The first bullet hit Milk's right wrist as he tried to protect himself. White continued firing rapidly, hitting Milk twice more in the chest, then fired a fourth bullet at Milk's head, killing him, followed by a fifth shot into his skull at close range.

White fled the scene before Feinstein entered the office where Milk lay dead. She felt Milk's neck for a pulse, her finger entering a bullet wound. Rumours about what had happened circulated, but were not confirmed until about 11:20 a.m. At that time, Feinstein addressed the assembled media which had expected the announcement of Don Horanzy as the new District 8 Supervisor. Feinstein was shaking so badly she required support from the police chief while speaking "As President of the Board of Supervisors, it's my duty to make this announcement. Both Mayor Moscone and Supervisor Harvey Milk have been shot and killed."Gasps, cries, and curses from those assembled interrupted Feinstein briefly before she continued. "The suspect is Supervisor Dan White."

White left City Hall unchallenged. He took the keys of his former aide's car from her desk and drove that car to a diner, where he called his wife from a pay phone, and they met at a nearby church.[19] Approximately 30 minutes after leaving City Hall, White turned himself in at the Northern Station SFPD precinct, at which he had previously served as a police officer, to Frank Falzon and another detective, both former co-workers. In a police interrogation room that afternoon, White confessed to shooting Moscone and Milk but denied premeditation. Part of the taped confession became public in 2014.

An impromptu candlelight march started in the Castro leading to the City Hall steps. Tens of thousands attended. Joan Baez led "Amazing Grace", and the San Francisco Gay Men's Chorus sang a solemn hymn by Felix Mendelssohn. Upon learning of the assassinations, singer/songwriter Holly Near composed "Singing for Our Lives", also known as "Song for Harvey Milk". Moscone and Milk both lay in state at San Francisco City Hall. Moscone's funeral at St Mary's Cathedral was attended by 4,500 people. He was buried at Holy Cross Cemetery in Colma. Milk was cremated and his ashes were spread across the Pacific Ocean. Dianne Feinstein, as president of the Board of Supervisors, acceded to the Mayor's office, becoming the first woman to serve in that office.

The coroner who worked on Moscone and Milk's bodies later concluded that the wrist and chest bullet wounds were not fatal and that both victims probably would have survived with proper medical attention. However, the head wounds brought instant death without question, particularly because White fired at very close range. White's resignation and all subsequent events including the shootings caused positional changes inside San Francisco city government. At the top two levels, these were: Mayor of San Francisco: George Moscone, killed in office November 27, 1978, was immediately succeeded by Board of Supervisors President Dianne Feinstein as Acting Mayor, until elected as Mayor in a vote of 6-2 among remaining active Supervisors (excluding herself) on December 4. Feinstein would serve out the remainder of Moscone's term, then be elected to her first full term as Mayor in November 1979.

White was charged with first-degree murder with two special circumstances, both of which had been passed into law through 1978 California Proposition 7 only three weeks before White carried out the killings of Moscone and Milk. Specifically, the victim(s) were elected officials of a local government of California and the killing was intentionally carried out in retaliation for or to prevent the performance of the victim(s) official duties; and, more than one murder was committed. Murder with special circumstances meant if convicted, White could face the death penalty. White's defence team claimed that he was depressed at the time of the shootings, evidenced by many changes in his behaviour, including changes in his diet. Inaccurate media reports said White's defence had presented junk food consumption as the cause of his mental state, rather than a symptom of it, leading to the derisive term "defence"; this became a persistent myth, despite the fact that neither defence lawyer had argued junk food caused him to commit the shootings and had only mentioned Twinkies in passing. Rather, the defence argued that White's depression led to a state of mental diminished capacity, leaving him unable to have formed the premeditation necessary to commit first-degree murder. The jury accepted these arguments, and White was convicted of the lesser crime of voluntary manslaughter.

The verdict proved to be highly controversial, and many felt that the punishment so poorly matched the deed and circumstances that most San Franciscans believed White essentially got away with murder. In particular, many in the gay community were outraged by the verdict and the resulting reduced prison sentence. Since Milk had been homosexual, many felt that homophobia had been a motivating factor in the jury's decision. This groundswell of anger sparked the city's White Night riots.

The unpopular verdict also ultimately led to changes by the legislature in 1981 and statewide voters in 1982 that ended California's diminished-capacity defence and substituted a somewhat different and slightly more limited "diminished actuality" defence. White never made a direct statement of remorse, and only one relayed as hearsay was given by a prison duty nurse who attended to White in 1983. He was paroled in 1984 and served this parole in the Los Angeles area, away from San Francisco. Frank Falzon, the homicide detective who took White's statement the day of the murders, said in 1998 that he met with White in 1984, and at that meeting, White confessed that not only was his killing of Moscone and Milk premeditated, but that he had actually planned to kill Silver and Brown as well. Falzon quoted White as having said, "I was on a mission. I wanted four of them. Carol Ruth Silver, she was the biggest snake ... and Willie Brown, he was masterminding the whole thing."[After serving his parole, White moved back to the San Francisco area in early 1985 and committed suicide there that October. *San Francisco Weekly* has referred to White as "perhaps the most hated man in San Francisco's history".

Late 1990s, Frank Falzon showed a KTVU reporter some of the evidence that still existed in police custody, including the clothing Dan White had worn, a tape of his police interrogation, Moscone's liquor bottles and glasses from the site of his shooting, and White's original resignation letter to Moscone. The revolver used in the murders, serial number 1J7901, was for a time assumed missing from police evidence storage. An SFPD clerk later confirmed that he had destroyed it "in 1983 or thereabouts" while witnessed by his supervisor,[42] and under a 1982 court order to do so.[43] Its parts were melted down in a foundry that produced manhole covers.

In 2003, the story of Milk's assassination and of the White Night Riot was featured in an exhibition created by the GLBT Historical Society, a San Francisco museum, archives and research centre to which the estate of Scott Smith donated Milk's personal belongings that were preserved after his death. "Saint Harvey: The Life and Afterlife of a Modern Gay Martyr" was shown in the main gallery in the Society's former Mission Street location.

In 2008 the film *Milk* depicted the assassinations as part of a biographical story about the life of gay rights activist and politician Harvey Milk. The movie was a critical and commercial success, with Victor Garber portraying Moscone, Sean Penn playing Milk and Josh Brolin playing White. Penn won an Oscar for his performance and Brolin was nominated. In January 2012, the Berkeley Repertory Theater premiered *Ghost Light*, a play exploring the effect of Moscone's assassination on his son Jonathan, who was 14 at the time of his father's death. The production was directed by Jonathan Moscone himself and written by Tony Taccone.

CHAPTER 15.

THE ROAD TO RUIN.

Possibly the crescendo assassinations in the 20th century, where martyrs are most noteworthy,   was that of **Monsignor Oscar Romero**, Archbishop of Sam Salvador on 24th March 1980. He is unofficially the patron saint of Latin America and is one of the ten martyrs from across the world depicted in stone above the Great West Door of London's Westminster Abbey. In 1997 his passage to sainthood began when he was proposed for beatification and canonisation. The process of Canonisation is a solemn declaration by the Pope in which a deceased member of the faithful is proposed as a model and intercessor to the Christian faithful and venerated as a saint on the basis of having lived a life of heroic virtue or having remained faithful to God through   .

Oscar Romero was the most widely admired religious figure of the last century, for he dared to speak out against oppression and torture. His death at the hands of a gunman, though e widely predicted, eventfully took place while he celebrated Mass in g his cathedral in San Salvador.

Although Romero had been considered a conservative before his appointment as archbishop in 1977, he denounced the regime of dictator Gen. Carlos Humberto Romero (no relation). The archbishop also refused to support the right-wing military-civilian junta that replaced the deposed dictator. Further, his outspoken defence of the poor—who were powerless victims of widespread violence—brought repeated threats to his life. In the face of those threats, Romero declared his readiness to sacrifice his life for the "redemption and resurrection" of El Salvador. His unreserved advocacy for human rights made him a hero to many, and he was nominated for the 1979 Nobel Prize for Peace by a number of U.S. congressmen and 118 members of the British Parliament. The following year Romero was assassinated at the hands of an unknown assailant while saying mass. The Comisión de la Verdad para El Salvador ("Truth Commission for El Salvador"), approved by the United Nations, later concluded that Romero's death had been carried out by a right-wing death squad. During his funeral a bomb or bombs went off outside the Metropolitan Cathedral of San Salvador, where tens of thousands of mourners were gathered at what has been considered one of the largest demonstrations in the country's history. Gunfire then rained down on the panic-stricken crowd, leaving an estimated 27 to 40 people dead and more than 200 wounded from the violence and subsequent stampede.

Romero's focus on the church's "preferential option for the poor" principle and his call for an end to their oppression by the regime led some Latin American Catholic theologians who were associated with the liberation theology movement to view him favourably. It is unclear, however, how closely Romero associated with the movement, which integrated social justice philosophy with Catholic social ethics and emphasised the struggle of the poor for justice. In 2015, 35 years after Romero's death, Pope Francis declared him a martyr. Romero was beatified later that year. In March 2018, following the medically inexplicable cure of a terminally ill Salvadoran woman whose husband had been seeking Romero's intercession, Pope Francis approved the miracle necessary for Romero's canonization, which took place at the Vatican in October 2018. According to canon law, martyrs require only one miracle for sainthood rather than the standard two.

By 1981 Mohammed Anwar al-Sadat, the President of Egypt, had seemingly achieved the impossible. He had united and strengthened Egypt in the ad aftermath of the death of President Nasser, the father of modern Egypt, and concluded a peace treaty with the nation's implacable energy, Israel. It was an achievement that astonished and delighted the non-Arab world. He was shunned, however, by his former Arab allies, and became a prime target for Arab radicals, and he ultimately fell victim to the most bizarre and bloody assassinations of modern times.

Mohammed Anwar al-Sadat was born in 1918 to a poor Egyptian-Sudanese family, on elf 13 brothers and sisters. Sadat graduated from the Cairo Military Academy in 1938. During World War II he plotted to expel the British from Egypt with the help of the Germans. The British arrested and imprisoned him in 1942, but he escaped two years later. In 1946 Sadat was arrested after being implicated in the assassination of pro-British minister Amin Othman; he was imprisoned until his acquittal in 1948. In 1950 he joined Gamal Abdel Nasser's Free Officers organisation; he participated in its armed coup against the Egyptian monarchy in 1952 and supported Nasser's election to the presidency in 1956. Sadat held various high offices that led to his serving in the vice presidency (1964–66, 1969–70). He became acting president upon Nasser's death, on September 28, 1970, and was elected president in a plebiscite on October 15.

Sadat's domestic and foreign policies were partly a reaction against those of Nasser and reflected Sadat's efforts to emerge from his predecessor's shadow. One of Sadat's most important domestic initiatives was the open-door policy known as *infitāḥ* (Arabic: "opening"), a program of dramatic economic change that included decentralisation and diversification of the economy as well as efforts to attract trade and foreign investment. Sadat's efforts to liberalise the economy came at significant cost, including high inflation and an uneven distribution of wealth, deepening inequality and leading to discontent that would later contribute to food riots in January 1977.

It was in foreign affairs that Sadat made his most dramatic efforts. Feeling that the Soviet Union gave him inadequate support in Egypt's continuing confrontation with Israel, he expelled thousands of Soviet technicians and advisers from the country in 1972. In addition, Egyptian peace overtures toward Israel were initiated early in Sadat's presidency, when he made known his willingness to reach a peaceful settlement if Israel returned the Sinai Peninsula (captured by that country in the Six-Day [June] War of 1967). Following the failure of this initiative, Sadat launched a military attack in coordination with Syria to retake the territory, sparking the Arab-Israeli war of October 1973. The Egyptian army achieved a tactical surprise in its October 6 attack on the seemingly impenetrable Israeli fortifications along the east bank of the Suez Canal, and, though Israel staved off any advance by Egypt to recapture the Sinai Peninsula, it sustained heavy casualties and loss of military equipment. Sadat emerged from the war with greatly enhanced prestige as the first Arab leader to have actually retaken some territory from Israel. (*See* www.britannica.com / Arab-Israeli wars.)

After the war, Sadat worked toward peace in the Middle East. He made a historic visit to Israel (November 19–20, 1977), during which he travelled to Jerusalem to place his plan for a peace settlement before the Israeli Knesset (parliament). This initiated a series of diplomatic efforts that Sadat continued despite strong opposition from most of the Arab world and the Soviet Union. U.S. Pres. Jimmy Carter mediated the negotiations between Sadat and Begin that resulted in the Camp David Accords (September 17,

1978), a preliminary peace agreement between Egypt and Israel. Sadat and Begin were awarded the Nobel Prize for Peace in 1978, and their continued political negotiations resulted in the signing on March 26, 1979, of a treaty of peace between Egypt and Israel—the first between the latter and any Arab countryWhile Sadat's popularity rose in the West, it fell dramatically in Egypt because of internal opposition to the treaty, a worsening economic crisis, and Sadat's suppression of the resulting public dissent. In September 1981 he ordered a massive police strike against his opponents, jailing more than 1,500 people from across the political spectrum. The following month Sadat was assassinated by members of the Egyptian Islamic Jihad during the Armed Forces Day military parade commemorating the Arab-Israeli war of October 1973. t was on that

In October 1981, President Sadat of Egypt was murdered by persons who were opposed to his policy of reconciliation with Israel and his close links with the United States. Sadat shared the Peace Prize with Israel's Prime Minister Begin after having taken the initiative to negotiate a peace treaty between the two countries. The so-called Camp David Accords came about thanks to the mediation efforts of US President Jimmy Carter. and Sadat.

The continuation of assassinations of political figures raged for the remainder of the decade. Not the least of these was **Benigno Aquino**, a Filipino Politician on 21st August 1983. The popular politician known as 'Ninoy' stepped cautiously through the plane door into the bright sunlight of the Manilla International Airport. The aircraft had just brought the defective leader of the political opposition back to his native Philippines for the first time in three years. News that the country's dictator, President Marcos was near death had encouraged him to return. Aquino's aim was to try to secure the Philippines' return to democracy should the autocrat finally expire. Aquino has d stated to the press on his flight " I have returned to join the ranks of those struggling to restore our rights and freedom."

Tragically Aquino got no further than the airport tarmac. He was accompanied by several foreign journalists invited along partly to ensure safety, plus a nearby convoy of security guards, all assigned to him by the Marcos government. In addition, there was a contingent of 2,000 military and police personnel at the airport. Despite all this security 'Ninoy' was shot in the back of the head as he defended the steps of the aircraft. It was later claimed that he was assassinated by a lone gunman, one Rolando Galman who had conveniently shot dead by airport security seconds after Aquino was shot.   No one actually identified who killed the assassin but an Aquinos; a fellow passenger later testified that she had been a man in military uniform pointing a gun at Aquino on the stairs, his head turned followed by the sound of gunfire. It was speculated that the First Lady, Imelda Marcos, a former beauty queen who had survived an assassination herself, was behind Aquino's assassination. She was after all shrew and a ruthless political operator in he own right. On recovery, President Marcos commissioned an investigation. The result was a predictable whitewash; a number of military officers who had come to the airport tarmac to greet Aquino were found guilty, and they are still serving sentences at the National Bilbid Prison A recent appeal against their sentences claimed that a business partner of the Marcos family,, ordered the assassination, even though he had been cleared by official investigation.

Two million people lined the streets at Aquino's funeral on 31st August 1983, and national protests didn't go away. Cory Aquino, Ninoy's wife, campaigned tirelessly across the country in a bid to vindicate her late husband's brave stance. Pressured by his US allies, Marcos was forced to reintroduce the semblance of democracy. in the general election of 1986, Cory Aquino- to Marcoses' incredulity- won a sizeable victory Marcos rigged the elector; the commission attempted to reverse the result, but much of the Filipino electorate had witnessed countless undeniable instances of blatant electoral fraud.   Marcos's attempt to retain power was condemned by the US Senate and the Filipino Church Most critically, the Filipino army began to defect from its elsewhere master. The Marcos, recognising their power grasp was fatally undermined, fled in exile in Hawaii, where Ferdinand Marcos, indicted for embezzlement but never tried, died of kidney failure in 1989. The Marcos, having given up the throne, Cory Aquino was declared the 11th President of the Philippines.

The Manila International Airport has now been renamed the Ninoy Aquino International Airport. Nimoy's image is printed on the country's 500,m peso bill, and the day of his assassination is now a public holiday. His memory is now revered by political factions across the country, and a bronze statue in Makati City has become the customary venue for anti-government rallies and demonstrations- a development Nimoy would have applauded.   And across the world, the assassinations continued. Just three years after the Aquino assassination, in The Philippines, **Indira**

Gandhi, one of India's most remarkable amid controversial political leaders, as well as the daughter of the country's first prime minister, Jawaharlal Nehru, and mother of the seventh prime minister **Rajiv Gandhi** fell victim to the assassin's bullet. By 1991 both mother and son and fallen victim were determined assassins. India's politics had claimed two more of its brightest stars. Indira's maiden name was, of course, Nehru who has no relation to 'Mahatma' Gandhi who was. shockingly assassinated in 1848. She married a common one in India, Feroze Gandhi, a Congress Party radical whom she wed in 1942. Following Indian independence in 1947 Indira Gandhi moved with her children to New Delhi to assist her father, now prime minister. She became her father's confidante, secretary and nurse, and managed his re-election campaign in 1951. Her absence from her marital home however prompted the effective end of her marriage. Feroze Gandhi himself, after a brief career as an anti-corruption crusader died of heart failure in 1960.

In 1959 Indria Gandhi was elected president of the INC div whereas alter following the death pdf her beloved father, she was appointed to the government as minister for information. Her rapid political ascent was delayed when in a confused aftermath of the Indo-Parkistan War of 1965, she finally became the fourth person to lead India as prime minister. The first electoral test for Gandhi was the 1967 general elections for the Lok Sabha and state assemblies. The Congress Party won a reduced majority in the Lok Sabha after these elections owing to widespread disenchantment over the rising prices of commodities, unemployment, economic stagnation and a food crisis. Gandhi was elected to the Lok Sabha from the Raebareli constituency. She had a rocky start after agreeing to devalue the rupee which created hardship for Indian businesses and consumers. The importation o wheat from the United States fell through due to political disputes.

For the first time, the party also lost power or lost its majority in a numbe of states across the country. Following the 1967 elections, Gandhi graduall began to move towards socialist policies. In 1969, she fell out with senio Congress party leaders over several issues. Chief among them was her decision to support V. V. Giri, the independent candidate rather than the offi cial Congress party candidate Neelam Sanjiva Reddy for the vacant posi tion of president of India. The other was the announcement by the prime minister of Bank nationalisation without consulting the finance minister Morarji Desai. These steps culminated in party president S. Nijalingappa expelling her from the party for indiscipline Gandhi, in turn, floated her own faction of the Congress party and managed to retain most of the Congress MPs on her side with only 65 on the side of the Congress faction. The Gandhi faction, called Congress, lost its majority in the parliament but remained in power with the support of regional parties such as DMK. The policies of the Congress under Gandhi, before the 1971 elections, also included proposals for the abolition of the Privy Purse to former rulers of the princely states and the 1969 nationalisation of the fourteen largest banks in India.

In the 1971 Lok Sabha elections the New Congress group won a sweeping electoral victory over a coalition of conservative parties. Gandhi strongly supported East Pakistan (now Bangladesh) in its secessionist conflict with Pakistan in late 1971, and India's armed forces achieved a swift and decisive victory over Pakistan that led to the creation of Bangladesh. She became the first government leader to recognize the new country.

In March 1972, buoyed by the country's success against Pakistan, Gandhi again led her New Congress Party group to landslide victories in a large number of elections to state legislative assemblies. Shortly afterwards, however, her defeated Socialist Party opponent from the 1971 national election charged that she had violated the election laws in that contest. In June 1975 the High Court of Allahabad ruled against her, which meant that she would be deprived of her seat in the parliament and would be required to stay out of politics for six years. She appealed the ruling to the Supreme Court but did not receive a satisfactory response. Taking matters into her own hands, she declared a state of emergency throughout India, imprisoned her political opponents, and assumed emergency powers. Many new laws were enacted that limited personal freedoms. During that period she also implemented several unpopular policies, including large-scale sterilization as a form of birth control.

Public opposition to Gandhi's two years of emergency rule was vehement and widespread, and after it ended in early 1977, the released political rivals were determined to oust her and the New Congress Party from power. When long-postponed national parliamentary elections were held later in 1977, she and her party were soundly defeated, whereupon she left office. The Janata Party (precursor to the Bharatiya Janata Party) took over the reins of government, with newly recruited member Desai as prime minister.

In early 1978 Gandhi and her supporters completed the split from the Congress Party by forming the Congress (I) Party—the "I" signifying Indira. She was briefly imprisoned (October 1977 and December 1978) on charges of official corruption. Despite those setbacks, she won a new seat in the Lok Sabha in November 1978, and her Congress (I) Party began to gather strength. Dissension within the ruling Janata Party led to the fall of its government in August 1979. When new elections for the Lok Sabha were held in January 1980, Gandhi and Congress (I) were swept back into power in a landslide victory. Her son Sanjay, who had become her chief political adviser, also won a seat in the Lok Sabha. All legal cases against Indira, as well as against Sanjay, were withdrawn.

Sanjay Gandhi's death in an aeroplane crash in June 1980 eliminated Indira's chosen successor from the political leadership of India. After Sanjay's death, Indira groomed her other son, Rajiv, for the leadership of her party. She adhered to the quasi-socialist policies of industrial development that had been begun by her father. She established closer relations with the Soviet Union, depending on that country for support in India's long-standing conflict with Pakistan.

During the early 1980s, Indira Gandhi was faced with threats to the political integrity of India. Several states sought a larger measure of independence from the central government, and Sikh separatists in Punjab state used violence to assert their demands for an autonomous state. In 1982 a large number of Sikhs, led by Sant Jarnail Singh Bhindranwale, occupied and fortified the Harmandir Sahib (Golden Temple) complex at Amritsar, the Sikhs' holiest shrine. Tensions between the government and the Sikhs escalated, and in June 1984 Gandhi ordered the Indian army to attack and oust the separatists from the complex. Some buildings in the shrine were badly damaged in the fighting, and at least 450 Sikhs were killed (Sikh estimates of the death toll were considerably higher). Five months later Gandhi was killed in her garden in New Delhi in a fusillade of bullets fired by two of her own Sikh bodyguards in revenge for the attack in Amritsar. She was succeeded as prime minister by her son Rajiv, who served until 1989.

CHAPTER 16.

THE FINALE

The first two decades of the 21st century have been no less affected by the assassination of a political leader, not to mention people of influence in social justice issues and attempting to work for peaceful solutions to wars and potential wars. The stakes can be high for political leaders. Looking back over the past twenty years, a number of leaders have been assassinated either while in office or after having stepped down. In the following list, we take a look at the presidents and prime ministers who have been killed since 2000.

There have been 10 world leaders assassinated since 2000. and a host of attempts on other well-known people in positions of leadership within and outside governments have been targeted to assassins worldwide. The rules of the game in the 21st century have changed in the methodology used to take out a life. No gun, no knife and no bomb was used in the killing of Alexander Litvinenko. Twenty years after the Cold War was supposed to nee over, a a Russian agent turned political refugee was murdered using a method most would have thought outlandish even it appeared in the pages of Ian Fleming: the secret application of a radioactive poison. it was no click Bond-style operation, however, but a clumsy yet chilling crime that caught the public attention.in world headlines.

Former Japanese **Prime Minister Shinzo Abe**, 67, was assassinated on Friday (July 8in 2022) during a campaign speech in western Japan. In a country where gun control laws are stringent, the attack is the first the country has seen since before World War II. The suspected killer is reported to have said he held a grudge against an organisation he believed the premier was connected to, yet police say investigations into the claims are ongoing.

last year, Haitian **President Jovenel Moïse** was reportedly tortured before he was killed by a group of hired assassins in an overnight raid. A few months earlier, Chad's President Idriss Deby had been killed while fighting rebels in the north of the country, just hours after having won re-election. The chart then shows a ten-year lull, where no presidents or prime ministers were killed. In that time, however, high-profile leaders such as Tunisian left-wing opposition leader Chokri Belaid and Mohammed Brahmi lost their lives. Benazir Bhutto, the sole female on the list, and the first female prime minister of Pakistan was shot and then hit by a suicide bomber's blast at a political rally in the city of Rawalpindi. In 2011, Libyan dictator Moammar Gaddafi was captured and killed after his government was overthrown by a NATO-backed rebellion.

Congo's President Kabila and Guinea-Bissau's João Bernardo Vieira were each shot by inside men, the first by a child soldier who had become his teenage bodyguard, and the second by a soldier in his presidential palace. Meanwhile, Nepal's King was murdered by his own son, who massacred nine members of the family - including the king - in the royal palace, reportedly over an argument about the prince's marriage.

Now the instrument of death by assassins has changed somewhat. No gun, no knife, and no bomb were used in the killing of Alexander Litvinenko. Twenty years after the Cold War was supposed to be over, a Russian agent turned political refugee was murdered using a method most would have thought outlandish even if it appeared in the pages of an Ian Fleming plot, the secret application of a radioactive poison. it was no slick Bond-style operation, however, but a clumsy yet chilling crime that caught the world's attention.

Alexander Valterovich "Sasha" Litvinenko 30 August 1962 was a British-naturalised Russian defector and former officer of the Russian Federal Security Service (FSB) who specialised in tackling organized crime.[1] [4] A prominent critic of Russian President Vladimir Putin, he advised British intelligence and coined the term "mafia state".

In November 1998, Litvinenko and several other FSB officers publicly accused their superiors of ordering the assassination of the Russian oligarch Boris Berezovsky. Litvinenko was arrested the following March on charges of exceeding the authority of his position. He was acquitted in November 1999 but re-arrested before the charges were again dismissed in 2000. He fled with his family to London and was granted asylum in the United Kingdom, where he worked as a journalist, writer and consultant for the British intelligence services.

During his time in Boston, Lincolnshire, Litvinenko wrote two books, *Blowing Up Russia: Terror from Within* and *Lubyanka Criminal Group*, in which he accused the Russian secret services of staging the Russian apartment bombings in 1999 and other acts of terrorism in an effort to bring Vladimir Putin to power. He also accused Putin of ordering the assassination of the Russian journalist Anna Politkovskaya in 2006.

On 1 November 2006, Litvinenko suddenly fell ill and was hospitalised after poisoning with polonium-210; he died from the poisoning on 23 November.[6] The events leading up to this are well documented, despite spawning numerous theories relating to his poisoning and death. A British murder investigation identified Andrey Lugovoy, a former member of Russia's Federal Protective Service (FSO), as the main suspect. Dmitry Kovtun was later named as a second suspect.[7] The United Kingdom demanded that Lugovoy be extradited, however, Russia denied the extradition as the Russian constitution prohibits the extradition of Russian citizens, leading to a straining of relations between Russia and the United Kingdom.[8]

After Litvinenko's death, his wife Marina, aided by biologist Alexander Goldfarb, pursued a vigorous campaign through the Litvinenko Justice Foundation. In October 2011, she won the right for an inquest into her husband's death to be conducted by a coroner in London; the inquest was repeatedly set back by issues relating to examinable evidence A public inquiry began on 27 January 2015,[10] and concluded in January 2016 that Litvinenko's murder was carried out by the two suspects and that they were "probably" acting under the direction of the FSB and with the approval of president Vladimir Putin and then FSB director Nikolai Patrushev. In the 2021 case , the European Court of Human Rights ruled that Russia was responsible for his death and ordered the country to pay 100,000 euros in damages.

Alexander Litvinenko was born in the Russian city of Voronezh in 1962. After he graduated from a Nalchik secondary school in 1980, he was drafted into the Internal Troops of the Ministry of Internal Affairs as a Private. After a year of service, he matriculated in the Kirov Higher Command School in Vladikavkaz. In 1981, Litvinenko married Nataliya, an accountant, with whom he had a son, Alexander, and a daughter, Sonia. This marriage ended in divorce in 1994 and in the same year Litvinenko married Marina, a ballroom dancer and fitness instructor, with whom he had a son, Anatoly.

After graduation in 1985, Litvinenko became a platoon commander in the Dzerzhinsky Division of the Soviet Ministry of Internal Affairs. He was assigned to the 4th Company of 4th Regiment, where among his duties was the protection of valuable cargo while in transit.[2][20][21] In 1986, he became an informant when he was recruited by the MVD's KGB counterintelligence section and in 1988, he was officially transferred to the Third Chief Directorate of the KGB, Military Counter Intelligence.[20] Later that year, after studying for a year at the Novosibirsk Military Counter Intelligence School, he became an operational officer and served in KGB military counterintelligence until 1991.

In 1991, Litvinenko was promoted to the Central Staff of the Federal Counterintelligence Service, specialising in counter-terrorist activities and infiltration of organised crime. He was awarded the title of "MUR veteran" for operations conducted with the Moscow criminal investigation department the MURLitvinenko also saw active military service in many of the so-called "hot spots" of the former USSR and Russia. During the First Chechen War, Litvinenko planted several FSB agents in Chechnya. Although he was often called a "Russian spy" by the western press, throughout his career he was not an 'intelligence agent' and did not deal with secrets beyond information on operations against organised criminal groups.

Litvinenko met Boris Berezovsky in 1994 when he took part in investigations into an assassination attempt on the oligarch. He later was responsible for the oligarch's security.[20] Litvinenko's employment under Berezovsky and other security services created a conflict of interest, but such practice is usually tolerated by the Russian state.In 1997, Litvinenko was promoted to the FSB Directorate of Analysis and Suppression of Criminal Groups, with the title of senior operational officer and deputy head of the Seventh Section.

During his work in the FSB, Litvinenko discovered numerous connections between top leadership of Russian law enforcement agencies and Russian mafia groups, such as the Solntsevo gang. He wrote a memorandum about this issue for Boris Yeltsin. Berezovsky arranged a meeting for him with FSB director Mikhail Barsukov and deputy director of Internal affairs Ovchinnikov to discuss the corruption problems;[28] however, this had no effect. Litvinenko gradually realized that the entire system was corrupt from the top to the bottom. He explained: "If your partner bilked you, or a creditor did not pay, or a supplier did not deliver - where did you turn to complain? ...When force became a commodity, there was always demand for it. "Roofs" (*krysha*) appeared, people who sheltered and protected your business. First it was provided by the mob, then by police, and soon even our own guys realized what was what, and then the rivalry began among gangsters, cops, and the Agency for market share. As the police and the FSB became more competitive, they squeezed the gangs out of the market. However, in many cases competition gave way to cooperation, and the services became gangsters themselves."

On 25 July 1998, Berezovsky introduced Litvinenko to Vladimir Putin. He said: "Go see Putin. Make yourself known. See what a great guy we have installed, with your help."[29] On the same day, Putin replaced Nikolay Kovalyov as the Director of the Federal Security Service, with help from Berezovsky.[29] Litvinenko reported to Putin on corruption in the FSB, but Putin was unimpressed.[29] Litvinenko said to his wife after the meeting: "I could see in his eyes that he hated me."[29] Litvinenko said that he was doing an investigation of Uzbek drug barons who received protection from the FSB, and Putin tried to stall the investigation to save his reputation.

On 13 November 1998, Berezovsky wrote an open letter to Putin in *Kommersant*. He accused four senior officers of the Directorate of Analysis and Suppression of Criminal Groups of ordering his assassination: Major-General Yevgeny Khokholkov, N. Stepanov, A. Kamyshnikov, and N. Yenin. Four days later, on 17 November, Litvinenko and four other officers appeared together in a press conference at the Russian news agency Interfax.

All officers worked for both FSB in the Directorate of Analysis and Suppression of Criminal Groups.[20] They repeated the allegation made by Berezovsky.[20][32] The officers also said they were ordered to kill Mikhail Trepashkin who was also present at the press conference, and to kidnap a brother of the businessman Umar Dzhabrailov.[32] In 2007, Sergey Dorenko provided the Associated Press and *The Wall Street Journal* with a complete copy of an interview he conducted in April 1998 for ORT, a television station, with Litvinenko and his fellow employees. The interview, of which only excerpts were broadcast in 1998, shows the FSB officers, who were disguised in masks or dark glasses, claim that their bosses had ordered them to kill, kidnap or frame prominent Russian politicians and business-people.

After holding the press conference, Litvinenko was dismissed from the FSB. Later, in an interview with Yelena Tregubova, Putin said that he personally ordered the dismissal of Litvinenko, stating, "I fired Litvinenko and disbanded his unit ...because FSB officers should not stage press conferences. This is not their job. And they should not make internal scandals public."Litvinenko also believed that Putin was behind his arrest. He said, "Putin had the power to decide whether to pass my file to the prosecutors or not. He always hated me. And there was a bonus for him: by throwing me to the wolves he distanced himself from Boris [Berezovsky] in the eyes of FSB's generals."

In October 2000, in violation of an order not to leave Moscow, Litvinenko and his family travelled to Turkey, possibly via Ukraine.[35] While in Turkey, Litvinenko applied for asylum at the United States Embassy in Ankara, but his application was denied.[35] With the help of Alexander Goldfarb, Litvinenko bought air tickets for the Istanbul–London–Moscow flight,[36] and asked for political asylum at Heathrow Airport during the transit stop on 1 November 2000.[37] Political asylum was granted on 14 May 2001,[38] not because of his knowledge on intelligence matters, according to Litvinenko, but rather on humanitarian grounds.[20] While in London he became a journalist for Chechenpress and an author. He also joined Berezovsky in campaigning against Putin's government.[39] In October 2006, he became a naturalised British citizen with residence in Whitehaven.

In 2002, Litvinenko was convicted *in absentia* in Russia and given a three-and-a-half-year jail sentence for charges of corruption. According to Litvinenko's widow, Marina Litvinenko, her husband cooperated with the British security services, working as a consultant and helping the agencies to combat Russian organised crime in Europe.[5] During the public inquiry started in January 2015, it was confirmed that Litvinenko was recruited by MI6 to provide "useful information about senior Kremlin figures and their links with Russian organised crime", primarily related to Russian mafia activities in Spain

Shortly before his death, Litvinenko tipped off Spanish authorities on several organised crime bosses with links to Spain. During a meeting in May 2006, he allegedly provided security officials with information on the locations, roles, and activities of several "Russian" mafia figures with ties to Spain, including Zahkar Kalashov, Vitaly Izguilov and Tariel Oniani.

Litvinenko allegedly converted to Islam in Britain and was rumoured to have told his father he had converted to Islam on his deathbed. Litvinenko said his father commented about it: "It doesn't matter. At least you're not a communist."This account has been strongly denied by close family and friends.Visitors to Litvinenko's deathbed included Boris Berezovsky and Litvinenko's father, Walter, who flew in from Moscow.

Mikhail Trepashkin said that in 2002 he had warned Litvinenko that an FSB unit was assigned to assassinate him.[47] In spite of this, Litvinenko often travelled overseas with no security arrangements freely mingled with the Russian community in the United Kingdom, and often received journalists at his home.Litvinenko published a number of allegations about the Russian government, most of which are related to conducting or sponsoring domestic and foreign terrorism.

Litvinenko stated that "all the bloodiest terrorists of the world" were connected to FSB-KGB, including Carlos "The Jackal" Ramírez, Yasser Arafat, Saddam Hussein, Abdullah Öcalan, Wadie Haddad of the Popular Front for the Liberation of Palestine, George Hawi who led the Communist Party of Lebanon, Ezekias Papaioannou from Cyprus, Sean Garland from Ireland, and many others. He said that all of them were trained, funded, and provided with weapons, explosives and counterfeit documents to carry out terrorist attacks worldwide and that each act of terrorism made by these people was carried out according to the task and under the rigid control of the KGB of the USSR.[48] Litvinenko said that "the centre of global terrorism is not in Iraq, Iran, Afghanistan or the Chechen Republic. The terrorism infection creeps away worldwide from the cabinets of the Lubyanka Square and the Kremlin"

When asked in an interview who he thought the originator of the 2005 bombings in London was, Litvinenko responded by saying, "You know, I have spoken about it earlier and I shall say now, that I know only one organization, which has made terrorism the main tool of solving of political problems. It is the Russian special services."Litvinenko also commented on a new law that "Russia has the right to carry out preemptive strikes on militant bases abroad" and explained that these "preemptive strikes may involve anything except nuclear weapons." Litvinenko said, "You know who they mean when they say 'terrorist bases abroad'? They mean us, Zakayev and Boris and me."[33] He also said"It was considered in our service that poison is an easier weapon than a pistol." He referred to a secret laboratory in Moscow that still continues development of deadly poisons, according to him.

Litvinenko accused the Main Intelligence Directorate of the General-Staff of the Russian armed forces of having organised the 1999 Armenian parliament shooting that killed the Prime Minister of Armenia, Vazgen Sargsyan, and seven members of parliament, ostensibly to derail the peace process which would have resolved the Nagorno-Karabakh conflict, but he offered no evidence to support the accusation.[20][53][54] The Russian embassy in Armenia denied any such involvement, and described Litvinenko's accusation as an attempt to harm relations between Armenia and Russia by people against the democratic reforms in Russia

Two weeks before his poisoning, Alexander Litvinenko accused Vladimir Putin of ordering the assassination of the Russian journalist Anna Politkovskaya and stated that a former presidential candidate, Irina Hakamada, warned Politkovskaya about threats to her life coming from the Russian president. Litvinenko advised Politkovskaya to escape from Russia immediately. Hakamada denied her involvement in passing any specific threats, and said that she warned Politkovskaya only in general terms more than a year earlier.[74] It remains unclear if Litvinenko referred to an earlier statement made by Boris Berezovsky, who claimed that Boris Nemtsov, a former Deputy Prime Minister of Russia, received word from Hakamada that Putin threatened her and like-minded colleagues in person. According to Berezovsky, Putin stated that Hakamada and her colleagues "will take in the head immediately, literally, not figuratively" if they "open the mouth" about the Russian apartment bombings. Litvinenko also said, "Trofimov did not exactly say that Prodi was a KGB agent, because the KGB avoids using that word."Shortly before his death, Alexander Litvinenko alleged that Vladimir Putin had cultivated a "good relationship" with Semion Mogilevich (head of the Russia mafia) since 1993 or 1994

In a July 2006 article published on Zakayev's Chechenpress website, Litvinenko claimed that Putin is a paedophile and that the KGB knew about it since Putin's graduation from the Red Banner Institute. Litvinenko asserted that the FSB had possessed video footage which documented sex between Putin and minor boys and that Putin destroyed it while FSB director.[86] Litvinenko also claimed that Anatoly Trofimov and Artyom Borovik knew of the alleged paedophilia.[87] An article in the *New York Times* described the allegation as "without evidence"

Litvinenko made the allegation after Putin kissed a boy on his stomach while stopping to chat with some tourists during a walk in the Kremlin grounds on 28 June 2006. The incident was recalled in a webcast organised by the BBC and Yandex, in which over 11,000 people asked Putin to explain the act, to which he responded, "He seemed very independent and serious... I wanted to cuddle him like a kitten and it came out in this gesture. He seemed so nice. ... There is nothing behind it."

Vladimir Bukovsky, a close friend of Litvinenko, said he was angry when he published the article, as he had strongly urged him against it. Bukovsky noted that despite his ferocious hostility toward the Kremlin, Litvinenko still had the mind-set of a security officer and "could not understand the difference between truth and operational information.

On 1 November 2006, Litvinenko suddenly fell ill. On 3 November, he was admitted to Barnet General Hospital in London.[91] He was then moved to University College Hospital for intensive care. His illness was later attributed to poisoning with radionuclide polonium-210 after the Health Protection Agency found significant amounts of the rare and highly toxic element in his body. Litvinenko met with two former agents early on the day he fell ill – Dmitry Kovtun and Andrey Lugovoy, in the Millennium Hotel's

Pine Bar where high polonium contamination was found.[93][92] Though both denied any wrongdoing, a leaked U.S. diplomatic cable revealed that Kovtun had left polonium traces in the house and car he had used in Hamburg.] Before his meeting with Kovtun and Lugovoy, Litvinenko had lunch at Itsu, a sushi restaurant in Piccadilly in London, with an Italian acquaintance Mario Scaramella,[94][95] who had claimed to have information on the assassination of Anna Politkovskaya, forty-eight, a journalist who had been shot dead on the doorstep of her Moscow apartment building only three weeks previously.

On his deathbed, Litvinenko claimed that Putin had directly ordered his assassination.[93] After his death, Marina Litvinenko, his widow, accused Moscow of orchestrating the murder. Though she believes the order did not come from Putin himself, she does believe it was done at the behest of the authorities, and announced that she would refuse to provide evidence to any Russian investigation out of fear that it would be misused or misrepresented. In a court hearing in London in 2015, a Scotland Yard lawyer concluded that "the evidence suggests that the only credible explanation is in one way or another the Russian state is involved in Litvinenko's murder".

Before his death, Litvinenko said: "You may succeed in silencing one man but the howl of protest from around the world, Mr. Putin, will reverberate in your ears for the rest of your life." On 22 November 2006, Litvinenko's medical team at University College Hospital reported Litvinenko had suffered a "major setback" due to either heart failure or an overnight heart attack. He died on 23 November. The following day, Putin publicly stated "Mr Litvinenko is, unfortunately, not Lazarus". Scotland Yard stated that inquiries into the circumstances of how Litvinenko became ill would continue. On 24 November 2006, a statement was released posthumously, in which Litvinenko named Putin as the man behind his poisoning.[1 Litvinenko's friend Alex Goldfarb, who was also the chairman of Boris Berezovsky's Civil Liberties Fund, claimed Litvinenko had dictated it to him three days earlier. Andrei Nekrasov said his friend Litvinenko and Litvinenko's lawyer had composed the statement in Russian on 21 November and translated it to English. Goldfarb later stated that Litvinenko, on his deathbed, had instructed him to write a note "in good English" in which Putin was to be accused of his poisoning. Goldfarb also stated that he read the note to Litvinenko in English and Russian and Litvinenko agreed "with every word of it" and signed it.

His autopsy took place on 1 December at the Royal London Hospital's Institute of Pathology. It was attended by three physicians, including one chosen by the family and one from the Foreign Office.[102] Litvinenko was buried at Highgate Cemetery (West side) in north London on 7 December. [103] The police treated his death as a murder, although the London coroner's inquest was yet to be completed.

On 7 December 2006, Litvinenko was buried in a lead-lined casket at Highgate Cemetery with Christian, Jewish and Muslim rites, including a Christian and Muslim prayer being said by an imam and Orthodox priest in line with Litvinenko's wishes of a non-denominational service at the grave. A Times report of his funeral, of 1st December 2006, noted that his coffin must not be opened for 22 years owing to the high dosage of polonium in his body. His killers continue to evade justice.

Here's a global look at other high-profile assassinations in the 21st century:

- Oct 15, 2021: British lawmaker **David Amess** is stabbed to death by an Islamic State supporter while meeting with voters.- July 7, 2021: Haitian President **Jovenel Moise** is assassinated by gunmen who also wound his wife Martine in an overnight raid on their Port-au-Prince home. More than 40 people have been arrested in Haiti for the attack, including high-ranking police officers and a group of former Colombian soldiers.- April 20, 2021: Chad President **Idriss Deby Itno** is killed while battling rebels in the north. Hours earlier he had been declared the winner of an election that would have given him another six years in power.- Feb 13, 2017: **Kim Jong Nam**, the estranged half-brother of North Korean leader Kim Jong Un, is killed by VX nerve agent at a Malaysian airport. He had been seen as a possible threat to his brother's rule and reportedly had met with US intelligence agencies.- Dec 19, 2016: Russia's ambassador to Turkey **Andrei Karlov** is shot dead by a Turkish policeman shouting condemnation of Russia's military role in Syria, in front of a shocked gathering at a photo exhibit. The gunman was later killed in a shootout with police.- June 16, 2016: British lawmaker **Jo Cox** is shot and stabbed to death by a far-right supporter in the English village of Birstall, part of her constituency.- Feb 6, 2013:

Tunisian left-wing opposition leader **Chokri Belaid** is fatally shot outside his Tunis home. His killing - followed six months later by that of another left-wing leader, **Mohammed Brahmi** - plunged Tunisia into political chaos with effects reverberating to this day. No one has been convicted in either case.- Sept 11, 2012: U.S. Ambassador **Chris Stevens** is killed when militants storm the US diplomatic compound in Benghazi, Libya. Another three Americans died.- Oct 20, 2011: Longtime Libyan dictator **Moammar Gadhafi** is hunted and summarily killed by insurgents after being toppled in a NATO-backed uprising.- March 2, 2009: Guinea-Bissau President **Joao Bernardo Vieira** is killed by renegade soldiers in his palace, hours after a bomb blast killed his rival in the West African nation.- Dec 27, 2007: **Benazir Bhutto,** the first female prime minister in a Muslim-majority country as well as Pakistan's second nationally elected prime minister, was shot at and then attacked by a suicide bomber at a political rally in Rawalpindi, Pakistan.- Feb 14, 2005: Lebanese Prime Minister **Rafik Hariri** is killed by a suicide truck bomb on a seaside boulevard in Beirut. Another 21 people died and 226 were wounded in the attack, which is seen by many in Lebanon as the work of neighbouring Syria- Dec 29, 2003: Archbishop **Michael Courtney,** the pope's ambassador in Burundi, is shot by gunmen as he was returning from a funeral and died during surgery.- March 12, 2003: Serbian Prime Minister **Zoran Djindjic** is shot dead in front of the Serbian government headquarters in Belgrade. He was a key leader of the revolt that toppled former President **Slobodan Milosevic** in October 2000. Twelve people were convicted in connection with the killing, which was carried out to halt his pro-Western reforms, according to a Serbian court ruling.- May 6, 2002: Populist Dutch politician **Pim Fortuyn** is gunned down in a northern Netherlands city, days before a general election in which he was a candidate, by an animal rights activist.- June 1, 2001: Nepal's **King Birendra** is killed when his son, Crown Prince Dipendra, opens fire on his family in the royal palace. The dead include **Queen Aiswarya,** a prince and five others. Officials said the shooting followed a dispute over the prince's marriage.- Jan 18, 2001: Congo President **Laurent Kabila** is assassinated in the presidential palace in the capital, Kinshasa, by one of his bodyguards, who was killed minutes later by security forces

So it is that the forces of Lucifer and his army of angels of death are alive and well in the 21st century. To the wind of change for today would be assassins, as much as the original assassins of the 12th century Levant, political murders, can be both sanctioned by God and governments. In this sense, humanity has not as it appears to date, progressed much throughout the centuries. It has been chillingly prophesied by the assassin Mohammed Bouyeri of Dutch filmmaker Theo Van Gogh in 2004; " Now you know what you people can expect in the future." It is hoped the words of past Prime Minister Gordon Brown might give us hope when he responded to Theo Van Gogh's killer remark: 'This atrocity strengthens our resolve that terrorists will not win, there or anywhere in the world.'-will prove to be a more prescient prediction for the remainder of the 21st century than that Bouyeni menacing forecast.

\

The Eagle does not fight the snake on the ground. It picks it up into the sky and changes the battleground, and then it releases the snake into the sky. The snake has no stamina, no power and no balance in the air. It is useless, weak and vulnerable unlike on the ground where it is powerful wise and deadly. Take your fight into the spiritual realm by praying and when you are in the spiritual realm God takes over your battles.

Don't fight the enemy in his comfort zone, change the battle grounds like the Eagle and let God take charge through your earnest prayer. You will be assured of a clean victory

Rumi, 13th century poet.

Doug McPhillips, poet, singer, songwriter, and author, commenced his journey of discovery over a decade ago after life-changing experiences.

The many tracks he has traversed throughout the Northern Hemisphere and down under in New Zealand and Australia has resulted in the facts and fiction of this novel.

Doug has recorded and sung songs interrelated to this work with majestic melodies in a true Australian style.

Doug has written ten novels, a book of poems, a travel guide and two albums of his songs all inspired by his adventurers.

www.caminoway.com.au

Doug is an adventurer who divides his time between creative pursuits, family and friends, and those who may benefit most from his efforts and experience.

International Publishers

IngramSpark
1 La Verge TN37086
Nashville Tennessee

Printed in Australia
Lightning Source
76 Discovery Road South
Scoresby, Victoria 3179